S0-DVE-539

GETTING NEAR THE END

* * ANDREW WEINER * *

ROBERT J. SAWYER BOOKS ARE PUBLISHED BY
Red Deer Press
813 MacKimmie Library Tower
2500 University Drive N.W.
Calgary Alberta Canada T2N 1N4
www.reddeerpress.com

CREDITS
Edited for the press by Robert J. Sawyer
Cover illustration and design by Marilyn Mets &Peter Ledwon
Text design by Erin Woodward
Printed and bound in Canada by Friesens for Red Deer Press

ACKNOWLEDGMENTS
Financial support provided by the Canada Council, the Department of Canadian Heritage, the Alberta Foundation for the Arts, a beneficiary of the Lottery Fund of the Government of Alberta, and the University of Calgary.

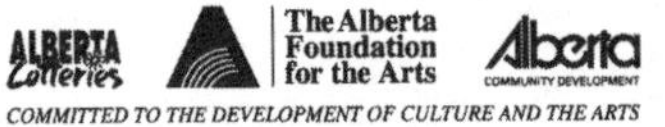

NATIONAL LIBRARY OF CANADA CATALOGUING IN PUBLICATION
Weiner, Andrew, 1949–
Getting near the end / Andrew Weiner.
ISBN 0-88995-307-4
I. Title.
PS8595.E4195G48 2004 C813'.54 C2004-903968-7

5 4 3 2 1

"Hurry up please, it's time."

—T. S. Eliott, "The Waste Land"

"Surely some revelation is at hand."

—W. B. Yeats, "The Second Coming"

* * DEDICATION * *

To André-François Ruaud
who believed in this book

✶ ✶ INTRODUCTION ✶ ✶

If you want to understand a writer, find out what other authors he or she admires. For instance, I'm an Arthur C. Clarke and Isaac Asimov fan.

Not Andrew Weiner. Oh, he's hugely familiar with the classics of hard SF. But his favorite writers are J. G. Ballard, Barry Malzberg, and Philip K. Dick—literary talents on the borderlines of the genre, shading toward the mainstream.

Ballard is the British author of *Empire of the Sun.* Like Weiner, he's fascinated by apocalyptic visions. And both prefer inner space to outer space; they're more fascinated by the human mind than the devices we make (and, indeed, both have very little faith in the enduring power of technology).

Barry Malzberg, meanwhile, is best known for a trio of novels ending with *Beyond Apollo,* about dispirited space travelers who stand as symbols not for humanity's loftiest goals, but for our own alienation from ourselves. There's no doubt that Wyatt, Denning, and Chang—the astronauts in this powerful new novel by Andrew Weiner—are descendants of Malzberg's spacemen.

In one of Weiner's many insightful critical essays about SF (which have appeared everywhere from *Books in Canada* to *The New York Review of Science Fiction),* he lauded Barry Malzberg as "the first true prophet of SF Postmodernism." Weiner himself defines Postmodernism, in part, as, "A feeling that there's no future, that everything has been done, that nothing lies ahead except repetition or degeneration." That sense certainly echoes throughout this book, although in the end, I think, Weiner is ultimately more optimistic than Malzberg.

And then there's Philip K. Dick, who, now that he's gone, has become one of Hollywood's hottest properties, the movies *Blade Runner, Total Recall, Minority Report,* and *Paycheck* were all based on his work. Dick was fascinated by our inability to draw clear-cut lines between illusion and reality, between sanity and madness, between cause and effect. All three themes echo loudly in Weiner's new novel, a story of a rock singer whose seemingly prophetic songs are either glimpses of an inevitable future or the force that is actually shaping the way the future will be.

Neither Ballard nor Malzberg nor Dick really liked having their work called science fiction. Andrew Weiner certainly fits that mold. Indeed, in 1993 he wrote a memorable essay called "SF—Not!" that concluded, "I do wonder whether some people might prefer at least a quiet and dignified obscurity to one involving publication with spaceships on the cover. And I wonder whether those people might include me."

Ultimately, though, despite his obvious literary antecedents, and despite statements like the above, in which he himself seeks to find what group he belongs in, Andrew Weiner is very much his own writer, with a unique, witty, sardonic voice. His work as a rock journalist certainly shaped this novel of superstar Martha Nova, but his vision is also strongly informed by his many years as a writer of feature articles about business.

Indeed, Weiner is one of the very few writers of science fiction who pays serious attention to economics, which Thomas Carlyle famously dubbed "the dismal science." It is indeed the dismal, the decaying, the unraveling, and the falling apart that fascinate Andrew Weiner. He sees where it's all going, and he knows we're getting near the end.

Robert J. Sawyer

✶ ✶ P R O L O G ✶ ✶

The Hour Is Getting Late
December 2023

* * 1 * *

They were in the hotel, the singer and her companion, on the thirty-second floor of the hotel that was said to be the finest in the city.

They had come to the hotel direct from the airport, through the secured private subway link. They had been in the hotel for five days, and still they had not stepped outside on to the streets of the city. Neither did they plan to.

The singer had an engagement scheduled for New Year's Eve, which was five days on, but otherwise they had no plans. The singer's companion had passed through that phase of his life in which it was important to him to have plans. The singer had never seemed to make them at all.

The singer's companion, whose name was Robert Duke, would have liked to have seen the action in the streets as they entered the city, the huge crowds gathering near the hotel to celebrate the singer's return. But the streets were not safe.

* * * * *

The private subway system that carried them from the airport to the hotel was of recent construction. Duke had scanned a couple of newsbites on it a few months before, and it more than lived up to its publicity. It was almost worth the trip in itself, to a city which he had never much cared for, to sit there strapped into the thickly upholstered velvet-covered seat in their private car, sipping his mineral water as they raced into town through the steel-lined, blast-resistant tunnel at 300 kilometers an hour. It was a new thing, in a world where there were all too few new things, and Duke was momentarily enthralled.

He gazed out through the thick bulletproof glass of the porthole at the walls of the tunnel. The walls were lined with the fiber optic cables which connected the city to the world. Information was racing past them in both directions: news and sports and entertainment but above all financial information. For all its recent difficulties, this city was still a major international financial center. The money rushed by, pulsing into the global electronic funds transfer webs, and Duke could almost feel the breeze.

It was to protect these communication links, the newsbite had told him, that this blast-resistant conduit had been conceived. Premium subway service had been an add-on, but a lucrative one, now that ground travel in this city had become more dangerous than the old public subway system.

"Terrific, huh?" Duke said to the singer's child, Daniel.

"Sure," Daniel had agreed, not looking up from the display screen of his seat-tray. "Really terrific." The boy was watching an old *Road Runner* cartoon, selected from the subway car's vast entertainment menu.

Any normal seven-year-old, Duke thought, would have been at least a little impressed. But the singer's child was anything but a normal seven-year-old.

* * * * *

In the hotel, the singer and her companion passed the time. They accessed the latest music and skimmed the latest movies and scanned the latest ideas. They ate and drank and played with the singer's child. They looked out on the city through the high wide windows of their suite and watched the disturbances.

The disturbances were bad. The singer and her companion had seen worse disturbances in different cities at different times, but they agreed that the disturbances were very bad this year in this particular city.

Security forces battled deviant groups. Distant mortars kicked up clouds of dust. Ambushed automobiles exploded in mined streets. Sometimes the sky burned red at night. The noise of all this failed to penetrate through the thick, soundproof windows of the hotel, but they could see that the disturbances were very bad.

The hotel could have been in Nepal and it could have been in Beirut and it could have been in St. Petersburg. It could have been anywhere the big hotels still stood, but it was in New York. The singer and her companion were in town for the New Year, another New Year in another big hotel. Except that this year, the New Year's Eve of 2024, the party would be something special.

This year, the party would be held in honor of the singer, whose name was Martha Nova. She was about to release her first new collection of songs, in audio, video, holo and other formats, in five years. The party to celebrate its release would be shown both in real-time and in endless reiterations on entertainment channels around the world.

For years now, the singer had been in seclusion from the world, steadfastly ignoring the pleas of her recording company and her fans for new songs, or for even the most fleeting personal appearance. And through all that time, her legend had grown. Anthologies of her old songs, endlessly recombined and re-permutated with unreleased outtakes and alternate versions into apparently new commodities, were downloaded into millions of home entertainment systems.

The singer was adored everywhere, in Tokyo and in Stockholm, in Cairo and in Winnipeg, in Seoul and in Reykjavik. At only thirty-three years old, she was said to be the most popular singer in the history of the world.

The party would be for the singer, and Robert Duke was merely tagging along. He would be careful to remain in the background. He had no wish to compete with the singer. It would be no contest in any case.

Duke himself had once been a famous singer. Although never as celebrated as Martha Nova, his name and his voice had been known almost everywhere. But these days he hardly thought of himself as a singer at all. These days, he saw himself more as a dancer.

Once, his voice had burned deep, penetrated the soul. Now, as he slumped past his fiftieth year, his voice was to all intents gone. But there was still the dance. The dance was in his style, in the way he moved through his life, moved on and moved up. It had always been the dance, as much as the voice, that people had paid to experience, and that much was still left to him, there was still the dance.

* * * * *

It was an old hotel, built in a period of great confidence and expansiveness. The ceilings were high, the carpets were thick and hardly worn-down, the dining rooms hushed and well-mirrored.

Robert Duke had always liked this hotel. He had first stayed here many years before, at that juncture in his career in which he had begun to really make it, to break through all barriers, to take this and all the other cities by storm. It was here, too, that he had honeymooned with his second wife, a leading indie screenqueen of that long-ago year, while the reporters and *paparazzi* had clustered outside the door of their suite.

Martha Nova had no memories of this hotel, only powerful premonitions, the strongest she had ever felt. In her memories of the future, the hotel loomed enormous.

* * * * *

The singer believed that she could see the future. She had been seeing the future since she was five years old.

The visions had come to her one night as she lay sleeping, and in the beginning they had driven her into madness. But eventually she had learned to live with them, even to take a certain comfort in them. Eventually, through her music, she had found that she could comfort other people too.

She often sang about what she saw up ahead. What she saw, above all else, was decay, dissolution, the approach of the end-time.

She liked to sing, she adored her child, she loved Robert Duke. These were not small things. Her enjoyment of them was intensified by the knowledge that they were getting very near the end.

* * * * *

Duke sat on the couch in the living room of their hotel suite, looking over a printout showing Martha's itinerary for her forthcoming west coast promotional tour. The flack from RealTime, Martha's record company, had dropped it off that morning along with the voucher for a private jet to L.A. They would be leaving the day after New Year's Day, according to the itinerary.

"Heavy duty tour," he said. "Press conference, talk shows, personal interviews."

Martha was sitting on the couch with Daniel, playing Go on the room's wallscreen. She looked away from the display of winking colored lights and smiled. "Yeah," she said. "They really laid it on. But I thought, if it makes them happy. It's not as if I'm going to *do* any of this stuff."

She looked to him for his response. He looked away.

Martha did not expect to be making that west coast trip. She expected to die here, in the hotel. She had told him that months before: *"It's where it ends. Where it all ends."*

Martha expected to die. And by now Duke knew enough to believe her predictions. But he didn't believe this one, wasn't yet ready to believe it. He continued to hope that this one time she would be wrong.

* * * * *

Martha screened her video-messages.

"Martha, I need to see you. Really."

The man on the screen was pale, beyond fashionably pale, sickly pale. His gray hair was short but wild, and his eyes were wilder, dancing from side to side. He was sweating visibly. His voice shook. He clawed at his face with his fingernails as he spoke.

"Who is that?" Duke asked, looking over her shoulder. "Is that . . ."

Martha, still intent on the screen, nodded without turning her head. "Yeah," she said. "Abe."

Abe Levett. Martha's original manager. The one who had discovered her—if anyone really "discovered" a Martha Nova—and guided her to the top.

It had been years since Duke had heard anything of Abe Levett.

"I've got . . . a business proposition," Levett was saying, uncertainly. "We have some business we need to discuss." He licked his lips. "Really. So call me, Martha."

This was not the Levett Duke remembered. The one he remembered had been loud, aggressive, hyped-up, often flat-out obnoxious; not this pallid, halting shadow.

"Whatever happened to him?" Duke asked.

But he knew what had happened to Abe Levett. For a while, it had been the talk of the business. Martha and Levett had fallen out after he had signed her up to play Vegas. Martha had wanted to keep touring the country and playing to her real fans; Levett had wanted to go after the big bucks. Or so the story ran.

Soon after that, Levett was history. Martha fired him, and he had had some kind of breakdown. Martha had found a new manager, but Levett had never found another Martha Nova. Perhaps he had never even tried.

Duke had heard some of this from a woman who sung backup for Martha in Vegas that year. "Horrible gig. You could see Martha hated every minute of it. Abe had set it up, but he spent the whole time complaining. Screaming at Martha, ranting at the band, he was like in this constant *rage.* Then one night I look out the window of my hotel room and I see him running right into the traffic. Cars zipping all around him, but he doesn't seem to see them. Major freak-out."

Martha had frozen the message display.

"Abe had a . . . panic attack," she told him. "That's what the doctors called it, after they admitted him to the hospital."

Martha had never talked to him about what had happened to Abe. And he had never asked. He had sensed it was a touchy subject for her. But now she seemed to want to talk about it. "What set it off?"

"I did," she said. "*I* set it off. Abe became deathly afraid of me."

"Why?"

"I think you know why, Robert. Because I *am* scary, if you take what I say seriously. Abe never wanted to do that. But one day he couldn't deny it any longer. But he couldn't handle it either. So he broke down completely."

"And you never saw him again?"

"When they first admitted him, but not after that. The doctors thought I was a disturbing influence on him. And later, when he was well enough to have a say in the matter, so did Abe."

"But he wants to see you now."

He nodded towards the wall panel.

Martha unfroze the display. The screen darkened, lightened, and they were looking at Levett again. "Martha, I really need to talk with you . . ." And again. "It's real important . . ." And again. Each time wilder, more frantic.

"What do you think he wants?" Duke asked, when they had viewed the last of the messages.

"To see me."

"But why now?"

"You might say that we have some unfinished business.

"Are you going to call him back?"

"No. But I'll see him at the party."

"You invited him?"

"No. But he'll be there."

"You're not worried he'll pull some number?"

"*Que sera sera,*" she said.

It was of her favorite expressions, and the title of one of the few songs by other songwriters that she ever performed. *Que sera sera.* That just about summed up her attitude to life.

The singer's child, Daniel, looked up from his home-schooling work. "I remember Abe."

"You must have been, what, two years old?" Duke said. "And you remember Abe Levett?"

"I remember him," the child insisted. "I remember how he ran. Into the heat, into the traffic. Down among the cars, hard white and smooth, under the signs that burned all night. I remember how he ran."

* * * * *

Duke surfed the music playing on the webchannels, flipping restlessly from one station to the next. The music was terrible. The music was wretched, strangled, desperate. The music was of its time.

He looked from the wallscreen to the singer's child, who was playing on the floor, painstakingly building up towers out of hundreds of small magnetized plastic components, then blasting them down with the accompanying wrecking kit. In some ways the child seemed almost backward, socially and psychologically. In others he was almost unbelievably precocious.

"Hey Daniel," Duke said. "You want to watch the wallscreen with me? You want to watch the ship come down from Mars?"

The child considered. "I don't know if that would be very interesting. It isn't going to crash or anything."

He completed his latest construction project, then destroyed it again. "All right," he said. "Let's watch the ship come down from Mars."

* * 2 * *

Denning had dreamed of the fire, dreamed of it in deep slow dreams that oozed with heavy colors, dreams that surrounded him and enveloped him and cradled him and carried him through his most terrible nights. He had dreamed of the fire, and now, as the ship began to tumble, he remembered his dreams.

"I'm in a spin," he told Control.

"Say again?"

"I said, I'm in a spin."

The heat increased, became unbearable, as unshielded surfaces caught fire in the terrible friction.

I have failed, he thought, failed reentry.

He fell. Slipping and sliding, he fell. Through the web, through the space and through the time, he fell, all the way down, he descended to earth.

And woke, once again, screaming in his bunk.

* * * * *

He had first dreamed of the fire years ago, back when he was a shuttle pilot. He had dreamed it again, in the days and months that followed, until finally, mercifully, it had faded away.

Now it was back. Now, as the moment of reentry came closer and closer to hand, he dreamed it almost every night.

Once, on the way out to Mars, he had told Mike Wyatt, his mission commander, about the dream. They had been sitting around, talking, the way they used to do, before Wyatt became impossible to talk to. Wyatt had been telling him about a dream of his own, in which they had arrived on Mars and Mars was like heaven, green grass and trees and running water and gentle sunlight and houses made of crystal, Mars was like heaven or maybe just California, the way California used to be before the drought.

Then Denning had told him about his own dream. It had been a relief, finally, just to blurt it out.

"What do you think it means?" he had asked.

Wyatt had lifted one long elegant black finger and stroked his graying goatee. "You ever tell one of the agency shrinks about this dream?"

"What do you think I am, nuts?"

Wyatt nodded. "They would have thought you were afraid. Are you afraid, Jake?"

"No." He shook his head vigorously. "Not at all."

"Not at all?" Wyatt echoed, a faint grin playing around the corners of his mouth. "You must be a very brave man, Jake. Braver than me. But okay, you're not afraid. So what is it? You think you're psychic?"

"Psychic? I don't believe in that stuff at all."

"Some say everyone is psychic . . . if they allow themselves to be. That the future is there for all of us to see, if we can bear to look."

"You think I'm seeing the future? My future?"

"You're seeing *a* future. Maybe the one that's going to happen to you, maybe not. There are many futures, Jake, it all depends on how we live, how we choose."

"But if it's my future, it could be yours, too. You would die right along with me."

"You see me in this dream of yours?"

"No, but you would have to be there. Because this is for sure my last trip."

Wyatt had been unperturbed.

"I die in every future you could imagine, Jake. And so do you. The only question is how. And when."

* * * * *

Denning lay on his bunk until his heart ceased racing, then got up and crossed the tiny cabin to the bathroom.

At least he no longer had to queue for his first piss of the morning. There were some advantages to solitude.

Afterwards he breakfasted, hardly tasting the food, the same breakfast he had been eating for three years now: cereal with reconstituted dried milk, grayish lumpy scrambled eggs from powder, lukewarm coffee. Oh, it had been a long three years, very long.

Then it was time for his exercise period. He did not really feel like exercising. He could perhaps postpone it until after lunch, or even forego it altogether. At this point it would hardly make any difference. And yet the idea did not merit serious consideration.

Early on, Denning had decided to stick to his schedule, stick to it all the way down the line. Stick to a schedule and you always knew where you were, who you were. Get too loose, let the schedule slip, drift off aimlessly into unstructured time, and you could all too easily end up like Chang, end up completely flipped out. Because out here, way out here, crawling along through interplanetary space, a man needed something he could hold on to. And he was so very close to home now, it would be tragic if he were to slip up now.

One day, he thought. *One day.*

Mechanically, he worked out on the treadmill. Dutifully, he played the aerobics disc and went through the rest of the sequence.

He was in pretty good shape, all things considered. But he knew that the return to full gravity, as compared to the feeble artificial gravity of the ship, was still going to come as a shock.

After exercising, he sat in the pilot's chair. On the way out, this had been Wyatt's chair. Denning had been rated number-two pilot. Now there were no other choices.

He swiveled in the chair to scan the instrument panels. Everything, as always, appeared to be functioning correctly. The only major systems failure on this ship had been confined to its softest hardware, to the crew itself.

He got up, stretched, scratched his head. He began to pace up and down on the narrow floor of the cabin. Five paces and turn. Five more paces and turn . . . It was not the most interesting walk. On the way out to Mars, when this ship had held all three of them, it had been terribly cramped. Even alone, as he was now, Denning found its confinement oppressive. A man could use a little more space.

But that, as the boys and girls back at the Agency would be quick to point out, was the whole purpose of the exercise: space. Getting it and keeping it. That was the whole philosophical and economic imperative underpinning this entire mission. That was what had locked Denning and his dear departed buddies into this flying tin can and propelled them in a preprogrammed arc towards the miserable wastelands of Mars: space. Nothing less.

Oh, it was ironic, it was certainly very ironic. Denning had reflected often on such ironies during the long lonely hours of this voyage home. He had thought many deep thoughts, engaged in many fascinating speculations about the nature of infinity. And very soon now he would set them all down in his memoirs for the enlightenment of humanity. Memoirs which, he had frequently calculated, ought to pull in at least ten million bucks, what with first serialization and digital representations. Which was only the beginning.

Nearly home, he thought. So nearly home. If he cared to turn on the viewscreen he would be able to see Earth spinning around and around the ship, a ball of dirt steadily gathering size. But he knew that the sight would only make him dizzy.

He could kill the ship's spin, slip back into freefall for a while. But that wouldn't do. Zero-gee played hell with muscle tone, and he needed to stay in condition. And he hated how it made him look: all the fluids collecting in his upper body, bloating his face, distorting it to the point where he failed to recognize himself in a mirror. But what he hated most of all was how floating in free fall made him *feel,* like some sort of ghost. More than ever, now, he needed to hold on to some feeling of his own substance, existence.

Almost three years. And quite alone these last four months of the way home. Plenty of time to think. Too much time, really.

He had thought a great deal about Chang, whether or not he had been right to kill Chang. But that was over with now. He had resolved that question to his own satisfaction. There was no doubt about it. It had been a matter of self-defense. There was nothing else to be done.

Chang had needed killing, he had gone out of his way to provoke it. Denning had put up with all the screaming, all the ranting. He had hardly even flinched when Chang smashed the radio. But when Chang tried to fuck with the navigational program, that was really too much.

* * * * *

He had woken suddenly in the middle of the night, jarred awake by a dream that instantly receded from him, a dream of flying to Earth on beams of light. He had woken to find the cabin lights on full luminance.

"Chang," he said, "turn off the fucking . . . ." And then he saw Chang sitting at the control deck. The graphic on the screen showed the ship's course.

"Hey," he shouted, scrambling from his bunk. "What do you think you're doing?"

Chang swiveled in his seat. "Cold," he said. "I'm cold." His teeth were chattering.

Denning didn't need to look at the environmental readouts to know that the temperature in the cabin was its usual just-this-side-of-stifling 25° Celsius. It didn't matter how high he turned up the heat, because Chang was always cold. He had been complaining about it ever since Mars. It was as though the cold of the planet had seeped into his bones and chilled him right through.

"Going to warm us up," Chang said. He sat back, so that Denning could see the new program he had entered.

"My God," Denning said. "The sun . . ."

"Going to fly to the sun," Chang agreed. He grinned. "Heart of the sun."

"You don't want to do this. What you want is to get back to Earth." He took a step closer. "Earth, Doug. Think about that. Blue sky, running water. Animals, fish, children. Fast cars. And women, women everywhere."

Usually, when Chang got into one of his moods, Denning could talk him out of it.

Chang shook his head. "The sun," he said, through his chattering teeth. "Going to the sun."

"We don't have the fuel. Eventually we'll spiral in, but the food will run out long before . . ."

He realized that he was babbling. And that Chang was paying him no attention. "Listen Doug . . ." he began again.

And then he looked carefully into Chang's eyes and saw that it was hopeless. There would be no reasoning with Chang. Chang was beyond reason, and he was never coming back.

Denning took another step towards the control deck. Chang raised his arm in warning. He was holding a screwdriver. The point looked unnaturally sharp. "No closer," he said.

They were unevenly matched, even without the weapon. Chang was younger and stronger. And crazier.

"You're going to kill us," Denning said. He clenched his fists helplessly by his sides.

Then he had sensed a strange flickering across his retina. And he had known what he had to do. *You must kill him. You must kill him, or you will die with him. You must kill him and then you must return to Earth.*

Until that moment, strangely enough, it had not seemed so terribly important to him whether or not he made it back to Earth. But now he felt the strength well up in him, the sudden and surprising strength. And he was able to arouse himself at last from his long torpor, from the terrible paralysis that had gripped his will ever since they had lost Wyatt.

With no sense of transition he was across the cabin, gripping Chang's arm, wrenching it until he released his weapon. Then he was gripping Chang's neck, squeezing the air from his lungs.

The strength had carried him through what had to be done—killing Chang, dragging his body into the air lock, ejecting it into the blackness outside—until he could at last slump back exhausted in his bunk.

Denning had never killed a man before, not with his bare hands. He had been on bombing runs, sure, back in the terror wars. But that was different, that was just hitting the target on the screen, like one more simulation game. Putting your hands around a person's neck and choking the life out of him, that was something else again. He was surprised at how easy it was.

Afterwards, lying alone in the cabin, the whole thing began to seem like some weird dream. It was hard for him to believe that he had really done such a thing. But Chang was gone, there was no denying that. He had been here yesterday, and the day before that, screaming and shouting or else just slumped in some zombie-like trance. He had been here, and now he was gone.

Really, there had been no choice. He had done the right thing, killing Chang. And surely they would see that back in Houston. They would agree that he had acted in the best interests of the mission, of which he was the *pro tem* commander.

He had assumed that status months before, after Wyatt had gone off chasing shadows in the frigging Martian night with only four hours worth of oxygen strapped to his back.

It was really too bad about Wyatt. They had been good buddies once. They had been buddies until Wyatt had turned morose, and then crazy, and taken that long last walk. Looking for Martians, Chang had suggested, and probably that was right. Certainly it was difficult to explain it any other way.

Wyatt gone, floating off into the mystic. Chang lost, too: fragmented, shattered, broken in some unfixable way even before his death. Leaving only him. The last survivor, the lone hero. Jake Denning: hero. The man who looked infinity in the face and never blinked: spat right in infinity's eye, in point of fact. The unshakable Jake Denning.

Won't they be surprised, he thought, back on Earth. Won't they be surprised to see me?

They knew, of course, that the ship was coming home, following its preprogrammed cycle. But they had no information as to the status of its passengers, not since Chang had smashed the radio.

Almost home, he thought. And I hope my wife is dead. She ought to be, the way she was drinking before I left.

What a self-sacrificing bastard he had been. Six months going out, without even a fourth for bridge. A year and a half on that dirt heap, all the time dying for a woman or a drink or a chocolate bar or anything at all except another mouthful of dust. Another seven months coming home, at first with a madman, and then all alone. But soon it would all begin to pay off.

In his mind he reviewed yet again his long-awaited homecoming: the parades, the speeches, the dinners, all the riches and fame coming his way. It was a very pleasant fantasy, one that he worked through often, changing a detail here and a detail there, shaping it, perfecting it. What he would say to the President and what the President would say to him. What he would eat, and what he would drink. Which screen stars he would fuck, and in what rank order, specifying positions. Oh yes, the possibilities were almost endless.

* * 3 * *

In times of trouble and moral panic, when the conventional narratives organizing personal experience collapse, alternate mythological systems spring to the forefront, drawing upon ideas and archetypes embedded within the collective unconscious. We see an outpouring of the world-mind, an eruption of psychic energy, a reawakening of the archaic imagination. Images of death and transfiguration confront us: angels, goddesses, monsters, UFOs, crop circles.

This pattern repeated itself throughout the second half of the twentieth century, from the great 'flying saucer' scare of the 1950s to the apocalyptic rock culture of the 1960s, the upsurge of Gaian Consciousness in the 1980s, and the pre-millenial panic of the '90s, and has cascaded down without pause into our own century.

The emergence of Martha Nova and the so-called "Nova Children," who follow her every word as a prophecy of the days to come, is only the latest example. Her influence, however, has been vastly magnified by our own deepening crisis, providing as it does fertile ground for all kinds of signs, portents and occult prophecies.

History shows us that prophets tend to appear in periods of cultural disintegration, whether as priests, artists or musicians. Like other entertainers before her who were hailed as "superstars," but on a far greater scale, Martha Nova has become the repository of projection and identification, reflecting and confirming our hopes and fears both for ourselves and for the broader society.

(Murray H. Snow: "Martha Nova and the Children: A Preliminary Analysis," Journal of Social and Cultural Change, June 2019*).*

* * * * *

In the streets outside the hotel, the Children waited. They had been waiting, some of them, for weeks, since the first hint that the singer would be coming to this city. Some were as young as eight or nine, many more in their teens. Others were older, and a few might have been the singer's grandparents.

The Children were dressed, mostly, in the long white cotton robes that Martha Nova had once favored on stage, hoods drawn up to keep out the December chill.

At first there had been only a few of them scattered along the avenue, humming her songs softly as they maintained their vigil. They wandered back and forth, peering hopefully into the windows of arriving limousines, trying to snatch a glimpse past the wall of security guards who blocked the entrance to the hotel. They watched the giant display screens go up along the street in preparation for the party. They huddled for shelter from the wind and the rain under the tattered awnings of boarded-up buildings. At night, when the curfew came down, they would melt away, or else be picked up by police patrols as possible runaways.

But as the days went by, there were more and more of them, streaming into the city from across the country, until the sidewalks were crammed with the Children. The police would move them on, but they would come back again and again. And in the end there were just too many of them. The police had given up trying to keep the sidewalks clear, given up trying to enforce the curfew laws. Now the Children waited by day and night.

The media called them Nova Children, after the name of the one for whom they waited. It was not how they usually referred to themselves. They were only the Children.

* * * * *

The Children waited in the streets. Kevin waited with them. He was fifteen years old, and he had been listening to Martha Nova's music nearly as long as he could remember. He heard it now, in his head, as he stood shivering in front of the hotel, waiting.

He had lived, until the previous week, in the giant condo arcology that was New Brooklyn. He had never set foot in Manhattan before, and the city awed him. Many of the buildings were impossibly ancient, fifty or even a hundred years old, ancient and grimy under oppressive gray skies.

In New Brooklyn, everything was new. There was no sky, only the great glass roof of the mall to which everything else—the condo, school and office buildings, the sports arena and swimming pool and indoor golf course—connected via a labyrinth of pedestrian walkways. You could spend months inside the complex without ever setting foot into the world outside. There was no reason to. Everything you could possibly want could be found within its walls. Everything except Martha Nova.

The city was old and vast and open. Within it Kevin felt invisible. There were no videocam eyes, scanning you from every angle from the moment you left your apartment; no MentHealth workers pushing their pills at you, itching to diagnose you as antisocial and put you away in one of their Recovery Centers. In the city you could lose yourself easily, as Kevin had lost himself this past week.

* * * * *

The day before he left New Brooklyn, Kevin had cut school. He did that often, sometimes for weeks on end.

Kevin was enrolled in the Microsoft franchise high school within the condo arcology. The new laws, aimed at postponing youth unemployment, required all students to remain in school until their eighteenth birthday. But truancy was rampant, and never pursued. It was enough for the teachers to cope with the students who did attend.

Kevin had spent the day with his friends, Willie and Diane and Bill and Franklin and Jeanine, amusing themselves as best they could.

Kevin and his friends were bored in school. Often they were bored outside of it too, bored with themselves and with each other. But they knew that it would not be for much longer. They knew from Martha that the end was coming very soon, that they would at last be freed. Knowing that, they were able to wait.

In the meantime, there were things they liked to do. They liked to wander through the mall. They liked to examine the products in the store windows that promised to change their lives. They liked to sunbathe under the lights beside the artificial sea, to bodysurf in the simulated waves. They liked to play crazy golf in the indoor amusement park. They liked the gaming arcades and the virtual worlds and the fast-food restaurants.

But wherever they went, they were hassled by security guards. No more than four juveniles were allowed together in the public areas. Larger groups were permitted in the food courts, but not for very long. And even when the guards were not around, you were still being scanned by surveillance cameras.

So they had retreated to Willie's apartment. It was a favored hangout because of the full-wall screen in the media room, and because Willie's mother was rarely home during the day. She was a manager of building systems in one of the office towers.

Willie had dialed up some pizza and popcorn from the kitchen console and then they had sat around watching some of his Martha Nova videos. Willie had an excellent collection; he traded with other collectors around the country.

"All Saint's Eve, 2012," he said. "Trinity Church, Toronto. One of the earliest known Martha shows . . ."

It was an amateur video, murky, clumsily shot. But they were entranced all the same, watching Martha's face caught in the candlelight, listening to her voice echoing from the walls, transforming first the church and then Willie's mother's media room into a deep, dark cave where they could watch the future play out in the shadows on the wall.

"She's coming, you know," Franklin said, when the disc was finished. "Coming to New York. Real soon."

"You've been telling us that for weeks," Diane said.

"Well, it's firmed up now."

Franklin cruised the music industry boards on the web, using stolen account numbers, picking up scraps of news that he exchanged with other online Martha Nova fans.

"She's been in Nashville," he said, "putting down an album. Now she's coming here to promote it. The album is all new songs. I'm going to get the track listing tomorrow, from someone who knows someone who works at the studio."

"A new album," Diane said. "It's hard to believe."

They had grown so used to the old songs. It was hard to imagine new ones.

"She always said that she'd come back," Jeanine said. "When the time was right."

"You know what this means?" Franklin asked. "This is the end. Or something very close to it."

They sat in silence for a moment, savoring the thought.

"I hope so," Jeanine said. "I really hope so."

* * * * *

Afterwards, they had chewed some shrooms. Franklin knew a guy who grew them in the den of his apartment. Or anyway he had grown them, until he got busted by MentHealth enforcers. They had trashed his mushroom farm and hauled him off to a Recovery Center. Franklin would need to find a new supplier, once his stash ran out. But then, maybe it wouldn't run out, not now, not with the end so close at hand.

They had listened to an audio of Martha, a copy of a dub of a set of alternate takes from her second album. Kevin had rested his head in

Jeanine's lap and closed his eyes and he had seen Martha Nova's face, smiling out over a great grassy plain. And the sun loomed enormous and low, swinging from one side of the sky to the other and back again . . .

And then he felt himself falling, as if into a dark whirlpool, with colored lights flashing harshly at him, and a voice in his ear, Martha's voice maybe, but not Martha's words, not any of her words that he knew, and he knew them all. *I want to stop time* . . . crooned the voice.

His eyes jerked open, and he sat up, startling Jeanine.

"You okay?" she asked.

But he was already on his way to the bathroom to vomit.

* * * * *

Kevin's mother was out when he got home the next morning. She was often out—she had a lover ten floors above—and even when she was home she did not pay much attention to his comings and goings. Her MentHealth worker kept her on such heavy downers that she did not notice much of anything.

Kevin's father, a data entry manager in a bank processing center, had been killed in one of the great computer riots ten years before. Kevin and his mother lived in reasonable comfort on the proceeds of his father's company insurance policy. Accidental death in company service paid quadruple the face value of the policy.

Kevin programmed himself a plate of waffles and soy bacon and flipped up today's school agenda on to the kitchen wall panel. Games, Comparative Religion, Deconstruction 101. Special of the day in the cafeteria was a choice of cheeseburger or vegetarian chili with salad. Kevin had told Jeanine he would probably see her at lunch, but he wasn't really up for it, not for the chili again.

There was a tickler icon in the corner of the screen, a little toon gorilla waggling its finger. Kevin pointed his finger at it to activate it.

Kevin had been using this same icon set since he had been a little kid. He knew he ought to get a cooler set, but he was fond of the gorilla.

"Remember," said the toon gorilla, in its dopey voice. "MentHealth tonight at six."

"Shit," Kevin said.

Kevin saw his MentHealth worker twice a month, in the big shiny Mental Health Administration field office in the mall. Her name was Mary Whitestone. She was thin and dark, with a nerve in her face that sometimes twitched. "Wiggly" Whitestone, the kids called her.

Mostly when Kevin went to see her, she would ask him a bunch of dumb questions about his life and how he felt about it, or make him take tests on a touchscreen terminal. But sometimes—this was the part he really hated—she would make him put his head in the hood of a machine that shone lights in his eyes. It seemed to him that music played in his ears while his head was in the machine, and voices spoke to him, although afterwards he could not recall the music or the words.

After these sessions, his ears would be ringing, and he would feel woozy for hours.

Nearly all Kevin's friends had to see MentHealth workers. Most complained about the pointless questions and the stupid tests. But none of them were familiar with the machine with the hood and the lights.

"Must be that you're crazier than anyone else," Willie had suggested.

Eventually he had summoned up his courage and asked Mary Whitestone about it.

"It's for data collection purposes," she had told him, her face twitching powerfully. "We're tracking correlations between personality and retinal formations."

"But why me?"

"Random sampling. Are you refusing to cooperate?"

He had shaken his head vigorously. Noncooperation was a prime symptom of Antisocial Personality Syndrome. Everyone knew that. You had to know it, if you wanted to stay out of a Recovery Center.

"Good," she had said. And then he had placed his head in the hood and let the lights make him woozy once again. And afterwards, as always, she had handed him his pills, the ones he was supposed to take every day.

Kevin's pills were a different color from the ones his mother took, but the effect was the same. They numbed you out. That was okay, sometimes. It was even useful when you got the dread, the mall dread, that awful wrenching slip-sliding dread that could hit you anywhere, any time. But it made it hard to hear the music. Usually Kevin left the pills alone, flushing them down the toilet when too many accumulated.

Knowing that he had to see Mary Whitestone that night cast a pall over the entire day. Maybe he would just crawl into bed and watch some ancient sitcoms. The building pulled in hundreds of channels from its array of satellite dishes. They got the *Seinfeld* channel, *Friends Forever, Always South Park,* dozens more.

And then the urgent news icon had started to flicker on the kitchen screen, a toon paperboy holding up an antique broadsheet newspaper. "Read all about it," the toon said.

It was probably for his mother. Some hot news item about a soap-star screen queen. His mother liked to keep up on the lives of daytime screen stars. If one of them killed herself, or got married again, or rushed her poodle to the pet hospital, Kevin's mother wanted to know that. Her own life was so pointless and boring that she needed to fill up her head with such stuff, even though it only made her feel worse.

Then he realized that the news flash was for *him.*

"Big news for Kev Moore," the toon said. "Big, big news."

* * * * *

The toon did not lie. It *was* big news. The news report confirmed what Franklin had said. Martha Nova was returning from a long period in seclusion. She had recorded a new album, to be released to stores and download portals on New Year's Day.

The news report also showed how the Children had begun to gather in front of a great old hotel to wait for her. Her record company would not confirm reports that Martha was already staying there, or soon would be. But the Children interviewed in front of the hotel were convinced that she *was* there. And Kevin had known immediately that he would join them.

He did not wait for his mother to return. Neither did he think to leave a note. He could read well enough, screens and street signs and video menus, but he almost never wrote.

Nor did he call any of his friends. They would come, too, in time, or not. That was their choice: he had made his. He left no message and he called no one. He simply walked out the door and made his way to the hotel.

As for his appointment at the MentHealth office, he gave it not a second thought.

Kevin knew how it would go: When he failed to show up, Mary Whitestone would notify MentHealth enforcers. They would call his home and his school, then initiate a broader search, first within the arcology, then outside it. When they found him, they would drag him up in front of the local Mental Health Tribunal. And he would be on his way into the black hole of a Recovery Center. He had seen plenty of kids go in over the years. Few came back. Those who did return were not the same.

Kevin knew all this, but he did not think about it. His fear of what MentHealth could do to him was overwhelmed by a more urgent imperative.

Before he left, he took some money from the drawer in his mother's night stand. She always kept money there. And he took something else. He took the gun he had seen and passed over so many times before. It had been his father's gun. Kevin could not remember it ever being fired.

He was not sure why he had taken the gun. He did not believe in violence. He was one of the Children. But he had seen the gun, and without thinking about it he had stuffed it in the pocket of his robes. It was there still, banging against his side as he walked. He did not even know if it worked.

But he knew that it would become clear to him soon, why he had taken the gun. And in the meantime, outside the hotel, he waited. He waited for Martha.

* * * * *

There was a twenty-foot high advertising display screen on the vacant lot across from the hotel. Martha's record company had erected it to publicize her new album. Soon it would show her first performance in years. For now it was playing a mixture of ads, music videos and newsbites.

Kevin watched the screen for news of Martha Nova.

"Any comments, Mr. King? Mr. King?"

Up on the screen, a videographer was standing on the sidewalk in front of a large office building, waving an audio feed in the face of a silver-haired man.

"Comments on what?"

A caption identified the silver-haired man as Darren King, Director of the Mental Health Administration. Kevin had seen this man on the newsbites before. He was the second-most important person in the country, the newsbites often said. Maybe even the first—Kevin's friend Franklin thought so. "That crazy bastard King," Franklin would say. "He's the guy running everything, not that asshole President. And he's going to lock us all away, you'll see. There won't be anybody left outside."

Up on the screen, Darren King feinted to the left, then the right, trying to get past the videographer to the limo that waited at the curb. But the videographer hung in with him. "Your comments on the return of Martha Nova to the music business."

"Martha Nova . . ." King said. "An unhealthy influence. Morbid, self-pitying, catastrophically gloomy. She does her best to bring out the worst in today's youth. I think you know how we feel about Martha Nova."

"And if she's about to resume her career?"

"That's unconfirmed."

"But if it's true . . ."

"We would view that as an extremely unhealthy development. We simply can't afford a return to these extremes of youth cultism, just when things are starting to return to an even keel. It's time for the people who run the popular music industry to show some leadership here, rather than blindly pursuing the bottom line . . ."

"So there is a new Martha Nova album coming?"

King waved his arms in irritation. "Why talk about Martha Nova? Why not talk about something positive for a change? The suicide rate is down. Homelessness, down. Illegal drug use, down. Down, down, down. And mental health is on its way *up.*"

"But what if Martha Nova does come back?"

King's face flushed with anger. "We'll deal with her, don't worry about that. One way or another, Martha Nova's doomsaying days are *over.*"

* * * * *

"Now that you're mine / I want to stop time"

As Kevin stood shivering on the street outside the hotel, the words buzzed in his head like lines from some half-familiar song. It was the same song he had flashed on at Willie's, just before he had thrown up.

It was not definitely one of Martha's songs. Maybe it was some other song he had seen on the videos, or a poem he had heard in school.

"Live this one moment with you baby / Until eternity"

Colored lights sparkled in his eyes, and he felt suddenly dizzy. For a moment, he saw Mary Whitestone's face, twitching at him. He put his hand on the cold metal base of a nearby streetlight to steady himself.

"I want to keep your love forever / Send you to eternity."

"You all right?" asked a young girl standing beside him.

"I'm fine," he said. "Thanks."

His vision had cleared. The song, or whatever it was, had gone.

He took his hand off the cold base of the streetlight. He realized that his other hand was in his pocket, holding the gun. He took that hand out of his pocket and rubbed it against the other one to warm it up.

"Just fine," he said.

The young girl nodded, and then turned away from him, to look back towards the hotel.

Kevin, too, resumed his vigil. He went back to waiting.

Waiting for Martha.

✶ ✶ PART ONE ✶ ✶

Expecting to Fly

* * 4 * *

Levett, her Rasputin, her Epstein, her personal manager, grows animated as he recalls the day he discovered the brightest star in today's entertainment galaxy. His short, powerful looking arms stab out like pistons from his stocky body to punctuate his words.

"How did I meet her? You could say that I stumbled into her. I was ice skating—ice skating was real big that year, especially with the college crowd—I was skating in the city square, and I just stumbled into her.

"Now I was a very good skater. In all due modesty, I have to say that I was good. I wouldn't normally have stumbled. Seeing her, looking at her, that was what made me stumble.

"She had it, all right, she had that quality. I don't know what to call it, even now. Star quality? More than that, much more, that doesn't even begin to describe the effect she had on me. There never was a star like Martha Nova.

"Her eyes. People always talk about her eyes. But that isn't it. I mean, granted, her eyes are extraordinary. But it's not just her eyes, it's the way she sees. Her whole way of looking at the world.

"It's hard to find the right words to explain it. Detached? Yes. Amused? For sure. But it was more than those things. She had this whole quality of vision. Like she was seeing everything for the first time. Like she was some kind of alien who had just landed on earth and was

still looking around and observing everything, just checking things out, you know, not making any comment at all. Just looking around.

"That was the way she always was. That was her whole attitude towards life. She'd come from this very small town and moved on to the big city and she was just amazed at everything she saw and heard.

"And I knew that she was something special. In that very first moment. Long before I ever heard her sing . . ."

(From *"The Martha Nova Story,"* Sandra S. Lanski, Starline House, New York, 2015)

* * * * *

On the ice, Levett flew.

He loved to skate. He loved that feeling of irresistible motion. He loved to be doing something right, for once.

He was flunking out of business school that year, because he could no longer bring himself to believe in the great and pointless charade that the course would lead to any sort of job. There were no jobs in this year of 2012: not for business students or law students or plumbers or electricians, there were no jobs at all.

Recently he had been cutting classes almost every afternoon to come here when the ice was less crowded, although it was still more crowded than he would have liked. There were a lot of people with nothing better to do than to skate away the afternoon.

At first Levett had come skating with friends. Now he mostly skated alone. He had never found a partner who could match his grace. Off the ice it was usually the reverse.

Skating for him was yoga, it was Zen, it was hypnosis. He would fall into a trance-like state in which he seemed to fly, to float above the surface of the ice, his mind taking temporary leave of his body. He never stumbled. Except the day he met Martha.

She was skating towards him, and he was checking her out, how she looked, how she moved. Their eyes locked for a moment. And he felt a strange dizziness, almost a vertigo, as though he was looking down upon his life, and the profoundly different turn it was about to take.

And then he was falling directly into her path.

* * * * *

Great way to meet women, Levett thought. Falling at their feet. But whatever worked.

After she had helped him up they had skated together for a while, and skated perfectly, two people moving as one. Now it was time to move things along.

"You want to get a hot chocolate in the Eaton Centre?" Levett asked, nodding towards the mall down the street from the rink.

"I'm not so good in malls," she said. "Although I'm getting better."

"Not so good? How do you mean?"

"I get . . . nauseous, anxious. It's all the people. I can't help feeling what they're feeling."

"Which is what?"

"I don't know. Tired, aggravated, angry. Or else just sad, depressed."

He stared hard at her for a moment. "Are you telling me you can read people's minds?"

"No, but I can feel them."

I can feel them?

Levett felt a tingle of alarm. She's probably nuts, he thought, like my mother. Next she's going to tell me that she can read my aura.

Maybe, he thought, I should just walk away right now.

But instead he said, "How about that place across the street?"

* * * * *

Now he was sitting across the table from her in the restaurant, looking into her eyes.

Your eyes are beautiful, he wanted to say, except that it would sound like a particularly dumb line. And it was not really true. It did not do justice to her eyes to describe them as beautiful.

"I never do that," he said. "Fall like that."

"But if you hadn't, we wouldn't have met."

He wondered if that was true. Would he have talked to her anyway? Maybe not. He was depressed about school; his last relationship had ended badly. If he hadn't fallen, he might just have gone on skating, then gone home to wonder what he had missed.

They talked freely, easily, as they sat sipping their hot chocolate, as if they were already old friends. Martha had been talking to him that way since she helped him up from the ice, laughing away his clumsy apologies. She had a way about her, an ease with herself and with other people, that he envied.

She told him that she was from Kapuskasing. "It's a real small town."

That helped to explain it for him, how she was, at least partly. It was something he had noticed before about small-town people, that quality of knowing who you were because everyone else knew who you were. But it didn't explain all of it.

She had come to the city to study commercial art under a government program to mop up youth unemployment.

"Not that there are any jobs for commercial artists. It's all synthed now. But I like to draw, and play around with synth programs. And it was time for me to come to the city."

Later he would notice that she would often say that it was time for her to do this or that.

"Besides," she said, "I like to see music. There's a lot of music in this city, much more than back home."

They talked about music, discovering some tastes shared and some not. She mentioned that she sang herself.

"I promote shows at school," he said. "I should hear you play."

It was not a line, exactly. He did promote shows, it was one of the few things he did well. He knew what kind of music would fill a hall, how to balance out the booking fees and the rental costs against the probable gate, how to work the publicity, how to take care of every important detail.

"I'm always looking for new supporting acts."

It was unlikely that he would be able to use her. But he did want to hear her sing. He wanted to know everything there was to know about her.

* * * * *

She lived in a tiny third-floor studio in a large house that had been carved up into apartments. There was very little furniture: a table and a few chairs, a mattress on the bare wood floor, a compact sound system, an Indian bedspread on the wall, a pair of wrought-iron candlesticks, a cactus sitting on an ancient clanking hot-water radiator. But there was enough. Levett felt very calm in the room.

They sat at the table, as she played for him, picking out chords on a beat-up old electronic keyboard and singing in a high, clear voice.

The songs were almost all originals. Some of the tunes were momentarily reminiscent of other singers, but even these would soon twist off into entirely new directions.

Her lyrics were strong, almost too strong. They spoke of doom and despair, destruction and decay and pollution, burning cities and wasted lives. They should have been depressing, but in some strange way he found them exhilarating.

"Getting near," she sang, in what he recognized immediately as one of her most powerful songs. *"Getting near the end."* It was not so much a lament as a promise.

She was amazing, he thought.

It was possible, he knew, that his judgment was distorted by the fact that he was attracted to her. Ever since he had seen her on the ice, he had been thinking about making love to her. And yet, as she sang, that had begun to seem less important, or anyway less urgent. What was important was the music.

As she sang, he began to see his own future, at first vaguely, then in sharper and sharper detail. It was the future he had been looking for all this time, sitting in the classroom and staring out the window, thinking, plotting, planning, scheming. Musing on the poetry of money, the vectors of freedom. Looking for some way up out of the mud. Always he had stared through windows, searched for the way through.

He saw his future, which was to guide Martha to superstardom. And when she finished playing—for her last song she did an old Doris Day number, *Que Sera Sera,* a weird but wonderful little gem—he told her what he saw.

"Bigger than Helicopter Sam," he told her. "Bigger than Eminem, U2, the Beatles . . ." He felt high, soaring on some manic burst of energy, jabbering away. "Remember what I'm telling you. You don't believe it now, but I'm going to make it happen."

"I'll remember." She laughed. "All right Abe. Make it happen."

They shook hands on the deal.

Afterwards they made love on her mattress as the afternoon sun outside the window faded into night.

"That was nice," she said, stretching lazily. "That was very nice."

And it *was* nice, Levett thought. But at some level, he was disappointed. Martha had been affectionate, she had been responsive, she had clearly enjoyed herself. But a part of her had remained removed from him, some secret part he could not access and that he somehow sensed he never would.

* * * * *

"You want to know what it is I do to deserve all this?" Levett asks.

He waves his arms, as if to indicate his priceless art collection, his sculptures, his sunken bathtub with the solid gold handles, his tropical plant house, the multi-million-dollar mansion that holds these treasures and offers a breathtaking view over the canyon.

"I'll tell you what I do. I feel the changes. That's what I do. I'm an extremely sophisticated sensing mechanism. I feel these . . . movements out there. And I go with the flow."

(From *"The Martha Nova Story"*)

* * * * *

He went to see her perform in the basement of a bar near the university. Martha's appearance here had been publicized only by word of mouth, yet the room was packed. Already she had developed a following. In time, he thought, someone else would have discovered her, and perhaps they would known how to handle her. Perhaps.

The audience was enthralled with her, and Levett was enthralled right along with them. Which did not stop him from seeing what needed to be done.

"We have to fill out the sound. Synths, sound modules, samplers, wave programs . . ."

He took the remainder of his student loan and made a down payment on some secondhand equipment. They worked together to polish her act.

"You need stage clothes. How do you see yourself?"

She closed her eyes for a moment. "White. I see myself in white."

"Good," he said. "Purity. Blankness. Good. Now, about your name. We need to do something with your name."

Martha's family name was eastern European and unpronounceable.

"What did you have in mind?"

"I was thinking of Martha Nova."

He had been afraid she would object, but she accepted it readily. She seemed to trust his judgment completely.

"Martha Nova," she said, rolling the words on her tongue. "I like it, Abe."

She resisted him on one subject alone, her songwriting.

"I was thinking," he said. "You should write a song about nuclear war. People are freaking about it again, with all this shit going down in the Caucasus. And it would fit in nicely with everything else."

It was all over the news channels that month. One of the warlords on the fringes of the old Soviet empire had claimed control of some ancient ICBMs, and was using them to extort foreign aid.

Martha frowned. She shook her head. "I don't see it," she said. "I just don't see it."

* * * * *

He booked Martha as the opening act for a show at the college the following month.

"Bad idea," Tucker Williams said.

Tucker, a third-year physics major, was Levett's junior partner in promoting these events. Tucker organized the security, the sound system, the lighting, the backstage catering. He rarely ventured an opinion on Levett's choice of acts.

"You don't like her music?"

"I like it fine. In the right time and place."

Levett understood Tucker's doubts. Invariably, for these shows, he programmed bands: hardcore or triphop or postrock, but always bands. This was a time of the group rather than the individual performer. In the group there was power, or at least solidarity in powerlessness. No one wanted to be alone, to imagine themselves alone.

He understood Tucker's doubts, and to some extent he shared them. But he was not about to admit that.

"I haven't been wrong yet, have I?"

When he was younger, Levett would makes bets with friends on which songs would reach number one on the Hot Hundred. He had cleaned up. He had only to hear a new song once to decide its fate, and he was almost never wrong. It did not matter whether he liked the music or not. He felt himself to be a kind of human barometer, attuned at some deep level to popular taste.

Now he sensed that people were ready for Martha Nova.

But for all his careful preparation, all his belief in Martha, he feared disaster that night. The students, already half-blitzed on booze and downers, were in a raucous mood when Martha came out on stage. They were expecting the usual: a minor band to warm them up for the major band who would top the bill. They were expecting to find temporary oblivion in bone-crushing noise. They were not expecting a lone woman in a long white dress with a bank of computer equipment.

The booing and the hissing and the slow hand clapping began even as Martha moved towards the microphone. A bottle landed in front of her feet and skittered off across the stage. Another exploded to her left, sending glass flying all around her. And yet she did not flinch, or even glance down. She stepped up to the microphone and began to sing.

"You have to get her off, before she gets hurt," Tucker said.

Levett took a step towards the stage, then froze. He could not bring himself to end it. Martha looked so confident up there, so much in command. And he was not yet willing to admit that he had been wrong.

"One song," he said. "Let's give it one song. See what happens."

"It's going to take a miracle to turn this crowd around."

Levett did not believe in miracles. But he prayed for one all the same as he stood there in the wings, torn between hope and despair, willing Martha to succeed, anxiously scanning the crowd for the next piece of ugliness.

And then the mood of the crowd changed, the way he had hoped it would but not quite believed that it could. Slowly, slowly, as she sang, the booing and the hissing and the slow hand clapping began to die away. It did not die completely with the first song, or even the second, but by the time she reached the third she had them. And by the end of the set, they did not want to let her go.

For Levett, there was almost a dream-like quality to it. It was like watching some Hollywood biopic rather than actually being there. And later, of course, all this would be a biopic, the kind that he would once have sneered at on the late-late show.

That night the headlining band received a curiously muted reception. And the following month Martha Nova filled the university hall for a solo concert.

* * 5 * *

Entering the fifth-floor loft that had once been a garment factory but was now the offices of Levett Management, Martha found her manager sitting at his desk engrossed in a magazine.

"What are you reading?" she asked.

"About *you.*"

Levett showed her the cover of the magazine. It was called *New Light.* The cover artwork illustrated the feature article, "Ten Steps To Easy Astral Travel."

"They reviewed your album," he said. "Full-page spread."

He nodded towards the cartons stacked up against the wall. Each carton was packed with audio discs. They had recorded Martha's first album on a shoestring, duplicated it under easy terms from a desperate reproduction house, released it on their own private label.

No major retail chain would touch the disc, but Levett had sold it on consignment to independent record stores, book stores, health-food stores, boutiques, anyone who could be persuaded to take on a few copies. In two months, they had moved over five thousand copies.

He had also made the songs available, both individually and as a collection, through a number of indie web distributors. Already there had been over 10,000 downloads, huge numbers for a complete unknown.

"What do they say about it?"

"They love it," he said, frowning. "They're ecstatic about it."

"But?"

"But it's bullshit, what they've written. Nice bullshit, but bullshit all the same. It's not enough for them that you're a terrific singer. They've got to try to turn you into some kind of prophet."

"They call me a prophet?"

"Prophet, seer, visionary. Almost every other word. When they're not comparing you to William Blake or the Egyptian Book of the Dead. Like, you know that song where you sing *And the sun will dance in the sky . . .* ? They go on and on about how it relates to some ancient Mayan prophecy."

"Mayans are big this year," Martha said. "Because of the 2012 thing."

Levett snorted. "Don't tell me about any 2012 thing. It's just complete bullshit." There was general agreement among a wide spectrum of cultists and lunatics that December 21st, 2012, the end of the old Mayan long-count calendar, would mark the end of the world. "I mean, you don't believe that do you? That one day in December we'll wake up and the world will end, just like that?"

"No," she said. "I don't believe that."

"That's good," he said. "Because I've got big plans for you next year. And the year after that. And meanwhile we don't need this. We don't need to have you wrapped up in this mystic crap."

He tossed the magazine onto his desk.

"Anyway, soon they'll be reviewing you on *Entertainment Tonight.* And I'll be able to leave this stuff to a clipping service."

* * * * *

"You're her manager?" the record company executive asked, in the entrance hall of the club, as Levett held out his hand to shake.

"That's right," Levett said.

"You're the one who brought me down here?"

"Right."

"Jesus H. Christ."

"You have a problem with that?"

"How old are you anyway?" the executive asked. "Eighteen, nineteen?"

"I'm twenty-four," Levett said. "What difference does it make? This is a young people's business isn't it?"

"You got it wrong, kid. Young people, you *buy* the product. *We* make it."

The executive's name was Ken Winston. He was in his late forties. He had diamond-studded teeth and a gold nose-ring. He was wearing a purple Armani one-piece leisure-suit.

"I must have been crazy," Winston said, "coming down here to see some teeny folk singer."

"Martha is twenty-two," Levett said. "And she's not a folk singer. Didn't you listen to the album?"

"I played a few cuts, yeah. Sounds like folk to me, folk with a few samples and dance beats and maybe a little bit of a New Age vibe. But what's the difference what you call it? It's all poison. These days, you can't give it away."

"It's not folk or New Age. We're after a lot bigger audience than that. Martha transcends categories. You'll see."

"Transcends categories," the executive mimicked. "Next you're going to tell me she deconstructs them. I've dealt with college acts, kid. I've heard it all. And I always say, never again. But somehow you sucked me in anyway. So where do I sit?"

They sat at a table close to the stage of the club. Winston remained pokerfaced throughout. But he was watching, Levett knew. He was watching very carefully.

"You may have something here," Winston said, afterwards. "I don't know if it's anything we can use."

Levett shrugged. "If you can't, someone else will. We came to you first, because you're the biggest. But there are other companies."

"Not that many."

It was true enough. Conglomerization, globalization, the increasingly fierce battle for a piece of a fast-diminishing pie, had reduced the number of major players in the recording industry to a handful, meanwhile pushing the few remaining independents to the wall.

"I'm confident we can get a deal," Levett said.

"You're confident. It's good to be confident these days. I'm glad somebody is."

Winston appeared to think at length, although Levett knew that he had already made up his mind.

"I'm not supposed to make any new signings," he said. "Our last quarter results were so shitty. But maybe I could swing a development deal. Cut an audio single and a video, take it from there."

"An album," Levett said. "We want a contract for an album."

Winston laughed. "How about a five-year deal? You lost me, kid." He stood up.

"I don't think so," Levett said. "We want an album deal, with escalators tied to performance. We want a minimum of three videos. We want support for a national tour, just the major urban markets the first time out. We're willing to look at a three-album deal, but only if the bucks are there."

"You don't know what you're talking about," the executive said. "You don't know anything about this business."

"These are the figures I had in mind," Levett said, making notes on the back of a paper napkin and handing it over to Winston. "I'll need to hear from you by Tuesday. Then I start moving down the list."

"You're not listening to me, kid," Winston said. "You've got yourself a serious communications-skills deficit here. You really need a training course or something."

But he took the napkin. And a few days later, his assistant called back.

* * * * *

"You had a call from the Denver *Tribe,*" Tucker told him, as he came into the office.

"What the fuck is the Denver *Tribe?*" Levett asked.

"Weekly tabloid, kind of alternative."

"They want to do a feature on Martha?"

"It was a news guy that called."

"About what?"

"You remember that Senator who got iced?"

"McWhurter, you mean? Got shot down by a Nazi?"

Charismatic, controversial, a leading contender for his party's nomination, Ralph McWhurter had been gunned down in an Aspen ski boutique by a member of a far-right terrorist militia, in full sight of a local TV news crew. McWhurter had been pretty far to the right himself, but apparently not quite far enough.

"Actually the guy who did it was a nut," Tucker said. "Long history of psychiatric problems, discharged from hospital only two days before."

"Crazies everywhere. What about it?"

"The guy from the *Tribe* thinks Martha may have predicted the assassination."

"He thinks *what?*"

"You know that song on the album, *Masked Man,* where she sings, '*Well you know he burned the flowers, and the evidence too . . .*'? This guy who shot the Senator, he kept a journal about what he was planning to do. Tried to burn it in the wood stove in his motel room, along with a bunch of dried flowers."

Levett laughed aloud. "This is a gag, right?"

Tucker shook his head. "I'm telling you exactly what the reporter told me. There's more. '*See the masked man in the mirror*'—the guy was wearing a ski mask—'*chilly Colorado day.*' And, '*Watching him smile / in the lens of the camera/ sight of the rifle.*' And, '. . . *the mirror shatters / casting false reflections / in splinters on the floor.*' One of the shots broke the mirror on the wall of the store, covered the floor with shards."

"This is the most idiotic thing I ever heard," Levett said. "Where does he get off on concocting bullshit like this? We sell ten thousand copies of that album, and one of them has to end up with some fruitcake journalist."

"He'd never heard of Martha before. Told me he was just following up on a lead. The paper got a dozen calls from people who knew the song."

Levett laughed sourly. "So the good news is, Martha is big in Denver. The bad news is, her fans there are nuts."

"You going to call him?"

"You kidding? You think I want to encourage something like this? That would make me as big an idiot as him."

"They may print it anyway."

"Let them," Levett said. "It will blow over quick enough. I mean, whoever heard of the Denver *Tribe?*"

* * * * *

In the anteroom of the recording studio, Martha was watching an all-candidates debate for the US presidential nomination on the wall panel.

"What this country needs," one of the candidates was saying, "is a Mental Health Administration. And a Mental Health President to heal our wounds."

The candidate had graying hair and serious-looking eyeglasses. His face was pink, cherubic. But the mouth was small and mean.

"That guy could use some collagen," Levett said. "Hey, wait a minute. Isn't he that talk show host?"

Martha nodded. "Fred Carson. Runs a call-in show on the Health Network. They call him the video shrink."

"He's a psychologist?"

"Psychiatric social worker. Or he was, before he got into daytime TV."

"Now he's running for President? Only in America."

Levett watched Carson continue to mouth off. "The escalating incidence of mental illness . . . treating the causes, not the symptoms . . . a national commitment of resources . . . declaring all-out war on the madness that threatens to engulf our institutions . . ."

"This guy gives me the creeps," he said. "Fortunately he doesn't have a chance."

"Actually," Martha said. "He has an excellence chance. Particularly after what happened to that Senator."

"McWhurter, yeah. Hey, did some journalist try to call you from Denver?"

"No," Martha said. "Was I supposed to speak to him?"

"Absolutely not. Like I've always told you: anyone wants to get in touch with you, they come through me."

"I know that, Abe. But what am I not supposed to be talking about?"

"Nothing," he said. "Absolutely nothing."

* * * * *

"You want Martha to tour with Robert Duke in the fall?" Winston rubbed his chin. "I don't know that his people will buy that."

"You can make them buy it," Levett said. "What I hear is, you're underwriting his tour."

"Yeah, maybe I could at that. But why would you want me to? Duke draws a hard-rock crowd. His fans wouldn't go for Martha."

"I think they will, Ken. And it's exactly the kind of exposure we need."

"I'll see what I can do. But I'll tell you, that Duke tour is looking iffy."

"Because of the Boston thing?"

There had been a riot at a rock show in Boston the previous week: five deaths, many injuries, considerable property damage. Other cities had experienced similar, although less serious, incidents through the summer. The Boston city council had rushed through an ordinance banning all rock shows. Several other cities looked poised to follow.

"The Boston thing won't stand up in court," Winston said. "But it'll stand up for a while. Plus we've got juvenile curfews in Pittsburgh and Philadelphia. The kids are crazy out there this year. And just to ice the cake, it looks like there could be a war over this Brazilian thing. If that happens, everyone will stay home glued to their screen."

"If the tour goes ahead," Levett said, "we go with it."

* * * * *

"You want to use this one?" Tucker asked.

He was sitting on the floor of the office, surrounded by clippings and printouts, putting together a new promotional package.

Levett looked up from the spreadsheet display on his desk. "Which one?"

In answer, Tucker held up a printout from the *Village Voice* web site, a recent concert review. Levett recognized it from the title, "*Psyching Out With Martha Nova.*"

It was a favorable review. It said many nice things about Martha and her show and her independently released first album. It also referenced her supposed prediction of the assassination of Senator Ralph McWhurter.

Levett thought hard for a moment.

"Yeah," he told Tucker. "Why not?"

Dozens of alternate and New Age publications had picked up on the story in the *Tribe.* The *Voice* mention was the most prominent yet, but only that morning Levett had fielded an inquiry on the same subject from *Rolling Stone.*

At first, Levett had been annoyed by these articles. They were a distraction from the real story he wanted to get across, which was Martha's music. And it was ridiculous to suggest that Martha might be psychic. Ridiculous, but also disturbing, for reasons he did not care to examine too closely.

Lately, though, almost without realizing it, he had begun to accept the inevitable.

"We can't stop this stuff, we might as well go with it. I mean, if people want to believe that Martha is psychic, who am I to stop them? It can only help us, only add to the mystique. Martha Nova, prophet. Prophet of a new world for humankind."

He sat back in his chair, smiling slightly, knowing that he had made the right decision, puzzling over why he had taken so long to come around to it.

And wondering why he felt such an icy feeling at the pit of his stomach.

* * * * *

"This is totally unacceptable," Levett told the marketing manager, indicating the video on the wallscreen, the promotional video that had been made for Martha Nova's first audio single. "This is out-of-line with the image we want to convey. You'll have to re-shoot. And I think you should find yourself a new director."

"There's no one hotter than Teddy Marks," the marketing man said. "And we spent a fortune on this already."

The images on the wallscreen were in black-and-white. They showed bleak housing projects, boarded-up factories, burned-out buildings, actors with doomed expressions. Martha Nova was seen for only a few seconds at a time, singing alone on a stage, dwarfed by looming banks of equipment.

"It's dreary," Levett said. "He's fixated on the most downbeat elements in the music."

"But the music *is* depressing."

"You're wrong," Levett said. "The music is uplifting. This . . ." He pointed to the screen. "*This* is depressing. This warmed-over socialist agitprop shit."

"Socialist agitprop is this year's thing," the marketing man said. "Of course, we just call it 'realism.' And Teddy Marks is your *numero uno* realist."

"It's wrong for Martha. It's way too heavy-handed. We need a lighter touch."

"Trust us, kid. We know how to sell records."

"I don't trust anyone to sell Martha except me. You're going to re-shoot this. And before you do, I want to talk to whoever is going to do it and tell them how."

"We're over budget already. We can't re-shoot."

"You don't have a choice. We have approval on all video representations. I gave up plenty to get that put in our contract, and you can bet I'm going to use it. You put this out, we walk."

“We don’t like performers who get legalistic,” the marketing man said. “We may decide to write this off. Put the record out with no video support, or not put it out at all. We’ve done it often enough with people we couldn’t work with. We could decide to bury Martha Nova.”

“But I don’t think you will.”

The reworked video was built around full-color shots of Martha Nova in concert, with frequent pans over the ecstatic faces of her audience.

The video was played in heavy rotation on the music channels. Aural and video versions of the single went straight to number one. The album showed every sign of following.

Soon afterwards, the craziness began.

✶ ✶ PART TWO ✶ ✶

Changes

✶ ✶ 6 ✶ ✶

When his record company proposed Ricardo Sykes to produce his new album, Robert Duke knew no good could come of it.

"The neurosynth guy?" he asked his manager. "Is this some kind of joke?"

"It's absolutely serious," his manager, Mike Garfield, told him. "This Sykes guy is real hot right now. And he wants to work with you. He's an admirer from way back."

"I'm supposed to be flattered?" Duke shook his head. "I've heard what he does. He's not going to do it to me."

"Your call," Garfield said. "You can cut the album your way. The company will still release it. But they'll put it out with no advertising, no promotion."

"Like that would be some sort of change."

"They've lost faith in you, Robert. They don't think they can sell your kind of music anymore. But Sykes is hot right now. They're betting that he can turn things around for you. And they're willing to place some serious money on that bet. Advertising, tour support, the works."

A few years ago, Duke would have told the record company what to do with their ace neurosynth producer and their serious tour support. But in those days his ego had been much larger: like his record sales, like his net worth.

"OK," he said. "We'll try it their way."

* * * * *

Ricardo Sykes was tall, pale, rake-thin, strangely insubstantial. Duke could not seem to form an image of the man in his mind: Sykes' features blurred, became indistinct, even as he looked at him.

Sykes had been born in Hungary, grown up in Italy, lived for years in Britain. But his voice was flat, accentless, characterless.

"This is an honor, Mr. Duke. Truly it is."

Music was droning in the background, music that had been mixed and remixed, sampled and resampled, digitally sliced and diced beyond recognition. Sykes' music.

They called it neurosynth: Music programmed to operate directly on the human nervous system. Or so it was claimed. To Duke it all sounded like dance music for automatons.

Duke stared blankly for a moment at the walls of the office. They were blanketed with gold and platinum discs, Grammys, Producer of the Year Awards. He shook his head slightly.

"All right," he said. "Let's get on with it."

* * * * *

Duke looked over the itinerary for his forthcoming tour. It was an ambitious schedule. Eighty-five dates, sixty cities, more than three months on the road, mostly in the big arenas.

"Some of these dates will change," Garfield told him, "depending on the curfews and whatever other shit comes down. But we have some fall-backs lined up."

"And they think we can sell out all these places?"

"With the right promotion, yeah. And with the right product on the radio."

"I don't know," Duke said. "I don't know about the product." His own work in the studio was finished. But Sykes had not yet provided even a rough mix.

"Anyway," Garfield said, "you filled these places last time out, no problem."

"Yeah," Duke said. "But that was three years ago."

He had been off the road a long time. He had been meaning to get back to it sooner. It was not that he disliked performing. In some ways, it was what he liked best, what made him feel most alive. But there had been family problems to deal with, and personal problems, and business problems, and hassles with the IRS . . . The time had just slipped away.

"I hope we've got a strong support act.

"I hear good things about her," Garfield said. "The record company is very enthusiastic about Martha Nova."

"Who the hell is Martha Nova?"

* * * * *

Garfield left him with a bunch of clippings about Martha Nova, and an advance copy of her upcoming album.

The clippings were mostly from arcane magazines and websites that advertised power crystals and holograms of the Face On Mars. They were wildly enthusiastic, describing Martha Nova as some modern-day amalgam of Joan of Ark, Nostradamus and Joni Mitchell.

She had come out of nowhere, or the nearest equivalent, some backwoods Canadian town with an unpronounceable name. In the photographs, she looked blond and bland, although there was something strangely knowing about her eyes.

It was with deep misgivings that Duke played Martha Nova's album. It was called *Gaian Songs.* It was her major-label debut, scheduled for release the following week.

The music bore only the most tangential relationship to his own rock-blues roots. But neither did it resemble the songs manufactured by Ricardo Sykes and his fellow *trendmeisters.*

It was folk music flavored with a techno sheen, chiming and changing, full of chants and incantations and spells and stories, overlaid with the peeling of bells and the hum of electric guitars and the hissing of antique vinyl samples. Here and there he could hear traces of acid, trance, ambient, jazz, hardcore, metal, African, Amerindian, Chinese . . . But traces were all they were, mixed and compressed into something that was at once quite ancient and entirely new. It was music you might hear in a dream.

He listened until the disc reached its end, and then he played it again.

Martha Nova, he thought, had the magic. It remained to be seen what she would do with it.

* * * * *

When Phil Maslow called, Duke was about to leave for a meeting with Ricardo Sykes to hear the final mix of his album.

"It's been a while," Maslow said.

"Too long," Duke said. *Not long enough,* he thought.

They went back a lot of years, Duke and Maslow. They had played together in the same band, the Silver Barons, slogging around the alternative-rock circuit, playing bars and colleges and benefits. They had written songs together, got drunk together, picked up women together, become nearly famous together. But their paths had long since diverged.

The Silver Barons had recorded an album for a small independent label. They had sold it from co-op websites and indie download outlets. Part hard rock, part yearning folk-blues, part political and part romantic, it had become a rock critics' fave, a college radio staple. Soon the major labels had come sniffing around.

It was Duke they wanted, not the band. It was Duke who had the looks and the voice, who had written the most accessible songs. The band was just baggage, the major label scouts told him, the band was only holding him back, he really ought to ditch the band. But Duke had insisted: Either they signed the entire band, or there would be no deal.

A deal had been offered for the Silver Barons. And Maslow had turned it down flat. He wanted to stay pure, to stay out of the mainstream.

"You want to be a rock star, Bobby?" he asked. "Go right ahead. Speaking for myself, I'd rather have my heart ripped out on the stage of an Atzec pyramid and get thrown down the steps and eaten alive. But I guess someone has to do it."

That had been the end of the Silver Barons. Duke had signed with a major label as a solo artist. And quickly his life had changed beyond recognition.

Maslow had stayed out on the margins. Even now, all these years later, he was still playing in bars and clubs, still recording for indie labels, still wearing his ideals on his sleeve. Maslow was in many ways a living reproach to what Duke had become.

"We're planning this evening," Maslow told him now. "For the Brazil thing."

Rumors of war were in the air. The Organization of American States had issued a last warning to the Brazilian *junta.* It was understood that the US would spearhead the OAS police action.

"Who's playing?"

"Oh, the usual crew, you know. Lots of old friends."

It'll be just like old times. Maslow was too cool to come out and say it. But he would be reveling in the desperate nostalgia of it all the same.

To Duke's relief, the dates clashed. "Sorry. I'm going to be out on tour."

"Couldn't you take a night off?" Maslow asked.

"Can't let the fans down."

"Can't give up the big bucks, you mean. I don't know why I bother calling. You never come through."

"I came through for your farmers, didn't I? And your Castroite refugees, and your war vets . . ."

"But you haven't come through in a long time."

Lately, Duke had been laying off the benefits. He had been taking too much heat. First had come the drug bust. He had been clean more than a year, but they had found traces all the same, and traces were all they needed. That one was still going through the courts.

Then they had hit him with a tax audit.

Maybe it was coincidence, but he didn't think so. Similar things were happening throughout the entertainment community.

"I'm under a lot of pressure, Phil. I've still got the IRS on my case."

"The IRS?" Maslow hooted with laughter. "What have you got to hide from the IRS?"

Plenty, Duke thought. Dubious tax shelters, offshore deposits, suspected skimming, all the stuff that had gone down when he hadn't been watching closely. Millions in back taxes if the IRS really pushed it, millions that had long since slipped through his fingers. But he could not expect Maslow to sympathize. "It doesn't matter. They want to get you, they get you."

"You wouldn't have let them scare you in the old days."

It was true enough. But in the old days he had had less to lose.

"I'm sorry," he said. "Maybe next time."

* * * * *

"Well?" Sykes asked.

The disc was half-over. Duke had not said a word since it began. Now he looked up at the producer and shrugged. "It's what I expected."

"But you don't like it."

"Liking it wasn't part of the deal."

Another song began, perhaps the best thing Duke had written in years. Sykes had choked the life out of it.

"This is the new sound, Robert," Sykes said. "The old sounds are over. Finished."

"So I've been told."

"You don't understand what I've done for you," Sykes said, in his oddly accentless voice.

"Oh, I understand," Duke said. "I understand exactly what you've done." He stood up. "But right now I think I've heard enough."

"You'll thank me," Sykes said, "when this puts you back on the charts."

"Not even then."

* * * * *

A limo was waiting outside the studio to take him to the reception.

The reception was to promote the forthcoming tour, which would support a record he hated. But he would go along with it, the same way he had gone along with the choice of Ricardo Sykes. Increasingly, these days, he felt as though he were sleepwalking through his own life.

During the ride to the reception, one of Duke's old songs began to play on the radio. A song about war. It took him half a verse to recognize it, even longer to place it. Had that been the Gulf War or the Cuban War or some other war again?

He felt no connection with the singer. The singer's voice burned with rage, as though he believed what he was singing. But Duke knew it to be an impersonation.

Even back then, he had never known whether what he was singing was true, whether he believed it. He had simply soaked it all in, everything going on around him: the anger at the war, the rage at the government, the songs other people sang and the way they sang them, the rhythms of the street and the rhythms on the radio. He had soaked it all in like some kind of sponge. And then he had squeezed it out again, in those songs that sounded so true and so fine.

And the songs *had* been true. True to their time, anyhow.

Once, Duke had believed himself author of his own success, master of his own destiny. Only much later had he come to recognize that for all his energy and talent and ambition, all his courage and daring, he had been only an instrument of his times.

The times had moved on past him now. But he could live with that. Or so he liked to believe.

"You play the cards you're dealt," he would say, cultivating a philosophical attitude that he did not yet wear altogether comfortably.

Now the cards had dealt him Ricardo Sykes, the tour, the press reception. And Martha Nova.

* * * * *

He met her at the reception. They chatted politely, warily. The wariness was mostly on Duke's part. He was half-expecting to meet a monster.

Suddenly, Martha Nova was famous. Her first single had shot up the charts, propelled by hype and talent in equal measure, with her album following in its wake. Then her breakthrough performance at the Grammys had pushed the song up to the number-one spot. *Earth Angel,* they called her in her first newsmagazine cover story that same week. *Queen of eco-protest . . . She sings for a dying world.*

Suddenly she was famous. And Duke knew all too well what it could do to you, that first wonderful and terrible hit of fame. It could make you a monster. No matter what kind of person you had been before, it could make you a monster. He had seen it happen often enough to others. He had seen it happen to himself.

But Martha Nova was not a monster. She was actually very charming.

"I used to have a poster of you on my wall," she told him. "When I was fourteen."

He was both flattered and alarmed by this new reminder of the relentless spinning of the hands on the big clock that counted out his time.

"I thought you were great," she said. "And I still do. That's why I jumped at the chance to do this tour."

Duke saw a short young man moving across the room towards them. He walked rapidly, as if to prevent anyone from getting a fix on his progress.

"Abe," Martha said, as the young man materialized at her side. "Meet Robert."

This, Duke realized, must be Martha's manager, Abe Levett. He had expected someone older.

Levett was wearing an expensive Italian suit. His hair was cut short. He bristled with nervous energy.

"The great Robert Duke," Levett said. "What do you know?"

Abrasive, Duke thought. This kid was certainly abrasive.

"You got yourself one hell of a support act, Robert," Levett said. "I'm just waiting to see how you're going to follow it."

Now that Martha's record had broken big all by itself, Levett was unhappy to see his client locked in as Duke's support act. He had tried to back out of the tour, but Duke's management had stood firm.

"We could have got out of this tour, you know," Levett said. "Could have got a medical certificate."

"So why didn't you?"

"Because Martha wanted to do the tour," Levett said. A look of defeat flickered briefly across his face. He shook his head slightly. Then he put his arm around Martha's shoulder, and began to pull her away. "Got to go, Martha," he said. "The *Post* guy is waiting."

Martha squeezed Duke's hand. "I'm really looking forward to this. It's like a dream come true."

He liked the way she was unafraid to say something so corny: *A dream come true.* Of course, for all her poise, she was still very young. Only a few years older than his own daughter, who he would look up when the tour reached Washington, if he could summon the nerve.

* * 7 * *

At the stadium, Duke found the members of his band sitting around watching the widescreen in the bar. Bombers were taking flight.

"It's started?"

Roscoe, the bass player, nodded. "Bye bye Brazil," he said, anticipating tomorrow's tabloid headlines.

"Christ," Duke said. "Again."

"Maybe you should write a song about it," Roscoe said.

Duke shook his head. He didn't write songs about war anymore. He had said everything he wanted to say about war.

He stood for a moment, staring at the news of the latest war. It made him feel edgy, aroused, disgusted, sad. He looked away. "We've still got a show to do."

"But maybe not an audience." Roscoe grinned, showing the gaps in his teeth. "Tough to compete with a war." Roscoe was already comfortably drunk. But that would not stop him from holding down the beat.

Roscoe relished failure, defeat, disappointment, his own and other people's. He had seen plenty of both. He had been in a band that had topped the world's charts, and in another that had been big in Europe. Now he was lucky to have a paying gig.

It would probably delight Roscoe to start the tour playing to an empty house. "This business is dying," he would tell them, over and over again.

And Roscoe was dying right along with it. At the bar, coughing up blood as he drank, he would boast about his doctor's warnings. Another year, tops, if he kept this up. Which of course he would.

Once, hesitantly, Duke had suggested taking Roscoe to a meeting of his recovery group. Roscoe, naturally, had scoffed. "I get my higher power," he said, "straight from the bottle."

Duke had not pushed the point. A few years ago, he might have said something similar. Even now, even though the group had done so much to help him clean up, he didn't buy the rhetoric except as metaphor.

Nor could he bring himself to condemn Roscoe. He didn't use anymore, and he hardly drank, but he did not deny others the right to use what they needed. He had used many things in his time, and learned something from all of them. If he was clean now, that was because he could no longer handle other ways of being.

"We'll have an audience," he said. "Don't worry about that."

He had seen them as he drove into the stadium, thousands of kids, lining up hours in advance. He should have been pleased, but instead he was disturbed. This was not the crowd he usually drew. His fans were older, scruffier. Many of these kids looked barely into their teens. Children, really.

Martha's children.

It would be embarrassing if that was true. Embarrassing to be outdrawn by your support act. But it probably *was* true. Martha's album now stood at the top of the charts while his own languished in the lower reaches, selling worse than its immediate predecessors.

"They've come to see the holy Earth goddess," Roscoe said. "Come to get blessed before they get drafted."

Duke grinned. There *was* something a bit otherworldly about Martha. From a distance, anyway. So pale, so blond, so not-quite-here.

"Martha's okay, once you get to know her."

He hoped to know her better.

* * * * *

There was a journalist from *Time* waiting to interview him in his dressing room. But the journalist didn't want to talk about Duke. After a few perfunctory questions, she zeroed in on what really interested her.

"Martha Nova," she said. "What's your call? Flash in the pan or here to stay?"

"She's a huge talent," Duke said. "I'm just delighted to be doing this tour with her . . ."

"So do you think it's true, what they say about her?"

"I don't know. What do they say?"

"That she can see the future."

Duke blinked in surprise. Now that he thought about it, there had been something about Martha's supposed psychic powers in the articles he had paged through. But he had not taken it any more seriously than the advertisements for dream machines and Mayan Apocalypse Calendars.

"I think Martha is very talented. But she's not *that* talented."

The journalist shook her head slightly, clearly dissatisfied with this response.

"What about her predictions?"

"What predictions?"

"They say she predicted the assassination of that Senator, McWhurter. Now they're saying she forecast the war. Apparently she laid it all out on a cut on her new album."

Duke made an impatient gesture. "You're not telling me you *believe* that?"

"It's good copy."

Duke rubbed his eyes. He felt exhausted already, as though anticipating the next three grueling months. The road stretched out ahead of him in his mind. Every day or two a new plane ride, yet somehow the same, to a new airport like the one before, and into a limousine like every other limousine. Driving past billboards the same as every place else, to a hotel like the one he had just left, a wallscreen with the same programs, a restaurant with the identical food . . .

Once, the prospect of a tour had filled him with energy. And what did not come naturally could always be induced artificially.

"Why are you wasting your time with this bullshit? Why don't you talk about her music? Her music is really good."

"Martha Nova," the journalist said, "is a lot more than just *music*."

* * * * *

From backstage, Duke watched Martha's act.

There was, he thought, something about the blond young woman in the long white dress with the ethereal voice, almost walled-in by banks of equipment yet somehow soaring above them. Painting her crystalline pictures of one world about to end and another about to dawn. Something indefinable, yet extraordinary.

As Martha sang, the arena itself seemed transformed, becoming part church and part carnival. It was as if a field of energy pulsed from the stage, enveloping the audience, incorporating it into her act, turning them into a gigantic amplifier for her music. The kids were laughing, crying, singing, dancing, sitting in rapt attention, hugging their neighbors.

She had the magic, all right. As he had once. Although hers was far more powerful.

He noticed Abe Levett standing beside him, apparently equally transfixed.

"She's wonderful," he said.

Levett's face hardened. "You bet your fucking life she's wonderful. You ought to bow down and kiss the fucking stage she stands on."

Martha was winding up her act. "You've got a great treat in store," she told the crowd, as they begged for more. "A chance to see a living legend, the fabulous Robert Duke."

Duke wondered when he had made the transition to living legend. It must have happened after his records stopped selling.

* * * * *

The war news was playing on the clock radio when they got back to his hotel room after the show. OAS troops claimed control of key installations in Brasilia.

"Will it ever end?" he asked, as he flipped it off.

"Oh yeah," Martha said. "One day it ends. All the wars end." Her voice was quiet, dreamy.

"In a thousand years, maybe."

"It won't be that long. Not nearly that long before war stops. Before everything stops."

"Stops?" He frowned. "How do you mean, stops?"

She gestured with her arms, as though to take in the hotel room, the city that surrounded it. "All of this. This way of living. It will all come to an end. Everything will change."

"Just like that?" He snapped his fingers. "Suddenly a better world?"

"Maybe a better one. Hopefully a better one."

"You're a dreamer, Martha."

"Oh yes. Yes I am."

She sounded, he couldn't help notice, a lot like his daughter.

"Love and peace," he said. "They already tried that. Before my time, never mind yours."

"That was when the change started. Soon, we'll finish it."

He shook his head briefly. "I hope you're right."

There had been a time when he would have mocked her naïveté, done his best to make her feel foolish. There had been a time when he treated most people that way, particularly those who had somehow crossed him. And Martha, however unintentionally, had crossed him up in spades.

Better to play to an empty house than to watch half the audience walk out before you started your set. And probably he had been lucky that so many remained, whether out of politeness or sheer inertia. The remnants had applauded dutifully, even calling him back for a ritual encore. But for the most part they were not his people. There was no energy in the room. He had sounded hollow even to himself.

"One last dance," he had told his band, when he called them together to rehearse for this tour. With the country in the shape it was in, with the problems in so many cities, the riots and the strikes and the on-again off-again curfews, they had all understood that this could be one of the last big tours. "One last chance to dance."

But now it seemed that he would not be granted even that much. He had sleepwalked his way into disaster.

Once, he would have raged at the situation. He would have blamed his manager, the promoters, the record company, the radio programmers. And he would have taken his anger out on Martha.

But somehow he could not get mad at Martha, or even envy her success. He was only embarrassed, and she was obviously embarrassed for him. After the show, she had gone out of her way to be solicitous, supportive, admiring. And when he asked her to come back to his hotel room, she had agreed readily.

He wondered now, as she sat next to him on the bed, whether she was about to fuck him out of pity. But he did not wonder that hard.

* * * * *

On his way out of the hotel the next morning, Duke found Roscoe sitting in the hotel bar. Roscoe was drinking vodka and poring over a printout from the *World Inquirer* website, shaking with laughter.

"What's so funny?"

"Earthquake," Roscoe said. "Our Lady Madonna is calling for an earthquake in San Francisco. Also a major fire in Seattle. And chances are good that Atlantis will rise from the sea any day now."

"She said that?"

"In her songs. As divined by three leading Martha Nova interpreters."

"Amazing. Amazing what people will believe."

"Amazing hype," Roscoe said. "Priceless, really. I mean, how do you compete with a gimmick like that?"

"You don't," Duke said. "You don't compete."

* * * * *

Abe Levett was sitting on a couch in the lobby, engrossed in reading the same article.

Duke sat beside him. "Why don't you stop this bullshit before it gets out of hand?"

"Stop it?" Levett echoed. "Why would I want to do that? This is wonderful stuff. You can't buy this kind of publicity."

"And what happens when Atlantis doesn't rise from the sea?"

"Who's going to remember the details?" Levett asked. "What they're going to remember is the mystique."

"No wonder this business is dying. With people like you running it."

"You've got that wrong, Duke," Levett said. "*You're* the one who's going to be dying. A little harder every night. Talk about a glutton for punishment. How much more humiliation can you take?"

"I don't know," Duke said. "I really don't know."

* * * * *

Duke's daughter, Lilith, came to see him after the show in Washington. She was living nearby, in a commune in West Virginia. He had arranged a block of tickets for Lilith and her friends—her family, she called them.

Maybe they were her family now. He hoped for her sake that it was a happier family than the one she had been raised in. But on his only visit to her new home, standing in the mud surrounded by squawking chickens and screaming children, looking at the windmills and the satellite dishes and the sheet metal shacks and the geodesic domes, listening to the constant droning New Age *muzak* everywhere, he had felt like a man from Mars.

They were some sort of cult, Lilith's new family, some kind of techno-hippy-survivalist-religious cult. They were waiting, she told him, for the world to end. And to begin again. Meanwhile they prepared themselves for the changes to come.

Better, he tried to tell himself, a cultist than a junkie and semi-pro hooker. Better a live daughter you couldn't hold a conversation with than a dead one you couldn't talk to at all.

"Great show, dad," Lilith said, kissing him on the cheek.

Her new politeness was disconcerting. It almost made him wish for the old days, when she would spend her nights out on the Strip watching the hardcore bands, coming home only to change her clothes and curse him as a hopeless dinosaur. At least she had been honest with him, back then.

"You hear from your mother?" he asked.

"She called me a few weeks ago from Paris. Sounded good. Doing some power shopping."

He wondered, sometimes, how he could have made such a mistake as to marry Leanne. And how they could have compounded that mistake by having Lilith. It had been at a time in his life when mistakes had come easily to him.

Lilith had brought with her a gawky young man named Judd. "Thank you for inviting us, Mr. Duke," he said. "It was great. My parents used to play your records all the time. They'll be knocked out when I tell them about this."

"And how did you like Martha?"

Judd's face lit up. "Oh, she's fabulous. We've been listening to her and almost nobody else for months now. When Lilith told us she'd got tickets . . ." He trailed off at Lilith's warning glance.

Afterwards, Duke took them to meet Martha. They stood dumbstruck.

"I thought they were sweet," Martha told him later. "Yeah," Duke said. "Like molasses."

Seeing his daughter had depressed him. At least that much hadn't changed.

✶ ✶ 8 ✶ ✶

Levett's phone call woke them in the middle of the night.

"I need to talk to Martha," he told Duke. "We've got a serious problem."

After Martha had gone downstairs to confer with her manager, Duke turned on the screen and flipped through the news stations. The big story of the night came from Seattle. A fire starting in a downtown department store had run out of control, consuming ten city blocks. Casualties were already into the hundreds, property damage into the hundreds of millions. Arson was suspected.

And then, over the footage of the flames, they played a snatch of a song:

"City's burning, we're all burning, flames rise high, rise high / In the window, teddy's burning, wishes he could fly / City's burning, we're all burning, reaching for the sky."

Duke recognized the lyric. It was Martha's *Seattle Song.* She performed it most nights. He had wondered, sometimes, why it was called that: the city wasn't mentioned in the song.

The picture cut back to the studio, where the newscaster spelled it out. Not only had Martha apparently forecast the fire, she had pinpointed its location. According to Fire Department investigators, the locus of the fire was a pre-Christmas window display of children's toys. The display had included a giant teddy bear, dressed as a fairy with wings. Fairy teddy bears were a popular item this Christmas season.

The newscaster now showed the video used to promote Martha's *Seattle Song,* an impressionistic piece which crosscut several times to the image of a burning teddy bear. A teddy bear with wings.

"Did Martha Nova see the future?" the newscaster asked. "Or is this a case of life imitating art? Serious questions, either way, for the year's most popular new singer."

* * * * *

There was a press conference the next morning. Martha asked Duke to accompany her. She looked pale, nervous.

"This is going to be bad," she said.

At first Levett handled the questions, while Martha sat beside Duke, holding his hand.

"You think the song is a prophecy?" Levett said. "That's crazy. It's just a song."

"But it's about Seattle."

"Martha visited friends in Seattle. One day she saw a fire, and she wrote a song. It's history, not prophecy."

"But it even mentions the teddy bear."

"The teddy bear is a nice little image, that's all."

"I'd like to hear that from Martha Nova." Duke recognized the woman from *Time.*

"Martha never talks about her songs," Levett said.

That was true enough. Levett, as Duke had observed, kept his client away from all but the most superficial contact with the media. Duke had thought that to be a deliberate strategy, designed to build her mystique. Now he wondered whether Levett had something to hide, or thought that he did.

"We have a right to know," the woman from *Time* said. "Whether this thing came to her in a dream, or something. Or whether it's some psycho fan making her songs come true . . ."

Uproar in the room. Levett bellowed to be heard. "You print that, we sue. The Seattle cops are investigating the store owner. They're not looking for a fan."

Now Martha was rising to her feet. "It's okay, Abe," she said. "Let me talk."

The room grew hushed.

"Well, Ms. Nova," the woman from *Time* asked. "Did you see the Seattle fire in a dream?"

"No. I didn't dream it."

"There where did the song come from?"

"It just came to me."

"When you visited Seattle?"

"Yes."

"And you saw a fire?"

She seemed to hesitate. "I saw several fires in Seattle."

"What about San Francisco?" another journalist demanded.

"What about it?"

"They're saying you've predicted an earthquake in San Francisco."

"I don't make predictions. I write songs."

"Would you be worried if you lived in San Francisco?"

"Would I be worried? I can't answer that."

"Don't you think you have a responsibility to warn people?"

Martha turned, if anything, a shade paler. "My responsibility is to sing."

"What about the end of the world?" asked a woman from a local TV station.

"I'm sorry?"

"Isn't that what you've been trying to tell us? Your biggest prediction of all? That we're getting near the end?"

Getting Near The End. Another cut from the album. Duke hadn't really thought about what it meant until now.

Levett was signaling frantically to Martha, but she ignored him. "Getting near the end?" she echoed. "In a way, the world *has* ended. It's already been destroyed. You can feel the grief and panic all around us. Look at the wars, the pollution, the poverty, the violence. The mental hospitals are full, millions of people are on medication, we can't take it anymore, we can't take this reality we're living in. Everything has ended. We know it, but we can't face it yet. We need some kind of final jolt. And it's coming, real soon. Everything is starting to happen very fast . . ."

"So is it going to be by fire?" asked a young, dreadlocked videographer from InterCityNews. "Ice? Flood?"

Nervous titters from the back of the room.

"There *is* a flood," Martha said. "Like a tidal wave, maybe, rushing to meet us. Washing it all away, everything we believed in, everything that we are. We don't know who we are anymore, where we belong, how we should live . . ."

"Could we please get past the metaphors?" asked the woman from the local TV station who had started off this line of questioning. "They're very nice and everything, but could you please give us a straight answer? Do you believe that the world is literally coming to an end, or not?"

"I believe that, yes," Martha said. "I've never made any secret of it. We are getting near the end of something. Our world is nearly over."

Renewed uproar. Levett grabbed the microphone away from Martha. "That's all, folks," he said. "That's more than enough."

"What about you, Mr. Duke?" the woman from *Time* asked. "Do you think Ms. Nova is psychic?"

Duke took the microphone. "No, I don't. It's like my Daddy always told me . . . if people could see the future, there wouldn't be bookies."

* * * * *

Following the Seattle fire, the tour, for Duke, more and more resembled a gigantic circus. There were media people everywhere now: waiting at airports, camping out in hotel lobbies, crowding the backstage area at the stadiums. And more of Martha's fans in every city, many more than even the largest venues could accommodate. Thronging in the streets outside the hotel, spilling out of the parking lots around the stadium. And singing, always. Singing Martha's songs.

Nova Children, the media had s
their lead story for the week: *She f*
The *Time* writers did not take
could see the future. But they fo
same. As for the "children," that
mostly quite young, and that the
though she were somehow cor

"We're reaping the whirl
cy of rage, boredom, abuse, neglect, addict
age they have sustained as . . . a basis for identity." Or as
fans put it, in a prominently featured pull-quote from the *Time* story,
"They fucked us and they fucked our world. They burned it out, gutted it, left us the ruins, the wreckage."

Duke watched to see the effects of all this on Martha. At the press conference she had seemed badly shaken, barely holding together. Now he feared that she would fall apart completely under the pressure of this vast and still-escalating celebrity.

But Martha surprised him. She showed no further signs of vulnerability. If she felt the pressure, she hid it well. Mostly she seemed oblivious to the growing madness around her. It was almost as if she had seen it all before.

Duke was opening the show now. Switching their slots had seemed the only sensible thing to do.

Abe Levett did not seem much mollified by this concession. "Why don't you just go away?" he asked. "We don't need you. And no one wants to hear you."

"You've got some problem, Levett?"

"With Martha spending her time with a loser like you? Why would I have a problem with that?"

Levett was jealous of him, Duke thought. Perhaps he had once had something going with Martha himself, or had wanted to. But Levett was right nonetheless. No one wanted to hear him.

de the set shorter, acquiescing to the obvious s fans. Only the duets with Martha they had intro- his set seemed to hold the audience's interest. But even s would surely have preferred Martha undiluted.

oing down, man," Roscoe would tell him. "We're hanging by rtips."

scoe's drinking was getting even more extreme, so that some nights no longer held the beat. Or perhaps he no longer cared to.

"You play the cards you're dealt," Duke would say, like a mantra. He wondered when he would begin to believe it.

* * * * *

There was panic in San Francisco. People were selling their homes and possessions and heading for the hills. Airports and train stations and freeways were jammed to capacity. As many as fifty thousand residents were thought to have fled the city.

"Make you feel good, Martha?" Duke asked, as he flipped off the hotel room screen.

She flinched from his sarcasm. "No, it doesn't. But don't get angry with me, Robert. I'm a singer, that's all. I never claimed to be psychic."

"You never denied it, either."

"Would it make a difference if I did?"

Duke sighed. "I guess your fans will believe what they want to believe. Just as long as you don't start believing it yourself."

"You don't have to worry about me."

"I do worry. I know what it's like, this craziness, what it can do to you. You start to believe what people are saying about you. You lose any sense of yourself."

She touched his arm. "It's okay, Robert. I know who I am. I know what I'm here for."

It was true enough. Martha always seemed able to maintain a certain detachment. It was one of many things that he still found enigmatic about her. For all the time he had spent with her, all the talk and all the sex, he still did not feel that he really knew her. He enjoyed being with her, he admired her music, he found her both funny and profound. But finally she remained a mystery to him.

But that was his fault, he thought. He was just too wrapped up in himself, too preoccupied with his own success and his own impending failure, to really get to grips with Martha, with that curious vagueness at her center and with whatever it was that the vagueness might conceal.

* * * * *

Levett was staring down from the window of his hotel room at the street below. "Unbelievable," he said.

Duke followed his gaze. It was the usual scene. Thousands of the Children crowding the sidewalk, singing loud enough to be heard even through the thick glass of the window. The faces were too distant to see, but Duke knew they would all be wearing the same rapturous expression.

"I thought we were finished when the psychic bit blew up in our faces," Levett said. "Some guy torches his own store, and suddenly Martha's the prophet of doom. And then they had to drag in that end-of-the-world *shtick* . . . We should have left that song off the album. People don't want to hear about the end of the world. I mean, who wants to hear that?"

"Some people do," Duke said, nodding towards the scene outside the window.

Levett shook his head ruefully. "These kids, I just don't get it. Don't they have homes to go to? Parents who give a shit where they are? It's like they're crazy for Martha."

"I don't know if they're so crazy," Duke said. "Maybe they're like canaries in a coal mine. Maybe they know what's coming down better than we do."

"Which would be what exactly?"

Duke shrugged. "The stuff Martha sings about. The end of the world, I guess."

Levett snorted with laughter. "The end? This isn't the end of anything. It's just the beginning."

Levett, usually wound tight as a clock spring, was in an unusually mellow mood tonight. The end of the tour was in sight, without further misadventure. And *Gaian Songs* had just shipped quadruple platinum. It was the biggest-selling title in years, almost single-handedly rescuing a moribund recording industry.

"I really did it," Levett said. "I really pulled it off."

"Pulled what off?"

"Took Martha all the way. Made her a star, like I always said I would."

Duke shook his head slightly. "That's not how it works."

"Listen, I'm not trying to take anything away from Martha. I'm her biggest fan, everyone knows that. But she couldn't have done it without me."

"Or someone like you."

"There's *nobody* like me, Duke."

"Look, Abe. You didn't make Martha. Even Martha didn't make Martha."

"You're telling me the fans did?" Levett's voice dripped with contempt. "All the wonderful little people out there?"

"The times are making her. She's saying something that people need to hear right now. You need to understand that, Abe, if you want to help her ride this wave."

Levett shook his head. "No wonder you're washed up. *The times are making her.* You start to think like that, you might as well roll over and die."

"Okay Abe," Duke said. "You did it. You did it all. Now, was there something you wanted to talk about?"

"Oh yeah. Yeah, there was."

Levett crossed to the desk. "We're going out on the road again in the new year. Martha will be headlining. Twenty-eight dates in the south-western states. That was always a good market for you. We were wondering if you'd like to come along and open for us."

Duke stared at Levett in astonishment. "You want me on your tour?"

"We still need a warm-up act. So why not the legendary Robert Duke?"

Duke could hear the sarcasm, but it was somehow perfunctory, as though Levett were deliberately restraining himself.

"You'd be second on the bill," Levett said. "But we'd give you half the gate."

"Half the gate? The shape this business is in, you can have your pick of any act, a lot cheaper than that."

Levett nodded. "Maybe we could. But we want you."

"This is Martha's idea, isn't it?"

Levett looked uncomfortable. "We've had our differences, Duke. But I'm not blind, I can see how Martha is around you. She's much looser, happier. I think—" He coughed. "I think it's a good idea. For you, too. Being associated with Martha certainly isn't hurting you."

Duke was all over the tabloids and the gossip channels now, perhaps more famous as Martha's lover than he had ever been in his own right. Although it had done little for his record sales.

"I'm sorry, Abe. I can't do it. In a way, I'd like to. But I can't."

"Word is, you could use the money."

"I can always use the money. But not this way."

"I told her you wouldn't buy it," Levett said. "And I think she knew it, too. But she wanted me to try."

Duke had expected Levett to be pleased with his refusal. Strangely, he looked crestfallen.

"You did try, Abe," he said. "You gave it your best shot."

* * * * *

Duke and Martha barely talked on the limousine ride out to the stadium. It was the last night of the tour. Martha sat with her eyes half-closed, as though viewing some inner vision.

"I spoke to Abe," he said, finally.

"I know."

"I'm sorry, Martha. For me to keep on playing . . . it would just be prolonging the agony. I don't want to do this anymore. I've been on this treadmill for half my life now, churning out albums, touring behind them, never stopping to wonder what I was doing. It's time for me to step off for a while. It's just not fun anymore."

"You could still travel with me. Maybe do a few duets. That could be fun."

"No," he said. "I couldn't. It's your tour, Martha. You don't need me dragging along behind you. And I have things I need to deal with. Business stuff. And personal stuff. I thought I would go visit my daughter for a few days, try and figure out what that's all about . . ."

"I think that's a good idea, Robert. It's just that I'd like you to come with me."

"Look, maybe I'll hook up with you when you get to Atlanta. I've got some friends down there. Maybe I'll tag along with you for a few days."

"That would be nice," she said.

But her voice was cool, remote. She didn't believe him, he thought. Maybe she was right not to believe him.

"We didn't make any promises, Martha."

"I know."

"Anyway, we've still got tonight. These days, that's about as far ahead as I can plan."

There would be an end-of-tour party that night for the musicians and crew.

"Yes," she said. "We've still got tonight."

* * * * *

News of the earthquake came through soon after he finished his set. An 8.1 on the Richter.

Out on the stage, Martha was singing. He put on his leather jacket and headed for the exit.

"Where you going?" Roscoe asked.

"Out," he said. "Out of here."

"You're not staying for the party?"

"No."

"Going to be a zoo, man," Roscoe said, with some relish. "A fucking zoo. Reporters are going to be screaming for blood."

"I know."

"You're going to leave Martha to face it by herself?"

"She'll handle it."

Roscoe shook his head. "What are you, spooked? You can't handle the fact that she's psychic?"

"She isn't psychic, Roscoe. That's total bullshit."

"Tell that to San Francisco."

"Everyone knew there would be another earthquake one day."

"And a fire in Seattle?"

"You're missing the point."

"Am I? All I know is, you're blowing it."

"Maybe."

"She's something, Bobby. She's maybe the one."

"The one?"

"The one you've been looking for," Roscoe said, his face uncharacteristically solemn. "All your useless life."

"No," he said. "Or if she is, I'm not ready for her. I can't handle this right now."

He motioned back towards the arena, where the cheers were sounding like barely muffled thunder.

"You're blowing it," Roscoe said, again.

It was the last thing Duke heard as he left the stadium, the last thing he would remember Roscoe saying. Six months later, a little earlier than his doctor had predicted, Roscoe would be dead.

* * * * *

While waiting for his flight, he called Phil Maslow.

"I heard you're planning another benefit," he said. "I'd like to do it."

"I'll see," Maslow said. "I'll see if I can fit you in."

He laughed about that for a while, and then he called his daughter.

* * * * *

In her dressing room, Martha waited for Duke.

She had known she would wait for him. Just as she knew that he would not come; and that, quite soon, she would start to cry.

But she would not cry yet. Not until Abe came to tell her that Duke had gone. She brushed her hair and waited for Abe to knock on her door.

It would not be long now.

✶ ✶ PART THREE ✶ ✶

Maybe Tomorrow

* * 9 * *

"First, I want to express my sincere condolences to the people of San Francisco. I feel with you, I feel for your losses. There's nothing more I can say.

"Time plays tricks on us. On all of us. Yesterday, today, tomorrow, we're always juggling them in our minds. And sometimes we fall out of the now. We act like it's still yesterday, or maybe tomorrow.

"Some people think I knew what was going to happen in San Francisco. They think I can see the future, and that I tell them about it in my songs.

"But I don't predict the future. The future is already here. In all of us.

"Sometimes I think I'm just a mirror, reflecting what people hope for, what they fear. That I pick up things in the air that people are waiting to tune into.

"But I try to do more than that. I try to touch people's lives, to take the edge off their fear and their pain, to help them get through what's ahead. That's why I sing, why I'm going to go on singing, It's all I can do."

(Statement by Martha Nova released via Internet on 12 November 2015, the day after the San Francisco earthquake.)

* * * * *

Levett accompanied Martha to the airport to put her on her flight to Corfu. But the flight was delayed by a bomb scare. There always seemed to be such scares these days, Levett thought, despite the automated scanning systems and the artificial intelligence programs that operated them, despite all the armed guards and the plainclothes operatives swarming through the airport, despite all these precautions or maybe in part because of them.

Levett sat with her in the executive lounge, holding her hand. Her face was hidden by a large black floppy hat and aviator shades, yet she still attracted curious glances from other people in the room, tired-looking business travelers in brightly colored corporate uniforms. Levett was used to Martha attracting such attention. Usually he enjoyed it. But today it made him feel uncomfortable, made him wish that he was someplace else.

"It will blow over," he told her. "All this. And you'll be able to get back to making music."

"Sure, Abe," she said, absently. "Sure it will."

He wanted desperately for the flight to be called. He wanted Martha on the airplane, heading away from him, a long way away.

The business traveler seated across from him was reading the *New York Times*. Martha's statement had been reproduced there that morning, alongside a brief, huffy editorial condemning her for her *"ludicrous self-importance . . . narcissistic delusions . . . appalling taste."*

Entertainment Daily had been nearly as damning, finding Martha *"evasive . . . shilly-shallying . . . teasing us . . . a sphinx without a riddle . . . a psychic striptease revealing nothing."* There had been many more such reports stacked on Levett's desk that morning, but he had not had the heart to read them all.

Martha had written the statement herself. She had insisted on writing it herself.

"You'll have a great time in Corfu," he told her, as they waited for her flight. "Get away from all this bullshit for a while. Walk, lie in the sunshine, drink retsina . . . and, oh yeah, write me a few songs."

This trip had been planned months ago. Martha would be staying in a villa that Levett had helped her pick out from the travel company's website, to rest up after the tour and prepare to record her next album. As it turned out, the timing could not have been better.

"Yeah," she said. She pushed back her aviator shades and Levett could see that her eyes were rimmed with red. She had been crying: for Robert Duke, maybe, or for San Francisco, or for herself. He had no way of knowing, and he wasn't about to ask. "And you're going to come visit me."

"As soon as I can," he said. "Soon as I get some stuff cleared away." When he had helped her pick out the place, he had talked about dropping in to visit her. "I bet you've seen enough of me for a while, anyway."

"No, Abe," she said, squeezing his hand. "It's the other way around."

"You think I've seen enough of you? You're wrong. You couldn't be more wrong."

"It's all right, Abe," she said, as she released her grip on his hand. "Really it is."

And then the voice on the PA announced Martha's flight.

* * * * *

It did not blow over, not soon, not ever. Interest in Martha Nova reached new levels of intensity. Sales exploded worldwide.

Inquiries continued to flood into Levett's office. "Do *you* think she's psychic?" the journalists would ask. And he would continue to deny it. He denied it vigorously, and repeatedly, until his voice grew hoarse.

He did not believe that Martha was psychic. He had not believed it before and he did not believe it now. He could not afford to believe it.

Because if he believed that Martha could see the future, he would have to believe the rest of it. He would have to believe that the future was all written out, like the pages in a book or the scenes in a play. That nothing happened other than what was supposed to happen. That he had not discovered Martha and guided her to success, but only followed a preordained destiny. That all his work, all his hustling, had meant absolutely nothing.

If that was true then he might as well not exist: would not, to all intents and purposes, exist. Because he was the sum of his achievements, he was the mark he made on the world, he was that or he was nothing.

* * * * *

Levett booked the studios for Martha's next recording sessions. And then he set out on his own vacation.

He flew first to New York for a major art auction, featuring museum-quality work from private European collections at distress sale prices. Bidding was light. He picked up several paintings he had previously seen only in books.

While in New York, he looked up his father.

"You bought art?" his father asked, incredulous. "You should have called me. I would have told you, this is no time to buy art."

His father was a partner in a firm that traded commodities.

"We're very bearish, kid," he said. "We're shorting everything. The whole economy is looking terrible. It's being swept down into the trough of the K-Wave, and no one can say how deep it's going to go." The K-Wave was one of the statistical models that Levett's father's firm used in making investment decisions.

"We're calling for massive deflation. All that debt being sucked down into a big black hole, and taking us straight down with it. I don't know that we're ever going to climb up out of it."

"I needed some pictures for my house," Levett said. "I can't just stare at a blank wall."

"You're telling me you *needed* a Rembrandt?"

"The price was right."

"Ever hear of wallpaper?"

Levett enjoyed flaunting his success to his father. Not that his father appeared impressed.

"Right now, this singer of yours is hot. Next year, people won't be able to stand the sight of her. And where will that leave you?"

"You're wrong. Next year she'll be even bigger."

"And the year after that? The way things are going, you've got to plan for the future. Cash will be king, the harder the better. Only thing I'm buying is gold. But you never did have any common sense."

This lecture on fiscal responsibility was something of a ritual between them. The only difference now was that Levett was no longer asking his father for money.

"You can't look at gold," Levett said.

Afterwards they played squash at his father's club. This was another of their rituals, enacted every time Levett came to visit, going back to when he was twelve. His father always won, meanwhile ridiculing him mercilessly.

"You should be able to beat an old guy like me," his father said, as they took a breather after the first set. "I told you, you've got to work on that pussy backhand."

His father was in excellent shape for a fifty year-old. He looked better now than he had when he had walked out on Levett's mother. His body was leaner, his stomach harder. He worked out religiously every day. He had a wife twenty years younger, and two children under the age of ten to keep up with. And he was still a ferocious competitor.

"And I told you, I don't like this game."

"You never did like stuff that was right in your face. Always shying away from a challenge. I told Gertrude—" Gertrude was Levett's mother—"you got to stop trying to protect the boy. You got to let him get out there and compete, or he's never going to amount to anything."

"I'm competing," Levett said. "I'm out there, competing."

"Then we'll see," his father said, picking up his racket. "We'll see who's fittest."

His father, as Levett well knew, was deliberately needling him, knowing that his game would suffer as a result. But at some other level he was completely serious.

Stay cool, Levett told himself. Stay focussed.

This time his father beat him by a narrower margin.

"That was better," his father said. "That time I almost had to try."

* * * * *

After New York he went to visit his mother in Florida. He had not seen her in almost a year.

"Let me be honest with you," his father had told him, soon after he moved out. "Your mother, she's nuts."

They were having lunch at an expensive steak house. Levett put down his fork.

"Nuts?" he echoed.

"I tried to make it work. But she's nuts. She can't help it—I don't know, maybe she can help it—but that's the truth of the matter. She always was nuts, always saying crazy stuff, right from the day I met her."

"Then why did you marry her?"

"Because she was a great-looking woman. I wasn't paying attention to what was coming out of her mouth. Took me a while to catch on."

If she's nuts, Levett wanted to say, why are you leaving me with her?

But he knew why. His father had left them to move in with his twenty three year old executive assistant, Angela. She would have no use for an eleven year old boy. Neither, for that matter, did his father. It wasn't as if Levett saw less of his father now. For years, he had rarely been home. He had always been traveling on business, or working late at the office. Or so he had claimed.

"Ma is a little eccentric," Levett said, halfheartedly.

"That's all."

"Eccentric? She's crazy as a loon. I should have walked out years ago, you know. I only stuck around for your sake."

Maybe his father actually believed that. Levett didn't believe it for a moment, but he did believe the rest of it. His mother was nuts. Not just a little strange, not just a little weird, a little flaky. Flat-out nuts.

Actually, he had known that already. He had known it as early as six, when his mother had terrorized the guests at his birthday party by dressing up as a witch. He had known it when she held long conversations with invisible people, when she cooked his shoes in the microwave to kill the germs, when she gave him sushi and ketchup sandwiches for school lunches, when she opened the door naked to the mailman and the meter reader, when she read him to sleep with selections from *Science and Health.* He had always known it. He just hadn't cared to admit it to himself.

* * * * *

They were building a landing strip outside his mother's trailer camp. The workers were mostly sun-bronzed seniors who worked slowly but doggedly, pulling out weeds, hammering down the bare earth.

At the far end of the landing strip was a huge hand-painted sign. SPACEPORT EARTH, it read.

Oh boy, Levett thought.

It was not enough that Ken and Dena claimed communication with space people. Now they were getting ready for them to land.

Ken and Dena were the leaders of the church to which Levett's mother belonged, the Church of the Alien Ascendant. Ken was a former bodybuilder, Dena an ex-soap queen. They were massive buyers of direct broadcast satellite time, through which they hawked their church, which now claimed half a million adherents worldwide, along with Ken & Dena's Space Food.

Space Food was a series of vitamin formulations, based on recipes supposedly beamed down to Ken from the stars. Levett's mother popped dozens of these pills daily. She claimed—it didn't say so on the label, due to fear of the FDA, but it was a well-known fact all the same—that the pills retarded the aging process. Retarding the aging process was a major concern in these parts. Not yet fifty, Levett's mother was a babe-in-arms compared to the average resident of this trailer camp. But she always had been ahead of her time.

She had been living here for three years. At first, Levett had thought it would prove to be one more passing fad, like the Christian Science and the

Zen, the Scientology and the Jews for Jesus, the nudism and the macrobiotics and the orgone boxes, the pyramid tours and the dowsing lessons and the healing magnets, like all his mother's other fleeting enthusiasms. But if it was a fad, it was one built to last, combining as it did elements of so many other less comprehensive answer systems. If anything, his mother became more passionate about it with each passing year, as the world moved ever closer to the longed-for arrival of Ken and Dena's space people.

The space people were angels, according to Ken and Dena. When they came, the world would end. But the space people would reward the true believers. They would grow new bodies for them, immortal bodies. And they would transform the ruins of the Earth into a new Garden of Eden, in which the chosen would dwell until eternity. In the meantime, judicious use of Space Food would help keep the old bodies together.

It was from his mother that Levett had developed his highly sensitive antennae for bullshit of all varieties, along with his profound aversion for all things mystical.

He had a low opinion of Ken and Dena, in some ways lower than his opinion of their predecessors in his mother's life of spiritual search. But at least it kept her off the street.

After his father had left, his mother had gone on a long slow, downhill slide. Without Ken and Dena to hold on to, she might have skidded all the way down. She might be eating out of dumpsters and sleeping on heating grates. Or, maybe worse, interned in one of President Carson's new Mental Health Recovery Centers.

He found his mother in the kitchen area of her trailer, microwaving a pouch of seaweed.

"You look terrible," she told him. "Your aura is all fuzzy."

"I've been working hard," he said.

"Working hard selling your harlot. You want some food?"

He shook his head. His mother's cooking had always been dreadful, even when she used more conventional ingredients.

"I ate on the plane. What are you talking about, harlot?"

"Thirty-one essential minerals," she said, spooning seaweed into her mouth direct from the package. "Ken and Dena eat it every day. I'm talking about your singer. Who else would I be talking about?"

"Martha? You don't like Martha?"

He was surprised that his mother had even heard of Martha. She didn't exactly keep up with world events. She didn't even have a TV. Ken and Dana were against TV, except to reach the unconverted. And to sell Space Food.

"No," she said. "I don't."

"You should listen to her. You might even like what she's saying. She's into some of the same stuff as you. The end of the world, like that."

"I don't need to listen to her," his mother said. "I know what she is. She's a false prophet, sent by the forces of darkness to confuse and cloud people's minds." She picked up a poorly printed newsletter from the kitchen table. "It's all here. All about your harlot. Ken spells it all out."

It was a church bulletin called *The Starry Messenger.*

"The space people have been telling Ken about Martha?" he asked, grinning. "I didn't know she was that famous."

"You can laugh now. But one day you'll see how she has you duped, like all the other fools who worship her. One day, when you're no more use to her, she'll destroy you."

"Yeah, I'll see. Right about the time your space people come down that landing strip."

* * * * *

From Florida, Levett had gone to Vegas to play the tables, a 40-hour binge, losing massively. After that, Aspen, where he had picked up a vacation home once occupied by the president of a major bank. The president was in jail now, and his bank was being wound-up by the federal government, its few remaining assets available at fire-sale prices.

His father had been right about one thing: cash was king. And Levett had plenty of it. Martha's album had just become the biggest global seller of all time, shattering a decades-old record. The advance for her next album, based on the escalation clauses and incentives he had insisted on in her contract, would be fifty million dollars.

He was rich. And Martha was even richer. As the money began to pour in, he had encouraged her to spend some of it. She had bought a house for herself and a Florida condo for her parents, a car for her brother, some jewelry for herself and her friends, a Lipschitz statue for Levett. Then she had run out of ideas.

"I don't need all this money, Abe," she said. "I don't have any idea what to do with it."

"There must be something you've always wanted."

She shook her head. "Not really. I mean, it's nice having *things.* A nice house, a good sound system, a comfortable bed. It's nice riding in a car instead of taking the bus, dressing in good clothes, eating off real china. I'm not saying I don't like it. But material things come and go. Or you do. You can't hold on to them forever."

"You can enjoy them while you're passing through. Anyway, *I* can."

"What would you think if I gave some money away?"

"To charity, you mean?" He shrugged. "I think that would be fine. As long as you feel good about doing it."

Levett had given away some money himself, but it hadn't made him feel good. The harder he had looked, the more overwhelming the problems out there had appeared: all that poverty and disease, all those victims of war and other disasters, natural and unnatural. No matter how much he gave, he could hardly hope even to dent the problems. Just thinking about the sheer hopelessness of it all left him feeling empty and depressed. So he had stopped thinking about it. And he had stopped giving.

* * * * *

From Aspen, Levett moved on to Milan, to be measured for a dozen new suits. In Milan he inquired about flights to Greece. But instead of visiting Martha he went to Ibiza, to pick out a condo and check out a yacht and hang out in expensive night clubs getting hammered on designer drugs.

He had promised to meet up with Martha again in New Orleans, where she would be recording her next album. She would be working with a new producer, new backing musicians. She had asked him to be with her at the outset to lend moral support.

He showed up a week late. He emailed her about the delay from Paris, pleading urgent business. But he had not been in Paris on business. He had been there to buy sculpture for the lawns of his new house in L.A. Afterwards, instead of flying home, he had gone on to Prague to pick up some antique garden furniture.

He had not been ready to face Martha.

He was still not ready.

* * * * *

"You all right, Abe?" Martha asked, when he arrived at the studio. "You look a little pale."

"Some bug I picked up in Paris," he said. "But I'm fine. How about you?"

"Corfu was great. But I missed you. Why didn't you come to see me?"

"You know how it is," he said. "Always something. You have a good holiday?"

"Wonderful."

"Hear anything from Robert?"

"Not a word."

Levett wondered why he felt relieved. It was not as if he and Martha were lovers anymore. That side of their relationship had long since come to an end. Their destinies, he had recognized, were joined in a different way.

And yet he had felt threatened by Robert Duke, much more than by any of Martha's other lovers. With Duke it had been different, somehow. With Duke, at least some of the time, Martha acted as though she might be in love with him. Levett could hear it in her voice when she spoke of

Duke, see it in her eyes when she looked at him. At other times she seemed mostly amused with Duke, she seemed to see him for what he was. But the love part of it had shaken Levett. He had never seen her like that before.

He told himself he was afraid that the relationship with Duke would undermine her, even as she was breaking through to the success he had so carefully planned for her. But what he feared most was being shut out of her life.

In the end, Duke had proved no threat at all. He had gone, and he had not come back. And once again, it was just Levett and Martha against the world.

* * * * *

"This is what we've got so far," Martha said, slotting the disc into the deck. "The tracks still need some work."

They were sitting in the living room of the house that Martha had rented in New Orleans. The playback filled the room.

Levett had heard some of these songs before, in live shows and on rehearsal discs. Others were new to him. A couple of the new songs seemed to be love songs, almost. One, called *Flying Boy* ("*. . . glide on, slide on, move on, fly on . . .*") was maybe about him. But he didn't really want to think about that. Nor did he care to speculate about who the other songs were written for.

"So what do you think?" Martha asked, as the disc ended.

"I like it a lot. It's more musical, more personal. It's great work, Martha. And no prophecies that I can hear. Although that doesn't mean someone won't hear them."

"It really bothers you, doesn't it Abe? The prophecy thing?"

"Bullshit always bothers me. But it's more of a nuisance than anything else. It doesn't seem to have hurt us."

"Did you ever wonder if it was true, what they say?"

Her tone was casual, but her eyes were intense. *Ask me,* they seemed to be saying. *Ask me if it's true.* He looked away.

"No," he said. "I never wondered. I knew it was bullshit, all along." Now he looked back to her. His expression was pleading. "It is bullshit, isn't it, Martha?"

"Oh yes," she said. "It's bullshit."

He stood up. "I should be getting back to my hotel."

"You could stay here," she said. "We could talk some more."

He looked at her blankly for a moment.

"No. I mean, thanks, but all my stuff's at the hotel"

"Okay," she said. "I understand."

* * 1 0 * *

"The Children? The thing about the Children is, everyone lies to them, everyone except Martha. Everyone tells them that we're going to pull out of this mess, that the future is going to be just wonderful. They know that's bullshit. And they know that Martha is telling them the truth. In a strange way, she's giving them hope. Hope that all this will end, and something better will begin.

"What kind of something?"

Abe Levett shrugs, looks momentarily puzzled.

"Something better than this. Martha doesn't sing about it, but I can hear it in her music all the same. I think the Children hear it, too."

Speaking about his artist at this moment, Levett's expression becomes transfixed. He looks as though he were himself one more ordinary Martha Nova fan rather than the manager who had guided every step of her meteoric career.

(From *"The Martha Nova Story")*

* * * * *

"What is it you do, actually?" Joanne asked, sitting up in bed and picking up her wine glass from the night table

"Show business management," Levett told her.

"Really? Who do you manage?"

Sometimes Levett would lie when he was asked this question. It could get tiresome, answering all the questions that would inevitably follow, about what Martha Nova was *really* like.

But Levett really liked Joanne. She was bright, she was attractive, she even had a job. She was a lawyer, in this town on business, just as he was here on business, for final negotiations with the merchandisers for Martha's next tour. And, that evening in the hotel bar, Joanne had clearly been attracted to him, Abe Levett. Not to what he did, or who he did it for.

It was possible, he thought, that he would enjoy seeing Joanne again. He had not had a serious relationship in a long time, and lately he had begun to want one. So he decided to be open with her. It was an important fact for her to know, and one he was proud of.

"I manage Martha Nova," he told her.

"Oh," she said.

"Oh?"

She shrugged. "Nothing."

"You're not going to ask me what she's really like?"

"No. Unless you want me to, of course."

"I thought everyone was interested in Martha."

"I think she sings very nicely," Joanne said. "I just don't like to listen to what she sings. It's not what I want to hear."

"What don't you want to hear?"

"I don't want to hear that we're all doomed. I don't want to hear that I'm just wasting my time, trying to build a career. I don't need to hear that."

"Most people don't hear it that way."

"Most people have already given up," she said. "And Martha Nova is telling them that it's okay to do that."

"But I think in a funny way she gives people hope. Otherwise no one would want to hear it."

"We're not going to agree on this. I think maybe we should drop the subject."

"I can't drop the subject. You're talking about me, about what I do."

"I'm sorry. I wasn't trying to be critical. I was just explaining why I'm not very interested in Martha Nova. Please don't take it personally."

"But it *is* personal."

"It's not just business for you, is it?" she said. "It's some kind of crusade. I think that's nice. I think that's great for you and for her. If I was a performer, I think I'd like to have you for a manager." She got out of bed and began to dress. "I also think it's time I was leaving."

* * * * *

In his office, Levett switched on his PDA. "Robert Duke," he told the machine. "Last 60 days."

The machine hummed softly, as it scanned indices for the major news and entertainment lines. It would not take long, Levett knew. If he had said "Martha Nova" the search might have stretched up to half a minute as the machine compiled the multiple references. But Robert Duke, these days, took only moments.

A tone sounded. "Showing one item last 60 days," the machine said in its vintage-newsreader mode. Today's voice belonged to Dan Rather.

"Read it."

"*Billboard line, 28.3.16, page 8798.* Headline: *Old Friends Unite To Stop James Bay III.* Text: At a sparsely attended benefit concert in Madison Square Gardens, veterans of the folk-blues circuit reunited to raise funds for the Cree Indian Nation. Alongside such familiar names as Phil Maslow and Janie Sanchez, the show featured a surprise appearance by rocker *Robert Duke . . .*" the machine jumped the volume a notch " . . . who played a brief all-acoustic set.

"The Cree Nation are battling to stop Phase Three of the Republic of Quebec's James Bay project, designed to supply hydroelectric power to the northeastern states . . ."

"Enough," Levett said.

"Printout?"

"No printout."

Levett felt the usual mixture of pity and disgust. The disgust was mostly for himself, for doing once again what he had told himself he would no longer do: keep track of Robert Duke.

For months now, Levett had been using his news compiler to sweep up any shred of news about Duke. He was not sure why he felt compelled to do this. Duke was no longer any threat to him. Martha never even mentioned him now.

But Levett had continued to track Duke's progress, watching with an almost morbid fascination as the man had gone into a long downhill slide. Duke's record company had dropped his option, and no one had picked it up; the IRS was pursuing him for back taxes; he had let his band go and was now performing as a solo act, in clubs and small halls.

Levett had watched Duke's fall with mixed emotions. The man was a relic, clinging to the old ways, trapped in the black hole of his own musical past, incapable of progress or change. He was pathetic, actually, one more deer caught in the bright headlights of the juggernaut future bearing down upon him. He was everything that Levett despised about the old music business.

But he was also a performer with a genuine kind of class, one whose style the teenage Levett had secretly admired while affecting to scorn. And, in the end, for all his fear and all his envy, he had sort of liked the guy. Which only made matters worse.

* * * * *

Levett arrived during a break in rehearsals for Martha's forthcoming tour. He found her sitting on the edge of the stage, working her way through a quart of caramel-crunch ice cream.

Lately Martha had been eating with a new enthusiasm. Lately her face had begun to fill out, her waist to thicken. But it wasn't just the extra weight. There was something else different about her.

"You're pregnant," he said.

She put down the ice cream.

"Yes."

"How long?"

"Four months."

"Who's is it?"

"It's mine. The rest of it doesn't matter."

"I didn't know you wanted a kid."

"Oh, I always thought I'd have one. At the right time."

"You think this is the right time? I don't know Martha, this may not be such a terrific career move."

"It will work out. *Que . . .*"

"I know," he said. "*Que sera, sera.*"

"How do you feel about this, Abe? I don't mean professionally. As my friend."

"Fine," he said. "I feel fine. If it's going to make you happy . . . I mean, we'll always be friends, right? No matter what happens."

"Sure," she said, her voice oddly flat. "Sure we will."

"You don't sound so sure."

She hesitated for a moment. When she spoke, she seemed to be choosing her words carefully.

"Oh," she said, "we'll have our ups and downs, I guess. Some longer than others. But not because of this child. And in the end . . . in the end we'll still be friends."

Somehow it was not that reassuring. But it was as much reassurance as he was going to get.

* * * * *

Who was the father of Martha's child? As far as Levett knew, there hadn't been anyone important in her life since Robert Duke.

He did the math. Martha, he figured, must have got pregnant during the southwestern swing of her most recent tour, possibly during her three-night stand in Houston. He had joined her on tour there, and gone with her to the party for the astronauts.

Details of the plan to send a mission to Mars had been announced only a few weeks before. The actual launch would not take place for several years, but clearly the space agency, and the government, were determined to milk every possible ounce of publicity out of the venture.

Martha Nova was one of a number of certified celebrities—rock stars and politicians and screenqueens and sports stars—invited to meet the team of astronauts in training for Mars. It was strange, Levett thought, that they would invite the songstress of doom to witness the preparations for this achingly nostalgic enterprise, this desperate reaching back to an earlier era of vigor and confidence in American life. No doubt they hoped that Martha would help focus attention on the Mars mission. It was so hard to get people's attention these days.

The party for the astronauts was held out at the Space Center. Levett remembered little about it afterwards, except being profoundly bored. Martha had quickly disappeared from his view and had not returned. In the end he had given up looking for her and gone back to the hotel alone.

The only thing that had really impressed him about the astronauts was that they were so small. He was taller than all of them and he was not very tall himself.

"Oh sure," said a journalist, when he remarked on this. "Weight counts, you know, especially on a long trip like this one. They love these itty-bitty types."

The singer's child would be small, too, only six pounds at birth although perfectly formed, and afterwards consistently small for his age. This was less than conclusive evidence, but Levett wondered, all the same. He wondered whether it might not have been an astronaut who had fathered the singer's child, and if so what she could possibly have seen in him.

The media, of course, also wondered at the identity of the child's father. But despite the most intensive investigation, they were unable to reach any conclusion.

Martha took a year off to give birth to the child and to get to know him. And then she resumed her career. She continued to ascend to the very top of the show business ladder, and then she kept right on ascending. And Levett climbed up with her.

In that sense, everything was as it had been before. But Levett and Martha now spent less time together than ever. The child demanded a great deal of her attention. And though Levett would visit, he found the child very hard to deal with, the more so as he grew older. No matter how hard he tried, he could not really warm to her son. Few people could.

* * 11 * *

Levett made plans for Martha to tour the Pacific Northwest. It was a short tour: six cities, a dozen dates. And the Pacific Northwest cities were still relatively calm, posing few of the crowd-control problems experienced in the larger urban centers.

Even so, it was torture to arrange. Insurance was virtually unobtainable. Crowd-control regulations were arduous and expensive to meet. Most venues required the posting of large bonds. Levett thought about giving up the whole idea. Martha didn't *need* to tour anymore. People would still buy her records.

And yet he knew it was very important to her, that contact with her audiences. And he hoped that getting her out on the road again would inspire her to write some new songs.

Martha had written almost nothing since Daniel's birth. The record company was getting restless: They were making noises about Martha doing an album of cover songs, an idea Levett had so far resisted.

So he persisted with the tour arrangements. Despite all the difficulties, it began to fall into shape. And then the man from MentHealth appeared.

* * * * *

Levett was studying the contract for Martha's three-night stand in Portland in the fall, displayed on the screen in his desk.

"I wouldn't worry about that contract, Mr. Levett," a voice said, from behind his shoulder. "You won't be signing it."

Levett turned to see a man standing behind him. He was tall and heavyset, graying, dressed in an ill-fitting dark suit.

"Who the hell are you?" Levett asked. "How did you get in here?"

The man flipped open his wallet to display a hologram, the image showing the letters M and H superimposed over an eagle. "Your assistant let me in," he said. "I'm Cy Olson. With the Mental Health Administration."

He walked around the desk, and sat down without awaiting an invitation.

There had been a lot of talk lately on the news channels about the new Mental Health laws, and the powerful new federal agency that would enforce them. The talking heads all thought that the new laws were tough but necessary, given the current situation, the growing incidence of mental illness and suicide and illicit drug use and on and on. Levett had not thought about it at all.

"You're some kind of shrink? I don't need a shrink."

The tall man shook his head. "I'm not a shrink. I used to be a psychiatric social worker, but these days I'm in special operations. Onwards and upwards." He smiled. "What makes you think you *don't* need a shrink?"

Was that supposed to be a threat, Levett wondered? Somehow it sounded like one. As if Olson for some reason thought he should be scared of him. Although as far as he could see, Olson had no leverage over him.

"Special operations?" he asked. "What kind of special operations would the Mental Health Administration run?"

"This and that. Whatever needs doing."

"But what are you doing here? What do you want?"

"We want you to call off that tour," Olson said, nodding towards the display screen. "We want to keep Martha Nova off the road. We don't want her to tour the Northwest this fall. We don't want her to tour anywhere, ever again."

Levett blinked. "The Mental Health Administration is telling me how to run my business?"

"That's right, Mr. Levett."

"You can't do that."

"You're wrong."

"I don't understand what you're even doing here," Levett said. "Why would the Mental Health Administration care what Martha does?"

"Oh, we care a great deal. Or anyway, my senior managers do. They had a long report drawn up on her, but let me put it in a nutshell for you: She's overexciting the kids. Stirring them up with her prophecies of doom and gloom. Bad enough that she's on the music channels all the time. We don't want her out on the road too. And we're not going to allow it."

"This is ridiculous," Levett said. "You can't be afraid of Martha. She's just a singer. That's all she is."

"She's a highly successful cult leader," Olson said. "Millions of kids hang on her every word. And she's a bad influence on their moral fiber, as bad as Satanism and angel dust combined. She's one of the reasons why this country is falling apart."

"Come on. You don't really believe that, do you?"

"Me?" Olson asked. "You want my opinion, Abe? Generally I try not to have opinions. It's tiring having to form opinions on everything. But for you I'll make an exception. I don't think we need any help from Martha Nova. I think we can fall apart without her just as well. But what difference does it make what I think? The important thing is what my senior managers believe. And yes, sure, absolutely they believe that."

"You can't order me to call off this tour," Levett said.

"Actually we *could* get a restraining order. Get your lawyer to check out the Public Representations section of the Mental Health Act. We're empowered to ban 'creative and artistic representations potentially damaging to mental health.' Martha Nova's music falls within the definition."

Levett shook his head. "What kind of law is that? And why didn't I hear about it before?"

"There's been discussion about it," Olson said. "In the on-line entertainment newsgroups and so on. But it's still low-profile. There hasn't been any action under the section yet. You could be the first."

"We'll fight you," Levett said. "In every court we can. Martha as damaging to mental health? You can't make that stick. You'll make yourself look like idiots."

"We think we *can* make it stick. But we'd rather not let things go that far. We'd prefer you to call this tour off voluntarily."

"Right," Levett said. "Sure I'm going to do that."

"I don't know if you're hearing me," Olson said. "One way or another, Martha Nova has to be stopped. And we're going to make sure that happens. But we're not unreasonable. We'll let you make alternative arrangements."

"What kind of arrangements?"

"Vegas," Olson said. "You can get Martha Nova to play Vegas. Let her fans come to see her in a nice controlled environment. No unruliness, no threat to public order, no problem we can see. Just good, clean family entertainment."

"Vegas? Martha will never agree."

"But you can make her agree, Abe. And you will."

"Or?"

Olson stood up. "You'll find out," he said. "You go ahead with this tour, you'll find out."

* * * * *

They pulled in Levett's assistant, Tucker Williams, the following week.

MentHealth cops—they called themselves "Intervenors," Levett learned—called at his apartment one night. One of Tucker's neighbors had reported him for antisocial behavior: playing his home-entertainment system too loud after 10:00 p.m. When Tucker answered the door, the Intervenors performed a routine retinal scan for purposes of identification. The scan revealed signs of probable nonprescription drug use. Based on this finding, the Intervenors searched the apartment, finding small quantities of psychoactive substances.

They had taken Tucker away to a Recovery Center for treatment.

"Can't I bail him out?" Levett asked his lawyer.

"Not on a MentHealth rap, no," the lawyer said. "They can hold him indefinitely. Until he's 'well,' basically."

"But he isn't sick."

"His behavior is antisocial," the lawyer said. "Any kind of nonprescription drug use, that's an automatic commitment to a recovery program."

"Can't we do anything for him?"

"We can request a hearing in front of the local Mental Health Committee—basically a group of registered mental health professionals. We can ask that Tucker be released into an outpatient program. That's within their discretion."

"And will they?"

"I don't know," the lawyer said. "This is all new. Everyone is still feeling their way. Some of these tribunals have been relatively liberal. Others have been quite heavy-handed. Also, it depends on how badly they want him."

"Tucker? They don't want Tucker at all."

"Then what do they want?"

"To put pressure on me."

The lawyer stared intently at Levett for a moment. Then he nodded slightly. "I've heard stories like that."

"If I don't do what they want, they'll come after me. Or Martha . . ."

"You think they have grounds to commit you?"

"They can probably find grounds to commit almost anybody, if they want to badly enough. This is starting to scare the hell out of me . . . I don't understand. How did these MentHealth types get so powerful so fast?"

"Desperate times," the lawyer said, "call for desperate measures. Isn't that what the President said? And he delivered. But you can't give him all the credit. It was what people wanted, what we thought we wanted. We were tired, and pissed-off. Everywhere we looked, we saw lunatics and junkies and suicides and serial killers. We though the whole world was going nuts. We wanted someone to *do* something to stop it."

"We?"

"I voted for him," the lawyer said. "For Fred Carson and his Mental Health Administration, Fred the healer, Fred the defender of community values . . . I voted for him, God help me."

* * * * *

There was no picture on the videophone, only Olson's voice.

"Well?" he asked.

"I'm next, right?" Levett asked. "If I don't cancel the tour, I'm next."

"Martha is next," Olson said. "If we can't control her through you, we go right to the source. Martha goes into recovery. A *long* recovery. Her fans may never see her again."

"Recovery from what?"

"We'll think of something, don't you worry about that."

"Her fans will freak."

"Then we'll face the consequences. Better now than later. Like I already told you, this Martha Nova thing is going to be stopped. It's gone way too far already."

* * * * *

"Is that a real Frances Bacon?" the journalist asked, staring at the painting above the marble fireplace in Levett's living room.

"Yes," Levett said. "It's real."

"I though that one was in a museum."

"It was."

"And that one?" the interviewer asked, indicating the painting that hung above the couch where Levett sat.

"Yes," Levett said. "It's the original Magritte. From the Tate."

"The British government let it go?"

"I don't think they noticed, actually. They've got other things on their mind. You could make a good argument that there is no British government anymore. Not in the sense that they control any significant part of the country. Mostly it's gangs and tribes and travelers and rentacops."

"Magritte," the interviewer said. He shook his head.

"This is a good time to collect art. The museums are broke, governments are broke. Hardly anyone is buying."

"No rich people left?"

"Oh, there are still rich people. But it takes more than money to collect art. It takes confidence in the future. If you don't have confidence, you buy gold, or maybe small collectibles, antique watches and jewelry, things you can stuff into your pocket if you have to make a run for it."

"But you have confidence?"

"Oh yes," Levett said. "Every confidence. But even if I'm wrong, I figure, what can it hurt? At least I'll have owned these paintings for a few years."

He liked being interviewed, always had. And he especially enjoyed being envied for his possessions. It made him savor them all the more.

Of course, the interviewer was less interested in Levett than in Martha Nova. But Levett did not mind that. He liked talking about Martha nearly as much as talking about himself.

"Martha Nova is playing Las Vegas in the fall," the journalist said. "That's a new move for her. You're not worried that it might turn off her hard-core fans?"

"The time is right for Martha to do Vegas. And it's wrong for her to play anywhere else. She's got a young child to look after, it's difficult for her to make those cross-country tours, and it's getting harder and harder to find places to play. There are curfews in major urban areas in twenty-six states now, and then there's crowd-control legislation, and on and on. Even if we could put a tour together, it's just not safe anymore. It's not safe for Martha and it's not safe for her fans. But in Vegas the fans can come to her."

“Rich fans.”

Levett shrugged. “No one group of fans owns Martha Nova, not even the Nova Children. And that’s not to knock the Children because I love them. I love everyone who buys the product.”

In truth, Levett did not love the Children. He found the whole business of the Children more than a little spooky. Which did not stop him going with the flow.

“How does Martha feel about playing Vegas?” the interviewer asked.

“She’s looking forward to it,” Levett said. “She loves to perform. It’s what she does. It doesn’t matter who she’s performing to. She’s really excited about this, let me tell you.”

* * 1 2 * *

"You and Mommy, you're going to have a fight," the singer's child told Levett, as he entered Martha's Las Vegas hotel suite.

The child was sitting on the living-room floor surrounded by small trucks. It was nearly midnight, but from an early age the child had kept the same hours as his mother, staying up on the nights she was playing and then sleeping late the following morning.

The child's nanny was lying on the couch watching the wallscreen. Martha was not in sight.

"What?" Levett asked the child. "What did you say?"

"I said, you're going to have a fight. After you go into the bedroom to talk to her."

The child had begun to speak before his first birthday, and now, at little more than two, could string together words in a disconcertingly adult way. He was obviously very intelligent. But what came out of his mouth could sometimes be quite strange.

"Why do you say that?" Levett asked. "I never fight with your Mommy. We're friends. Friends don't fight."

"Sometimes they do," the boy said. "Sometimes."

But the child was obviously losing interest in the question. He turned his attention back to his trucks.

Martha was in her bathrobe when he entered her bedroom, toweling water from her hair.

"Abe," she said. "I'm glad you could make it." She hugged him briefly. "Did you get to see any of the show?"

"All of it. You should have known I would be here. This Vegas thing is important. It's a whole new audience for you."

"Maybe."

Martha had not been enthusiastic about these Vegas dates. Usually she went along readily with his plans, but this time she had been resistant, almost sullen about it. "I don't want to do it," she had told him, when he first broached the idea. "Please don't make me."

Martha had been looking forward to the Northwest tour, and was bitterly disappointed when he had told her they had to call it off. It had taken him hours to convince her that it was impossible, that no one could do that kind of tour anymore. And then hours more of pleading and wheedling to get her to agree to the alternative. He hadn't enjoyed it. But there had been no other choice, not for him or for Martha.

Martha had not been happy about playing Vegas. And judging by the performance he had just seen, she was still not happy. It had been just about the most lifeless show he had ever seen her put on.

"I thought it went all right," she said. "The show. They seemed to like it."

It was true enough. It had been all right, but only that. The audience had been attentive, they had applauded in the right places, but they had not been ecstatic. They were not, for the most part, real Martha Nova fans. And she had done nothing to change their minds.

It was so long since he'd had any criticism to make of her performance that he was not sure where to begin. And so he postponed beginning.

"I saw Daniel on the way in. He's getting to be a big boy."

"Not that big," she said. "I don't think he's ever going to be big."

"He said something funny when I came in. He told me that we were going to have a fight, you and me."

He laughed, a little edgily. She failed to join him. Her face seemed to whiten.

"Oh," she said. "It's now."

"Now? What's now?"

She shook her head. "Nothing."

She sat down on the bed and pulled the bathrobe more tightly around herself. She was shivering.

He sat down next to her and put his arm around her. He saw tears welling up in her eyes. He could not remember when he had last seen her cry.

"Are you all right, Martha?" he asked. "Are you sick or something?"

"I'm fine," she said. "Really. I'm just feeling a little sad." She wiped the tears off her face with the sleeve of her bathrobe.

"Maybe we should do this later."

"No," she said. "We should do it now. You wanted to talk about the show."

"That's right," he said, "but it will keep."

"You didn't like the show. You didn't think I was putting enough energy into it. You're afraid that I'm blowing it, blowing this Vegas gig. And you're starting to think that you made a big mistake booking me in here."

"What is this, a mind-reading act?" he asked, irritated.

"I'm saying these things for you, because you don't want to say them for yourself. You don't want to hurt me. But it won't hurt me, really."

"All right," he said, angry now. "The show sucked. Is that what you wanted to hear? You did a really good job of fucking it up for me. You punished me real good for making you play here."

"I wasn't trying to punish you. It's true I didn't want to come here, but I did try to put on a good show tonight, I really did. It's just that lately I've been feeling down, you know."

"About what? What should you be feeling down about? You're rich, you're successful, you've got a kid you love. What are you worried about? The end of the world?"

She winced slightly. "It's personal," she said. "Something personal."

"Is it about Daniel?"

"No. Daniel's fine. Daniel's perfect."

"I don't know, Martha," he said. "Lately you've really been letting yourself go. The record company keeps screaming at me for new product—product we *owe* them—and you can't seem to deliver . . ."

"I've tried, Abe. You know that. But the songs don't come."

Somehow, her pathetic expression only enraged him further.

"And now you can't even fucking perform." He was shouting. "So let me tell you what you have to do to shake it up. Tailor it to the audience. I want you to do some standards. Show tunes, classic rock stuff. Like, I don't know, *Stairway To Heaven.*"

"All right," she said. She sounded exhausted. "I could do that."

"And I want a little more glitz. A spangled jumpsuit or something. The white thing is getting tired."

"Fine. I'll go shopping in the morning."

The less she resisted him, the angrier he became, and the harder he felt compelled to push her. She was agreeing, he thought, only because she did not believe that he was serious about these demands.

"And when you do *Seattle Song,* I'm going to have you surrounded by a flame hologram. And we're going to have a whole bunch of flying teddy bears swooping out of the wings."

"I don't do *Seattle Song* anymore," she reminded him. "Not for years."

"I want you to do it now."

"All right," she said, again.

Except for the increasing outrageousness of his demands, it was the way their arguments had always gone. He would tell Martha something and she would listen the way she always listened: like she knew everything that he was going to say and it wasn't going to bother her in the least. In a sense they never really had argued, because an argument ought to have two sides.

"You don't care," he said. "You just don't care."

And then it hit him, finally, the recognition he had so long delayed.

"You don't care," he said, "because you heard all this already. You saw the fucking future."

"I do care," she said. "I do care about you, Abe."

But he was no longer listening to her. He moved away from her on the bed.

"Oh boy," he said. "Oh boy."

It was impossible to say what had finally led him to accept the knowledge that he had denied so long. But he knew now, and he was consumed by that knowledge. His whole world flipped over, and then flipped again. He put his hands to his head, as if to make his mind cease spinning.

"I should have known," he said. "I should have known from the very beginning."

He got up from the bed, still holding his head, and began to back away from her, to set a greater and greater distance between them. He was terribly afraid.

"It's all right," she said, softly, almost crooning. "It's all right, Abe. Take it easy. You're tripping, that's all."

"I don't do drugs. Not anymore."

"Then you're having a flashback. To when you used to do drugs."

Her face seemed to recede away from him, then loom closer. His vision became blurry.

"You saw the future," he said. "You can see it now."

"Stop it," she said. "Concentrate and you'll be able to stop it."

"You can see the future. The whole thing, every last detail of it." A new idea struck him, deepening his terror. "You can see me die."

"No. I never saw you die."

"You can." His heart hammered in his chest. "Tell me how. No, wait. Don't tell me."

He had backed all the way to the bedroom door.

"Don't go, Abe. You don't have to go."

"I do. And you know it."

She shrugged, as if in assent.

"How can you stand it?" he asked. "I couldn't stand it."

"You get used to it," she said. "It isn't as bad as you think."

And then he ran from the room. He ran from her, ran from his own recognition.

She called after him as he left. "I'll see you later. I'll see you at the party."

But he didn't think much about that as he ran. And he would not think about it afterwards. Not until they were very near the end.

* * PART FOUR * *

Life On Mars

* * 1 3 * *

A few days before the launch, Wyatt threw a barbecue at his house for the crew members and their wives and children. After dinner the three astronauts walked together in Wyatt's garden.

"It's going to be difficult," Wyatt said. "We know that. This is by far the longest voyage anyone has ever undertaken, in distance and in time. We have to promise each other now that we're going to support each other. We're going to have to keep our heads and show strength of will and try to maintain good relations between ourselves."

Wyatt was some sort of Baptist lay preacher, and he was given to speech making. Denning found it boring when he did that, although he liked Wyatt as much as any of the group of astronauts who had been selected to train for this mission. They were even buddies to the extent that, shut out from the inner circle formed by the others—Wyatt for his bible-bashing, Denning because of a quietness too easily mistaken for arrogance—they found a kind of solidarity in their mutual exclusion.

"Strength of will?" Chang echoed. "Where do you get this stuff, Mike? And what is this get-together bullshit, anyway? You know that Su-Li doesn't really get along with Mary"—Su-Li was Chang's wife, a former fashion model, while Wyatt's wife Mary was a prematurely gray and grandmotherly type—"and Hilda, well . . ."

Hilda was Denning's wife. As was her habit, she had drunk considerably before and during dinner, then asked if she could lie down somewhere for a while.

"The point is," Chang said, "we're not close friends, our families are not close, this is all a sham. And we're going to be spending enough time together as it is."

"This is how the Sovs used to do it," Wyatt said. "Before a mission, they would get together and talk it out, just between themselves. Maybe I shouldn't have invited the families, but I thought it would be nice . . ."

"We're not Sovs," Chang said. "Bunch of losers—lost a whole fucking empire."

"They knew a lot about space psychology," Wyatt said.

"Sure," Chang said. "They played tapes of bird songs. It's bullshit, it's got nothing to do with us. *We're* going to Mars, not them."

"He's got a point, Doug," Denning said. "We have to be able to get along. We're going to be an awfully long way from home."

"It'll be a breeze," Chang said. The youngest team member, he had never even flown the shuttle. "An absolute breeze."

Denning said nothing to this. There was no way he was about to admit his terror over what was to come.

* * * * *

Space. All too much of it. Even growing up, in that archetypal small town. There was the main street and there was the Interstate and then there was the desert, stretching away forever under the deep blue sky. Often he felt achingly lonely, as though the emptiness outside was somehow inside him as well.

In grade school he had seen an old video documentary from before his birth, from the days when astronauts had first walked on the moon. He was badly shaken even then, thinking about the sheer precariousness of it all. Going out there into infinite space, dragging your own life-support system behind you, muttering mantras about God and country and family to comfort yourself. Even watching it on the classroom TV, he had felt the fear grip him, the fear of falling and the fear of suffocating, those ancient genetically encoded fears.

He went to college and then he went to war. He was a good enough pilot, although flying did not thrill him the way it thrilled so many of his colleagues. He was operating a machine, and operating it skillfully, and he was able to repress thinking about what he was really doing, barreling through the empty skies within that thin metal shell.

Later he was a shuttle pilot, in the last days of the shuttle program, and he was able to do that too, although it disturbed him in a way that ordinary flying never had. It was much harder to blot out the blackness and emptiness out there. Particularly when you had to go outside and walk in it. Hanging there in that bubble-suit at the end of a tether, like a baby floating on the end of an umbilical cord, the earth below you or above you and the darkness all around you, terrified him.

But although he could not deny what he felt, he could and did deny feeling it to others. "Wonderful," he would say, just like his colleagues. "Fantastic. Just a wonderful sensation."

* * * * *

For years he worried that the Agency shrinks might catch him out. But they never did. Of course he never told them about his dreams of burning and his dreams of falling to earth. He filled out the tests, he chatted with the test-jockey, and they waved him on through.

Except for the last time, the time he was interviewed right after signing up for the Mars mission. That time the shrink had had something on his mind.

The shrink was an older guy, silver-haired, named Abrams. He wore a faintly disgruntled expression as he stared at the display screen on his desk. The display showed a stack of files, each marked with a date.

"These are your test scores," Abrams said, running his finger down the display. "From the day you joined the Air Force up to the day before yesterday." He tapped the most recent folder and it opened up to show a graph.

Denning craned his head.

"How did I do?" he asked.

"You did very well, lieutenant. As always."

"So that's it? I'm in?"

Abrams leaned forward, stared at him. "I don't like these scores, lieutenant. Not that there's been any huge change. But collated with all the previous data, there's a cumulative pattern through which you become even more of what you already are . . ."

Abrams waved his fingers so that the other folders at the bottom of the screen opened up, their wave forms superimposing themselves in different colors over the more recent scores.

"Which is what?" Denning asked.

"A man who is hiding his fear." Abrams indicated a huge multicolored surge in one corner of the chart. "Your tests present you as a man almost entirely without fear."

"And this is a problem because . . . ?"

"It's hardly uncommon, in your profession, to hide and deny fear. A little self-deception can be a very useful adaptive mechanism. But yours is an extreme case. It's a classic counter-phobia, with the denial in direct proportion to the underlying fear that fuels it. You're driven to do what you're most afraid of doing—like going to Mars."

Denning shook his head. "I didn't fake those tests, doc."

"You faked them. You may not know it. Or you may know it but pretend that you don't. Either way, you're in a massive state of denial."

"And you think, what? One day I'm just going to blow?"

"The possibility exists, lieutenant, or we wouldn't be having this conversation."

"You can check my records. I've never had a problem."

"Those were missions of much shorter duration. We could monitor your psychological state, manage our risks. If we send you to Mars, you'll be beyond our help. It will be up to you to keep it together."

"I always have."

Abrams shook his head slightly. "This Mars mission doesn't worry you at all? Going out there, so very far out and for so long, using largely unproven technology? With some huge question marks about the physiological impacts of the voyage, the intense solar radiation and the variations in gravity, not to mention the psychological stressors . . . You're saying you're not in the least afraid?"

"There's nothing I'd rather do. It's the dream of my life, doc."

"And you have no doubts about the successful outcome of the mission?"

"If the Agency says we can do it, we can do it."

"You're in this deep, lieutenant. After this, there's no turning back. I should flag this right now."

Something in Abrams' voice tipped him off which way it was going to play.

"But you're not going to?"

Abrams sighed heavily. "What the hell," he said. "If they do send you out there, maybe you can keep it together. I like your chances better than most of the other candidates. I hope to hell you can keep it together."

* * * * *

It could have been worse. Abrams could have got on him about his drinking, but the subject hadn't come up.

There had been a physical examination for the Mars program, too, and a raft of blood tests. Later there would be random urine checks. But Denning had known his way around them. He did his drinking only in windows of opportunity, although within the window he could put away an amount even he found alarming. As could his wife.

In the early years of his marriage he had got along with Hilda well enough. It was nice having someone at home, although they were never really close, he was never really that close with anyone.

His wife wanted children and he was willing to go along, although it was not something he had ever wanted for himself. He was willing to do his part, but it turned out that his wife could not. They talked about adoption, on and off. But with the birth rate in steep decline, and all the obstacles to foreign adoption, the immigration quotas and the health checks and the maze-like local bureaucracies, there were few enough kids available. You had to jump through a lot of hoops to have a shot at one, you had to give the matter a great deal of time and focus, and he had neither to give. And after a while he began to doubt that Hilda could pass the screening.

He knew that it was his fault, Hilda's drinking, because he had taught her to drink, and because he was not the husband she really needed. She was lonely when he was away and lonely when he was home. But he could not worry about that too much. He had his own problems, after all.

He never seriously expected that he would go to Mars. There were too many with better credentials. But there was a glamour attached to the project, and a good salary, and there were few enough other job opportunities.

It was not even certain that the project would get off the ground, the economic situation being graver each year. But it was one more way of priming an increasingly rusty pump, and in a time of growing troubles it was thought of as an important morale-builder.

Year after year, the appropriations slipped almost unnoticed into the budget, providing employment in key congressional districts. The funding was renewed and renewed until they were almost ready to do it, to actually send a ship to Mars.

And then the Chinese made it to the moon. And everyone agreed that we could not let them get to Mars first, we had to get a jump on the Chinese. Even more money flowed into the project, and the pace of preparation accelerated.

As the mission approached, Denning found himself unexpectedly propelled into the ranks of the front-runners. One candidate developed a heart murmur, another was in a bad traffic accident, still another was belatedly pulled as a security risk. And in the end he was selected.

* * * * *

She had told him he would go, of course, years before, that weird singer. He did not remember much about their time together, but he remembered that much.

He had met her at a party that the Agency threw to whip up interest in the mission. He had not been himself that night. He had fought with Hilda on the way out to the Space Center, about her drinking, and how she should be careful not to embarrass him. She had screamed at him, calling him terrible names she must have picked up from her new drinking buddies in the roadhouse taverns she had taken to frequenting.

He was furious by the time they got to the party. He had begun to drink methodically, throwing back one neat scotch after another. He had felt nothing but contempt for the politicians and the rock musicians and the screen stars and the hack science-fiction writers clustering around him. Let them go up there, he thought. Let them strap themselves on top of a rocket and go see what it was really like.

"It's all a show," he started to tell a junior congressman, before an Agency flack pulled him away. "A big fucking show. Bread and circuses, right?"

He realized that he was behaving badly, and that if he continued to do so they might throw him off the team. Perhaps that was what he wanted. But if it was, he was not prepared to admit it to himself. And so he had started a harmless flirtation with the singer. And then she had been swarming all over him.

There was a certain sort of woman who pursued astronauts, but the singer was not like them at all, and Denning was both flattered and puzzled by her attentions. He had heard her music now and again on the car radio. He did not much care for it, but he knew that she was very popular and successful.

She was good-looking enough, in a cold sort of way. But there was something a little spooky about her, as if she wasn't quite there, as if she was somewhere else at the same time.

"You're the folk singer, right?" he said. "I just love folk singing. *Oooooowoo, if I had a hammer . . .*"

And then, one or two drinks later, he made his move. "It's getting crowded. Would you like to take a walk? I could show you around the Center a little."

"Why don't we go back to my hotel?"

He had thought about that for a moment, glancing back towards the table where the astronauts' wives had gathered, where Hilda was presumably sitting. But he was drunk enough not to care too much about the consequences.

They had gone back to her hotel room. And after that things had gotten a little fuzzy. He must have been drunker than he thought, because when he woke up the next day he could not even remember fucking her.

He recalled arriving at her suite, and being impressed by its opulence. They had sat on the couch and begun to make out. But after that he remembered nothing until he woke up the next morning, stretched out almost fully clothed on the bed, with the singer sitting by the dressing table brushing her hair.

Well, not absolutely nothing. He could recollect having a fleeting sensation, as he sat on the couch with the singer, that someone else was in the room, flickering faintly at the edge of his vision. He had turned his head to get a better look. And then what?

He didn't know. The memory was too slippery. He could not get a grip on it. In truth, he did not want to.

He had got out of that hotel room as quickly as he could. But before he left, she told him that he would be going to Mars.

"Have a good trip," she said, as he was leaving.

"Trip?"

"To Mars."

"It hasn't been decided who's going to go," he told her. "There are twelve of us in the running. Only three will go. Right now I'm low down in the order."

"You'll go."

She had said it with absolute certainty, like some gypsy fortuneteller reading the cards. And in the end, of course, she was right. Later, he would sometimes wonder how she could have known. But for the most part, he tried not to think about her at all.

He knew enough about alcoholism to deduce that he had experienced some kind of blackout in the singer's hotel room. And he knew that blackouts were very bad news. After that night he had stopped drinking, cold turkey. All by himself, no bullshitting around with AA or the Agency shrinks. For a while, he was very proud of himself.

* * * * *

"This is about leaving," Wyatt said, towards the end of their last night on Earth. "One of the Apollo astronauts, Mike Collins, said that. *Space flight was about leaving.* That's even more true now. This is about leaving the planet before it's too late."

"Leaving it all behind, right?" Hilda asked. She had joined them, refreshed from her nap but still visibly buzzed. "All the mess. Leaving it for us to deal with."

"It's about heading out where we belong," Wyatt said. "Where God has destined us to go. Reaching for the stars."

"The way I see it," Chang said, "it's not so much about leaving as it is about coming back. Once we get back from Mars, we're going to be heroes, we're going to be like *gods.* There'll be nothing people won't do for us."

But that wasn't right, either, Denning thought. Or at least, it wasn't why *he* was going to Mars. He had never figured on being anyone's hero. Nor did he see anything terribly heroic in what they were about to do, climbing into that module and letting a giant firecracker blast them all the way to Mars.

What they were about to do was dangerous as hell, but it was hardly heroic. It was more of a stunt, like jumping over vats of boiling oil on a motorcycle, or going over Niagara Falls in a barrel.

"Right, Jake?" Chang was asking him. "Isn't that right?"

"Oh yeah," Denning said. "That's right. We're going to be famous."

They would be famous the way screen stars were famous, and serial killers, and relatives of the President. But perhaps he would enjoy it when the time came.

* * 1 4 * *

Pinball. As they blasted out towards Mars, Denning remembered his father's antique pinball table in the basement rec-room of his childhood home. Mostly he had been a Nintendo kid, but now and again he would hammer away at that old machine with the flashing lights. The display, as he now recalled, had shown the metal ball zipping around the solar system. In a way, it was destiny.

Pinball, he thought. That's what we're riding. A big chunk of metal careening our way out into the void.

* * * * *

The six-month-long flight from Earth to Mars was not quite as bad as Denning had feared.

In the close confines of the cabin he found it increasingly difficult to sustain the illusion that he and Wyatt were friends. And there were times when he felt like killing Chang. But there were ways of escaping them, escaping to his bunk to work on his bridge puzzles, or paging through the mystery novels that Control had thoughtfully dumped into the ship's computer.

It was more difficult to escape Control, with their routine check-ins and their equally routine media circuses in which the astronauts would talk to the President or to their wives and children. Denning was not sure what was worse, talking to Hilda or talking to the President. As the ship moved further from Earth, and the time lapse on these communications increased, these rituals became ever more strained and artificial, until they were discontinued entirely.

Afterwards, they would just send taped sequences. There was less media interest, in any case, as the voyage dragged on. The Agency had sold the right to mission coverage to the highest bidder, who then resold the footage to other markets. But the ratings, after their departure, had been a bust. There was just too much else going on in the news . . . if people could stand to watch the news at all.

Even heavily edited as it must have been, the news from Earth was clearly not good. The economic situation was terrible and the international situation was terrible. The cities were armed camps, there were psychos everywhere, crime was running even further out of control, there were terrorist attacks everywhere. There had been a limited nuclear exchange between India and Pakistan. The guerilla armies of the New Shining Path had swept through Central America and were knocking on the doors of Mexico City.

But somehow it was hard to get very excited about any of that, it was all so long ago and far away.

Perhaps he should have figured out earlier what was happening to Wyatt. The mission commander seemed normal enough for the most part, but he was spending an awful lot of time outside the ship. Any possible excuse and he would be out there, adjusting the telescope, taking readings, examining structural degradation. They were supposed to take turns, sharing exposure to hard radiation, but early on Wyatt had asked if he could go instead of Denning.

"I love it out there," he had said. "Looking on God's handwork. I just love it."

Denning had agreed readily enough. He had absolutely no desire to go out there if he did not have to. And the further they moved away from Earth the more he feared the vast emptiness that was swallowing them up.

At first he wondered whether Wyatt had somehow sensed his fear, and was covering for him. But as time went on, and as Wyatt badgered Chang into giving up his outside time as well, it became clear that the man really did love it out there.

"I'm not scared or anything, you understand," Chang told Denning. "But it's a drag, suiting up, going out, doing the checks, coming in . . ."

Chang was bored, that was the problem, he was bored already, with the voyage and with his companions. Eventually his boredom would start to drive him mad.

"Sometimes," Wyatt said, once, "I wonder what it would be like, suiting up and going out there and cutting the line. To float free, completely free . . . Do you ever wonder what it would be like?"

"No," Denning said. "No, I never wondered that."

* * * * *

It was pretty much an anticlimax, actually getting there. They left the mother ship in its preprogrammed orbit around Mars and Wyatt guided the lander down smoothly.

Denning was the second man out on to the surface, carrying the camera. Wyatt, of course, was first, and he had the flag. "We made it," he said, as he stepped out on to that sandy plain. "Thank you, Lord."

"Was that in the script?" Denning asked, curious.

"There is no script," Wyatt said. "Now shut up, we're transmitting."

"They'll be editing," Denning said. "What's another thirty second time delay?"

As Wyatt planted the flag in the ancient dust, Denning felt an almost overpowering urge to giggle. It all seemed absurd, suddenly.

"Well," he said. "I guess we can go home now."

"Shut up," Wyatt said, again.

"Yeah," Chang said, from behind him. "Try and be a little dignified, for chrissakes."

Chang was angry because he was third man out of the lander. Control had set down the order on a seniority basis. As if Denning gave a shit.

“Marvelous stuff,” Control said, hours later, after they had pitched camp for the night. They said this on the open channel. And on the other channel, the closed one, “What the fuck’s the matter with Denning?”

He was a long way from Control, but he was still afraid of what they could do to him when he returned.

“I’m sorry,” he said, over the coded channel. “Just a little clowning around. It won’t happen again.”

In retrospect, this too would seem comical.

* * * * *

There was a great deal of work to do, much of it very hard. At first Denning almost enjoyed it. It helped to keep his mind off where they were and how far they were from home. But after a while it really began to get to him.

It was cold, this planet, most of the time, colder than Antarctica, and just as bleak in its own way. But the worst of it was that it was so empty, so completely empty.

Sure there were mountains, lots of mountains that had once been volcanoes. There were gullies that had been river valleys when there had still been running water here, before the volcanoes had died and the carbon dioxide had thinned out and the water had frozen into the ground.

But that was just scenery. No matter how hard they looked, even trekking up to the pole to drill into the ice, they could find nothing living on this planet, not a single microbe. Nor was there any evidence that anything had ever lived here. It was so empty and dead, this world, it made his hometown feel like Manhattan.

And everywhere the dust . . . not even sand, just dust, everywhere, a reddish dust that piled up on everything, until it was blown up into the sky by the fierce storm patterns and you couldn’t see the glove of your suit in front of your face.

Day by day, he felt the emptiness and the deadness seeping into him, filling him up. In his dreams he would stand out there in the dust and scream and yet be unable to hear his own voice. Later, when Chang began to make a point of sleeping with earplugs, he realized that he must be screaming in his sleep.

His dreams were bad and his appetite was poor and his hands would sometimes shake uncontrollably. He no longer believed that he would make it back to Earth. It was just too far, impossibly far. He was sure that he was going to crack. And yet it was Wyatt who cracked instead.

In the beginning Wyatt had been commanding, driving them on relentlessly to build the base dome and to move through the endless sequence of other tasks that Control had set them.

At night, as Denning slumped exhausted on to his cot, drifting rapidly into sleep, he would hear Wyatt still awake, praying loudly. And in the morning when he awoke, Wyatt would already be up, pacing about in anticipation of the day's tasks. In retrospect Denning would realize that there was something manic about the way Wyatt drove himself and drove them. But at the time he was too fatigued and numb to think much about it.

Wyatt sustained this grueling pace for several months, the strain only occasionally evident in a twitching facial nerve, an unexpected burst of temper. And then one day he went mad.

"There were Martians," he told Denning and Chang over their final ration of the day. He said this in a conversational tone, as though remarking on the weather, so that it took a moment for them to understand what they had heard.

"What?" Chang said. "What did you say?"

"I said, there were Martians."

"You found something?" Denning asked, thinking of the tests that Wyatt had been running that day on the latest batch of soil samples. "You actually found something?"

"There were Martians," Wyatt said again, shouting now. "Are you people listening to me? I'm not talking about bacteria, I'm not talking about lichen. I'm telling you *there were Martians.*" And then, more calmly: "Until we killed them."

"Killed them?"

"By coming here," Wyatt said. "We came here and made them like they never existed. But there were Martians. Beings like *gods*, creatures of superior force and power. Or giants, giants at the very least. Old wise creatures, little green Martians, bug-eyed Martians. All kinds of Martians. Living in jeweled palaces, domed cities, ancient towns with narrow winding streets. With canals, canals a mile wide, brimming with cool blue water . . . *There were Martians.* Until we came here and made them dead."

Denning saw Chang get up from the table and move towards the medicine chest. Wyatt paid him no attention.

"Mike," Denning said, tentatively. "I read Burroughs, too, when I was a kid, I read Bradbury, all that stuff. It's a shame it isn't the way they said it would be. But we never thought it would be . . ."

"We killed them," Wyatt said, flatly. "We made them dead. We made them like they never had been. And all that was left was the emptiness, that's all that was left."

He began to cry then, in great racking sobs. He did not resist, or even look up, when Chang jabbed him through his shirtsleeve with a needle. He cried for a few minutes more. And then he put his head down in his arms and began to snore.

"Should we call this in?" Denning asked, after they had dragged Wyatt to his cot. "Should we tell Control now?"

"There's nothing Control can do for us, or for him," Chang said. "Let's get some sleep. We'll deal with this in the morning."

But in the morning Wyatt was gone.

* * 15 * *

"Hello, Robert."

As Duke came out of his dressing room and headed towards the stage, he heard an oddly familiar voice. He turned to see a woman with a large floppy hat pulled down over long blond hair, and antique mirrored shades over her eyes. She was holding the arm of a man with neatly trimmed gray hair and beard.

"It's good to see you," she said, taking off the shades.

He looked into those abnormally blue eyes, and the recognition dawned.

"Martha," he said, astonished to see her here, backstage in this tiny theater, on this cold March night in Montreal. "What are you doing here?"

"We were passing through, and I heard you were playing. It's a long time since I've been to a show. And Daniel has never seen one at all." She indicated the solemn-looking child trailing behind her. "Say hello to my old friend Mr. Duke, Daniel."

"Hello," the boy said, without enthusiasm.

He had heard that Martha had a child: the whole world had heard. The boy looked a lot like his mother. Perhaps he looked like his father, too, but Duke had no way of answering that question. No one knew who the boy's father was, despite the most frantic investigative efforts by the world's entertainment media.

"This is my friend Murray Snow," Martha said.

"A pleasure," the gray-haired man said, reaching out to shake his hand. A firm grip, a faintly British accent.

Behind this group hovered a muscular young man with watchful eyes, presumably Martha's bodyguard.

It was a tiny retinue for Martha. In the old days, she had traveled with an army of dressers and hairdressers, record company flacks and media hacks, protectors and advisers and hangers-on.

"Martha . . ." he began.

And then he was being waved towards the stage where the pickup band were playing the intro.

"I've got to go. Maybe we'll talk later."

"I'd like that," she said.

* * * * *

Duke had not seen Martha in years. But he had watched from a distance as her career arced ever upward. Until she had quit at the age of twenty-nine, at the very peak of her popularity.

Her management explained that she wished to spend more time with her child. The show biz oracles were quick to suggest that she could no longer sustain the pressures of her success, all that love and all that hatred pressing down upon her.

Duke doubted that. Martha, when he had known her, had seemed remarkably unaffected by it all. But he could have been wrong about that. He had not really known her that well.

They had shared a few bills, when she had been on her way up and he had been on his way down. They had shared a few bills, and a few hotel rooms, too, but it had never been anything serious. He had been too tied up with himself to really get close to Martha. And Martha had seemed mainly amused with him, amused but no more than that. It had never been serious on either side. Or so he had always told himself.

* * * * *

After the show, they walked to a restaurant a few blocks away. Despite the cold, it was a luxury for him to be able to walk the streets after dark. Back in L.A., it would be lunacy.

Along the way they passed a bar. Through the window of the bar, on the wide-screen TV, they saw a graphic of a spaceship heading towards the planet Mars. The caption read "41 days to planetfall."

It was months since the ship had departed, in a final gigantic burst of publicity. There had been a few follow-up items on the news, but then it had faded from view, and Duke had almost forgotten about it.

"What do you think of that, Martha?" Duke asked. "Soon they're going to be landing on Mars."

"What do I think about going to Mars? I think it's like the weather, you know, space exploration. You can't stop it. It's fate, somehow, that we keep doing it. Like we need to, whether it's really a good idea or not."

Martha was still staring at the screen, which now showed the astronauts inside the spaceship.

"I hung around a little with one of those guys," she said. She pointed at the white astronaut with the dark hair, next to the black astronaut. "That one. Jake."

"What was he like?"

"Frightened," she said. "Lost. You know, the usual."

* * * * *

They found their restaurant and sat at a table and ordered their food.

"So you're still on the road," she said.

"Sometimes. Actually, not that much."

This was the first time he had toured in nearly a year. Even in the twilight of his career, the nostalgia surrounding his name was sufficient to fill the smaller halls. But with the problems in so many cities these days, and the on-again off-again curfews, it was difficult to set up a tour. It was a little easier up here in Canada, where things had not yet run so far out of control.

"Supporting a new record?"

"Just playing. I get bored, sitting around back home."

He had not made a new record in years. His last record company had dropped his contract, and no one else had picked it up. They all shared the conventional wisdom that he was burned-out as a creative and commercial force. Duke was inclined to agree with the conventional wisdom.

He did not even enjoy performing that much anymore. He had little appetite for the endless recapitulation of a dead past. But it was the life he had grown used to.

These days he played solo, or with a local group. It was cheaper and less cumbersome to do it that way than to try to keep a band together.

"I miss it sometimes," Martha said. "Going up on stage."

"I heard you retired. I didn't understand why."

"I wanted to spend this time with Daniel. And I didn't have anything more to say."

That was Martha for you, he thought. It was always nice to have something to say. But there were plenty of times when you didn't. It had never stopped him from singing.

They talked about the past, and then they talked about the present: the riots and police strikes, the gang wars and citizen militias, the terrorist hits and fire bombings and assassinations and Mental Health laws and all the rest of it.

"Back in L.A.," he told her, "we've got street gangs as big as army divisions. We've got war zones, dead zones, whole city grids that belong to the gangs and the squatters and the junkies. Packs of wild children scavenging food scraps from dumpsters, ready to cut your throat for a five dollar coin or for your kidneys."

The wars overseas had played themselves out and had come back home. But the new wars were fought street by street and block by block between multiple contestants divided by ideology and nationality and religion. Islamic insurgents battled Vietnamese drug runners, the John

Birch Army fought it out with Trotskyist Brigades, you needed a scorecard to keep track of who was fighting who and why. But when they weren't fighting each other they turned their attention to fighting the established order, or what remained of it. Anyone and everyone was a potential target.

Whole cities were under permanent National Guard occupation, while others hired private mercenary armies to help hold the line.

"It's like everything is falling apart," Duke said.

"Yes," Martha agreed, almost absently. "Falling apart."

But she was removed from all that now. She lived, most of the time, in Corfu.

"That guy you introduced me to," he said. "Murray. Is he in the business?"

"Murray is a psychiatrist. Although right now he's on sabbatical. He's staying with us in Corfu while he writes his book."

"Book?"

"About the world in transition. About the disturbances. That's why he came to Montreal—he's speaking at a conference on civil disorder and the origins of the disturbances. We came along for the ride."

The disturbances. Everyone talked about them that way now, as though they were some kind of force of nature. When you called something a disturbance, there was always the hope that things would eventually return to normal, whatever that was.

"And what do the people at this conference think they are? The origins of the disturbances?"

She shrugged. "I haven't heard Murray's speech yet. But what I heard today was pretty much the usual. The breakdown of the family, the schools, the sense of community . . ."

"You don't sound convinced."

"It's all true enough, I suppose. But it's missing the point somehow. These disturbances . . . I think it's the Earth, Robert. The Earth on the brink of a nervous breakdown."

"The Earth? We're talking about riots and bombings. About things that *people* do."

"But we *are* the Earth, Robert. All of us, every living thing. And now it's like she's acting through us, trying to purge herself . . ."

"By burning everything down?"

"If that's what it takes."

"Same old Martha. All doom and gloom."

"I see a lot of hope, actually. But first we have to get through these times."

"You sound like you're starting to believe your own songs."

"I always believed them."

Still flaky after all these years, he thought. And yet, all the same, he found himself liking her all over again. He had forgotten how good it felt to be around her, to bathe in the immense tranquillity she radiated even as she discussed her most apocalyptic visions.

"Where are you heading now?" he asked, as they rode in the cab back to her hotel.

"We're going home tomorrow." And then she said something that surprised him. "Why don't you come along?"

"I'm playing in Toronto."

"Come on afterward."

"I might just do that," he said, not imagining that he would.

* * * * *

He was in his hotel room in Toronto after the show, watching a report on the latest terrorist bombing in Boston, when the record company executive came to call.

"Great show," he said. "Brought back a lot of memories. I was here for a sales meeting and I asked who was playing in town and they said 'Robert Duke.' And I said 'Robert Duke is my idol.'" He smiled, showing his diamond-studded front teeth.

The record company executive's name was Ken Winston. He was wearing the lurid green corporate uniform of RealTime Records.

Duke might once have been excited by the fact that a representative of a major label would want to speak to him. But he had long since given up hope of a new recording deal, and did not allow himself to hope for one now.

"So I'm sitting there thinking," Winston said, "what happened to Robert Duke? What the fuck happened to him?"

"This and that." Duke no longer even tried to recite the whole weary litany of crooked managers and persecutory IRS agents, crazy wives and gonzo tabloid journalists, drug busts and car wrecks, missed connections and lost opportunities. These days, it bored even himself. And he had come to see that what it came down to was basically a bunch of excuses. "Time, mostly. Catches us all."

Winston nodded. "But there's this great thing about time. Sometimes it loops around. Sometimes, what was old can become new again. That's what I said to myself . . . Maybe Robert Duke's moment is going to come again. Maybe I could help make that happen."

He stared hard at Winston. The executive stared back, unblinking.

"What are we talking about here?"

"We're talking about a new Robert Duke album," Winston said. "On RealTime Records. So what do you say, Robert?"

"That it sounds interesting," Duke said, carefully. "That you should talk to my manager."

"I'll do that," Winston asked. "We'll have the contract ready for you to look over when you get back to L.A. Or if you're somewhere else, we'll e-mail you there."

"Where else would I be?"

"Corfu, maybe. I heard you might be heading there."

Duke made the connection, finally, the one that had been eluding him, or that he had been eluding. RealTime was Martha's label.

"You heard that from Martha?"

"Martha? Martha doesn't talk to us. But she's still under contract to us, she's still a crucial asset. We keep an eye on her. We like to know what she's doing, what she's thinking. We know she invited you to Corfu, and we see that as a real positive step."

"Positive? How do you mean?"

"She's reaching out to her past. She wants to come back, but she's not ready to admit that to herself yet. She still needs a little push. Hopefully, you can give it to her. And we can have a new Martha Nova disc on the racks, right next to yours."

Since Martha's retirement, RealTime had been skillfully repackaging her old songs and newly discovered out-takes. But by now they would be desperate for new product.

"I see," Duke said. "What we're actually talking about is a new Martha Nova album."

"Listen, Robert. I was serious about what I said before: you *were* great. And maybe you could be again. But it's an iffy proposition, given the current market conditions. If we could get something new from Martha, it would make it a lot easier for us to take a flier on something like your album."

"And if spending time with me doesn't make Martha want to come back?"

"Then you'll persuade her. Tell her the whole world is waiting for her."

"She already knows that."

"It might make the difference, hearing it from you," Winston said. "Word is, she thinks a lot of you."

"What word?"

"Come on, Robert. You're in all the Martha bios. *The rock star who loved her* . . . Don't tell me you didn't read them."

"I skimmed a couple of them."

"Close associates say, you were the big romance in her life."

"Yeah, right. Her hairdresser. Her cook. Her driver. Some close associates."

"Maybe they weren't so far wrong. She did invite you to Corfu. And as far as we know, there's no one else in her life right now."

"What about Murray Snow?"

"A good friend," Winston said. "Also her shrink. She used to see him almost every day back in L.A. And when she moved out to Corfu, she took him along."

"What's he treating her for?"

"Creative block. That's his specialty. He treats all the big screenwriters, artists, game designers."

"Martha is blocked?"

"She hasn't written a new song in years."

"And has Snow helped her?"

"No, he hasn't. He doesn't seem to be helping at all. We're starting to think he may be hindering . . . deliberately keeping her blocked."

"Why would he want to do that?"

"Maybe because MentHealth asked him to."

"MentHealth? Why would they care about Martha's creativity?"

"MentHealth have been tracking her for years. They think she's a destructive influence on public morale. They were delighted when she left the country. And they sure as hell don't want her coming back."

"And you think Snow works for MentHealth?"

"He moves in the same circles, he probably thinks the same way. He may well be keeping Martha out of the picture for them. But we're hopeful that you can counter his influence. Persuade her to come back."

Duke shook his head. "Even if I could . . . there's no way I would do something like that. I mean, sure I'd like a new recording deal, but not that badly. How could I face Martha, if I agreed to something like that?"

"She need never know about it."

"But I would."

"Look, don't decide anything now. Go to Corfu. See for yourself what's going on with Snow, what you think would be best for Martha."

"But why should I? If I'm not taking your deal, why should I go?"

"You want to know your motivation? You think this is the Actor's Studio? You know, most people, most of the time, don't have the faintest idea why they do what they do. They just do it, then they try to figure out why. But you want a reason, I'll give you one. You should go because you want to see her. And because you don't have anything better to do with your life."

✶ ✶ 1 6 ✶ ✶

Towards the end of his life the psychoanalyst Carl Jung dreamed of the end of the world. He saw the oceans rising, inundating the land. He did not take this vision literally, but understood it to signify the inundation of the islands of individual human consciousness by an upsurge of the collective unconscious.

This same preoccupation is reflected in Jung's later visionary works, such as Flying Saucers: A Modern Myth of Things Seen in the Skies, *in which he engaged with contemporary symbols of transformation signifying a forthcoming end to time, or at least a great disruption preceding the coming of new times.*

Jung saw the flood coming. Now, the tide is rising. As our global information and entertainment networks coalesce, creating new tribal links even as they erode old ones, an archaic revival gathers force. Progressively we plunge beneath our thin veneer of modernity, down to the primitive yet sophisticated ancient mind, tuning in to transmissions from the deepest levels of our collective unconscious.

The popularity of the singer Martha Nova is a key signifier of this movement. With her songs of madness and destruction and a yearning for an end to time, she is both a spokesperson for the historical world moment and a harbinger of the times to come.

(Murray H. Snow: "Martha Nova and the Children: A Preliminary Analysis," *Journal of Social and Cultural Change,* June 2019).

* * * * *

"How do you find things back home?" Murray Snow asked.

Duke looked up from his plate. "Oh, the same I guess. Which is to say, worse all the time."

"You don't think the Mental Health laws are helping?"

Duke put down his fork and pushed his plate back. He was too tired from his long flight to enjoy it. He had arrived here at Martha's house in Corfu only two hours before.

"I don't know," he said. "Maybe it would be worse without them. But a lot of people don't like it very much, having some MentHealth worker come around to tell you that your kid is antisocial and has to start taking some pills. Or that people at work say you're becoming paranoid and you have to come in for testing . . ."

"Sometimes," Snow said, "you have to make a choice between civil liberties and public order. And yet I wonder whether we've made the right choice."

Duke looked at the psychiatrist in surprise.

"You don't support MentHealth?"

"I was all in favor at first. But the reality of it has been disappointing. MentHealth has become little more than a machine for drugging unruly children, for holding them in the trance of modern civilization. And a clumsy, insufficient machine at that. Because for all its efforts, the madness still grows." Snow shook his head ruefully. "And yet some of the best people in MentHealth are friends of mine, true idealists."

"Those are the ones you have to watch out for," Duke said. "The true believers."

Later, when the talk at the table turned to the past, Snow sat still as a statue while Duke and Martha swapped old road stories.

"So I told the promoter, either the band get *green* Fudgicles, the way it says in the contract, or there's no show. Purple and orange, forget it . . ."

Martha roared with laughter with him, at the way he had once been. "Crazy times."

"I guess you're well out of it."

"For the moment."

"For the moment? You're thinking about going back?"

"Oh sure. Sure I'll go back, when the time is right." She put her arm around Daniel. "Right now I'm happy to be here with my son and with my friends. But now isn't forever."

"I suppose in a few years," Duke said, "when Daniel will be more grown up, it'll be easier for you."

"Oh, it won't be that long."

Snow was frowning at Martha.

"You should think about this carefully," he told her. "You have to be sure you're ready to handle the stress."

"I'm not fragile, Murray. I'm not going to break."

"But these are dangerous times. You've seen the news: the riots, the fires, the terrorism, the gang wars, everything spiraling out of control. People are highly aroused, ready to flare up at the slightest cue. And you excite people, Martha, you stir them up. Some of your fans may not be so very well-balanced to begin with. You might excite someone a little too much. It would only take one . . ." Snow trailed off, as though unwilling to complete the thought.

"To kill me?" Martha asked. "That was always a risk."

"It's an even graver one now."

"Perhaps. But then, perhaps the music will help to calm people down. You know, back in the Middle Ages everyone sang together. Right across Europe, in every church, the same hymns at the same time. They knew something we've forgotten, that music is a way of tuning society. If you don't tune it right, everything falls apart."

"I admire your music, Martha. But you'll have to admit it hasn't made that kind of difference."

"I'm not talking about my old songs, Murray. I'm talking about the new music, the songs I'm *going* to write."

"You're working on something?" Duke asked.

"No," she said. "Not yet. I don't hear the new songs yet. Just the occasional snatch. But it sounds like quiet music. Real quiet and soothing."

Duke stared at her, intrigued. She talked as if songwriting for her was simply a matter of tuning in to some radio inside her head.

"Even a whisper," Snow said, "can be a shout. In the wrong ears." He turned to Duke. "I hope you won't encourage her in this foolishness, Robert."

"Martha will do what Martha will do," Duke said. "I don't think either of us can hope to persuade her to do anything else."

* * * * *

"I don't think he likes me," Duke told Martha afterwards.

"Murray? He doesn't even know you."

They were walking in the gardens. Snow had gone back to the guest cottage where he was staying, and Daniel had gone up to his room.

Duke's fatigue had lifted. He felt energized by the clear night air, by Martha's presence beside him . . . It was still hard to believe that he had come here, harder still to imagine what would happen now.

"He thinks I'm reminding you of the past, of what you're missing."

"He's a little protective," she said. "But he's just trying to do what he thinks is best for me. He's really a wonderful person. When you get to know him better, you'll see."

Martha led him down a path to the beach. They sat on the sand in the gathering twilight, watching the waves break on the shore.

"It's beautiful here," Duke said. "But don't you get bored?"

She shook her head. "I was so busy for so long . . . It's been great to just goof off, these past few years. I wasn't writing or recording, back home. I was hardly performing. I thought that I might as well be somewhere I could enjoy doing nothing. I always knew that it wasn't forever, but this has been a great place to wait."

"For what?"

"For what time brings. For my music to come back. For you, Robert . . ."

"For me?"

"Sure. I knew you would come here. That we would have this time together."

"You knew? How could you know?"

She put a finger to his lips. "Later," she said. "We can talk about that later."

* * 17 * *

Duke sat at a table on the back patio, talking into his notebook, setting down fragments of lyrics of songs he would probably never complete.

Glancing up, he saw Murray Snow returning from his walk along the cliff-top path. Snow was dressed in khaki shorts and shirt, binoculars around his neck, his bird watchers' manual in his hand.

Snow went bird watching every morning. You could set your watch by it. Every afternoon Martha went to Snow's cottage for their session. You could set your watch by that, too.

Duke wondered what Snow had been saying about him to Martha. Nothing good, he was sure. Snow could only see him as a bad influence on Martha: a living reminder of her wild past, a warning signal of a dangerous future. And no doubt he had told Martha as much.

But if Snow had been trying to undermine Duke's relationship with Martha, so far his efforts had been unsuccessful.

She had taken him to her bed the very first night, and they had picked up where they had left off so many years before. Or perhaps not exactly where they left off. He was in some ways a different person now. This time around, he was beginning to suspect, it could be something serious.

Duke watched as Snow reached the guest cottage, paused there, then started walking towards him.

"Would you care to join me for a cup of tea?" Snow asked. "We should talk."

"About what?"

"About Martha," Snow said.

Duke nodded slowly. "All right," he said. He closed his notebook, stood up.

Snow led the way to the guest cottage. It was quite Spartan: a bed, a dressing table, a couch, a desk, a toilet, a sink, an electric kettle. But the walls were covered with framed photographs of swirling patterns.

While Snow busied himself filling the kettle, Duke studied the photograph over the desk. It showed a giant circle that had been carved into intricate crescent shapes, surrounded by a cluster of half circles.

"Isn't that spectacular?" Snow said. "Truly a mandala for the ages."

Duke squinted at a caption-line underneath the photograph: *Alton Priors, Wiltshire, 20 April 2023.*

"Is that a crop circle?" Duke asked. "I haven't heard anything about crop circles in years."

"The media no longer pays them any attention. Yet they persist all the same, all over the world. This year is shaping up as one of the best ever, in terms of both numbers and aesthetics, although the latter of course is a matter of taste."

He pointed to the image over the couch, a complex mathematical figure of circles joined by intersecting lines.

"That one, for example, I find quite astonishing. Experts believe it to be a representation of the Tree of Life, as diagrammed by the Kabbalists . . . a Jewish occult tradition which in itself can be traced back to the ancient Sumerians. The circles are known as *sephira,* which literally means 'number.' In Kabbalistic tradition, the sephirot are emanations of God which, when combined, constitute the fullness of the godhead."

"Experts?" Duke echoed. "There are experts on crop circles?"

"There are experts on everything these days. Whereas I have merely an amateur's interest in these manifestations."

"An aesthetic interest?"

"But not only that. I regard these crop circles as important signifiers."

"Signifying what, exactly?"

"The end of time, Robert. The end of time."

"I'm not sure I follow you."

"I suppose it is quite a leap."

The kettle was boiling. Snow picked it up and poured hot water into a pair of mugs. He handed one to Duke. "I hope green tea is all right."

"It's fine."

Snow motioned for Duke to sit down on the couch, then swiveled around the desk chair to sit facing him.

Duke was still staring at the crop circles. "I thought they were a hoax."

"In what sense?"

"They were made by people . . . ordinary people."

"As opposed to little green men? Yes, I'm quite sure they were made by people, whether by conscious processes or in some other way. But that doesn't make them any less an expression of the world mind. They are symbols thrown up by the collective unconscious of humanity, symbols of transformation."

"World mind?" Duke echoed. "How do you mean, world mind?"

"For now it's only a metaphor. But it's emerging, all around us, growing stronger every day. Crop circles are only one of many signs that our collective unconscious is awakening. A historical disjunction is close at hand, perhaps an end to time as we know it. Would you care to read my paper on the subject?"

"Maybe later." Duke said. He sipped his tea. It was still boiling hot.

He wondered if Snow would be willing to keep talking about crop circles and the collective unconscious all morning. Quite likely so, he thought.

"You wanted to talk about Martha?" he asked.

"Yes," Snow said. "Martha is thinking seriously about resuming her former career. And I'm afraid you've been encouraging her."

Duke shrugged. "I don't have that kind of influence over Martha. But if she asked my opinion, I'd say, sure, she should go back. She's a great talent, Murray. She shouldn't be hiding herself away."

"I'm not sure how much you know about the circumstances surrounding her departure from the United States."

"Circumstances?"

"Martha left the country just hours before the issue of an Intervention Order by the Los Angeles office of the Mental Health Administration. Which is to say, basically a warrant for her examination and confinement. She has not returned to the United States since that time."

"MentHealth were going after Martha? On what grounds?"

Snow hesitated. "As her psychiatrist, I can't comment on that. Except to say that there *were* grounds."

"And Martha heard about this order?"

"She heard about it from me. I have friends in MentHealth—former colleagues, students, and so forth. Knowing of my interest in Martha, they informed me of what was about to occur. I was able to warn Martha in time."

"But why would they warn you? Unless they *wanted* you to tell Martha about their plans . . ."

"They warned me out of friendship."

"More likely they wanted to make her run. And you helped them do just that."

"I did what I thought was best for Martha. If I hadn't, Martha would be back home in some Recovery Center."

"You really think they would have gone that far, faced down all the outrage they would have stirred up?"

"Yes, I do."

"I think you did their work for them. You helped them scare off Martha. And you're still helping them, keeping Martha here like some kind of caged bird."

"I have strongly advised Martha against returning, that's quite true. I really don't think it's safe for her. MentHealth won't tolerate it. They regard her as a disruptive influence, a quasi-messianic leader of a dangerous cult. These are difficult times, Robert, what with the unemployment, and the rioting, and the increased incidence of mental disorder, and so on and so forth."

Snow seemed bored, reciting this wretched litany.

"Right now," he said, "there's a lot of restlessness back home, a lot of hunger, waiting to focus around something. Martha could be it. MentHealth are afraid that her return could blow the lid right off. If I can't persuade her to stay here, they'll take steps of their own. And this time, there may not be any warning."

* * * * *

Duke made his way from Snow's cottage, deep in thought.

"I bet you'd like to know."

He looked up to see Martha's son Daniel standing in the doorway to the house.

"Know what?"

"What they're saying about you, mommy and Dr. Snow. I bet you'd like to know that."

At this odd echo of his earlier thoughts, Duke felt a shiver travel up his spine.

"And why Dr. Snow thinks Mommy is crazy. You'd like to know that, too."

It was something Duke was still not used to, the *strangeness* of Martha's child. The boy was like no other child Duke had known. And sometimes he said the strangest things. If he had been enrolled in school back home, it was likely that he would already have been picked out by

MentHealth workers as potentially dysfunctional, already placed under some sort of treatment. MentHealth believed in catching them young. Which could be one more reason why Martha no longer lived back home.

Martha had made him strange. Dragging him around with her across the country for the first three years of his life. And then, after she had quit the music business, keeping him with her at home to share her self-imposed exile from the world.

Back in L.A. the boy had attended a play group when Martha's schedule had allowed. But since then he had rarely been exposed to other children. Oh, he logged into several virtual schoolhouses on a regular basis, learning music and mathematics and science alongside the holographic representations of other children scattered around the world. And sometimes, too, he would spend time on the net playing with a boy in Tokyo and a girl in New Delhi, the three of them engaged in some vastly recomplicated strategy game Duke could not begin to comprehend.

But mostly Daniel seemed to prefer to be alone, or else with his mother. Even alone he was often with his mother, listening to her songs or engaging her in long conversations in which he took both roles.

It was not the healthiest way to raise a child. But Duke could not criticize Martha for the way she lived. He knew the reasons for it well enough.

"Your mother isn't crazy," he said. "She has a creative block, and Dr. Snow is helping her with it. A creative block means that she can't write songs."

"I know what it means," Daniel said, "and he does think she's crazy. Look."

The boy picked up Duke's notebook from the table and began touching the screen.

"What are you doing, Daniel?"

"Dialing up Dr. Snow's notebook . . . See."

Duke's half-finished lyric disappeared. The icon for the notebook's built-in cellphone filled the screen. Then a series of file folders appeared. Denning scanned their labels. *Book. Current Case Files. Personal. Financial.*

"You got into his files? How?"

"It was easy," the boy said. "His password is CGJ. Like, for Jung, you know. Real hard to guess."

Daniel clicked on the file folder labeled *Book.* A title page appeared: *Psychological Origins of the Disturbances.* Duke found himself looking at Chapter One.

"*. . . the first great upsurge in the incidence of schizophrenia in the late 19th and early 20th Century—leading to a tenfold increase in reported rates—coincided with the stresses of sweeping global industrialization. The parallel, and even larger, increase in the early 21st Century must be tracked against the collapse of the old industrial economy, and its replacement by one based on information.*"

"Boring," Daniel said.

He closed the folder and selected *Current Case Files.* The files of "Martha N.," dating back some six years, comprised this entire folder. Daniel picked on one from early on in the time sequence, *Martha N.: 2017.*

7.10.17: Tentative working diagnosis: dissociative reaction, with etiology in early childhood sexual abuse . . .

Duke tore his eyes from the screen. "I don't want to read this. It's private."

"Not anymore," the boy said. "You should read it. It's real interesting. There's stuff about you, and about me. And lots of stuff about how mommy is nuts. About how her amnesia is all in her mind."

"Amnesia?" Duke echoed, startled. "There's nothing wrong with her memory."

"Sure there is," the boy said. He tapped his forehead. "She's forgotten the future."

* * * * *

7.10.17: Tentative diagnosis: dissociative reaction, with etiology in early childhood sexual abuse (note: the "dark man" may be a screen memory concealing her father . . . explore further). From this split arose two "Marthas": one a self-described "normal person" and another who could "see the future." In some ways akin to classic multiple personality disorder, except that the two coexisted in full knowledge of each other.

The second Martha, the one associated with her creative gifts, has now fallen silent. Subject believes that she will not recapture her creativity until she can again access her supposed psychic powers.

The songs are Martha, in other words, but Martha is not her songs. It is as if she has allowed this second self, this disowned part of herself, the use of a piece of her brain, to which she tunes in, periodically, for her new songs. And from which she currently hears nothing.

The construction of the second Martha represents the working out of an elaborate set of defense mechanisms developed in response to the damage sustained to her self-concept in early childhood. It is surely no coincidence that the second Martha fell silent with the birth of the child. The assumption of her role as a mother has permitted the original or primary Martha to reaffirm her feminine identity and at last set aside her defenses. In essence she has healed herself, although she is as yet unwilling to accept a cure that leaves her bereft of her creativity.

This analysis would suggest that Martha may never sing again. Perhaps this would not be such a bad thing. Although I enjoy certain aspects of her music, I find its overall tone depressing in the extreme. Moreover, its widespread popular acceptance both reflects and stimulates an extremely unhealthy mood among the youth of this country.

So Martha, Duke thought, had come to believe what her fans kept telling her, that she could see the future. Except when she tried to, she couldn't. And so she had rushed off to Murray Snow.

Duke closed the file, searched for the current year.

12.04.23: Asked if the subject had shared her belief in her supposed psychic powers with her old/new friend Robert Duke. Has not done so. Expects either disbelief or social rejection. Reference to painful past episode with her former manager, Abe Levett, but unwilling to discuss further.

14.04.23: Robert Duke a disturbing influence. Martha obviously nostalgic in his presence, talking for the first time in many years of writing new songs, resuming her career.

Duke himself a rather sad case: only partly reformed Don Juan, failed Peter Pan. Attempting to counterattack his influence. Potential consequences of comeback attempt highly damaging.

17.04.23: Persists in belief in forward amnesia. "Almost remembers" something of critical importance that will happen in this house, but cannot access it . . .

* * * * *

In the living room, Duke found the boy sprawled out on the couch in front of the wallscreen, watching a cartoon.

"Why, Daniel? Why did you want me to read those files?"

"So you'll understand."

"Understand what?"

But the boy did not seem interested in elaborating. He used the remote control in his wristwatch to surf through the channels, stopping when he reached the BBC World News logo. Up on the screen, men in bulky space suits were lumbering through the orange dust. One carried an American flag.

For a moment, Duke thought it was a history show. But it didn't look like the moon. Then he remembered.

Mars. They had made it to Mars.

"Hey," he said. "They did it. They really did it. Isn't that something?"

There would be many, of course, who would say that this was an utterly meaningless achievement, given the situation back here on Earth. But it was an achievement all the same.

"Something," Daniel agreed, in a matter-of-fact tone.

The boy was looking intently at the man with the flag, identified by the voice-over as mission commander Mike Wyatt. "He's not coming back," Daniel said, conversationally, pointing at the screen.

"What?" Duke said.

"Him. He's never coming back to Earth. He's going to die there on Mars."

Duke shook his head, unsure how to react. He had no interest in playing surrogate father: he had done poorly enough with his own children. And he knew that the boy would not accept it in any case. But there were some things you could not let pass by.

"That's not very nice," he said, weakly. "It's not nice to say things like that."

"He's going to die," Daniel insisted. "I know it."

The boy often claimed to know things. He knew when it was going to rain or when the local power grid was going to fail or when the cook was going to burn the kebab. The boy liked to play fortuneteller, but until now Duke had never given the matter any thought. Only now did it occur to him that the boy was invariably right. Which was absurd.

"You can't know that," he said. "Nobody can."

"*I* can."

Up on the screen, the Mars story had given way to coverage of a major fire in Liverpool. The fire followed a week of rioting in three northeastern cities. Maybe, Duke thought, the Brits needed their own Mental Health Administration. Or maybe they already had one. It hadn't exactly worked wonders back home.

The boy watched the flames impassively for a while. Then he used the remote to turn off the wall. He got up from the couch. "I know something else," he said.

"What?" Duke said, sharply. "What do you know?"

"There's going to be an accident. Someone in this house is going to have an accident."

"Accident?"

"A real bad accident. Someone could get killed. That's what mommy told Dr. Snow about: '*something of critical importance*' that she almost remembers."

Duke stared at him, momentarily at a loss for words.

"Don't you want to know who's going to have an accident?"

"No," Duke said. "No, I don't think I want to play this game."

"Maybe it's you," the boy said. "Maybe that's who it is."

Duke opened his mouth to form a reply. None came.

The boy left the room.

The kid is playing mind games with me, Duke thought. Trying to drive me nuts. To drive me away.

He had been under no illusion that Martha's son liked him. It was only natural that the boy would resent the stranger who had appeared so suddenly in his mother's life, after so many years in which he had commanded her exclusive attention. But until now, he had not fully grasped the depths of Daniel's hatred.

Someone could get killed . . . Maybe it's you.

Scary stuff, coming from a seven-year-old.

Scary in more ways than one, actually. Because no matter how hard he tried, he could not help thinking: *Like mother, like son?*

That was what they used to say about Martha, back in the old days. What Martha, according to Snow's notes, had come to believe herself, that she could see the future.

He had never thought that was true, when he had known Martha before, any more than it could be true of Daniel now. No one could see the future.

Why then did he feel such an overpowering sense of dread?

✶ ✶ PART FIVE ✶ ✶

Seeing

* * 18 * *

"Robert."

He turned to see Martha coming through the patio doors.

"I'm going into town to pick up a few things," she said. "Would you mind watching Daniel for a few hours? He doesn't want to come."

"What about Leila?"

Leila was the woman who came in from the nearby village to baby-sit Daniel.

"Leila has to leave early; she has a family emergency. Is it a problem?"

Someone in this house is going to have an accident . . . Maybe it's you. It was nearly a week since Daniel had made his strange predictions. Duke had still not mentioned it to Martha. It was something that he and the boy would have to work out between themselves. Although so far he had made no effort to work things out. So far, he had dealt with his discomfort by avoiding the boy.

"No," he said. "That's okay. It's no problem."

Martha drove off in the Land Rover, with one of her security staff following in the Jeep. Duke went to check on Daniel.

He found the boy in his room, sitting among a clutter of toys, deep in conversation with his Talkie machine, a small handheld device with a display screen from which Duke caught a flash of fast-shifting colors.

"My father is coming," Daniel was saying. "Coming back from outer space."

"Outer space," echoed the machine, in a startlingly deep voice. "Your father is in outer space, but he's coming home."

"Twice," the boy said. "He's coming back twice. First without his spaceship, and then again inside it."

Duke was interested to hear more about the boy's fantasy father. But the machine had its own agenda. "You need a spaceship," it said, "to travel in space."

Duke had heard about Daniel's new toy from Martha, but this was the first time he had seen it. It had been shipped in from Harrods of Riyadh a few days before. The Talkie was a child's version of an adult PDA with built-in educational enhancements. It was programmed to recognize over one hundred thousand words, and to make age-appropriate conversational responses. Through links to worldwide databases, it offered encyclopedic knowledge.

"No," the boy told the Talkie. "Not always . . ." He looked up, then, and saw Duke in the doorway.

"Hi Daniel," he said. "What's that you have on the display?"

The boy turned the toy around so that Duke could see the colored shapes and lines. "Weather program. I'm studying weather."

"Quite a gadget."

"It's not so smart. There's plenty of stuff it can't answer." Daniel put the Talkie down and looked at Duke expectantly.

"I came to tell you that your mommy went into town," Duke said.

"I know that."

"Well, if you want anything, just call."

Duke turned to leave. But he was surprised to hear the boy call after him. "I want to go for a walk."

"Where?" Duke asked.

"Along the cliffs," the boy said. "I like walking along the cliffs."

Around the headland from Martha's property there were steep cliffs, with a sheer drop to the waters some two hundred feet below. Duke never walked there. He had an aversion to heights, although he was not about to admit that to the boy.

"Are you allowed to walk along there?"

"Sure. Sure I'm allowed."

* * * * *

"What were you telling your Talkie?" Duke asked. "When I came in?"

They were strolling along the cliff path and watching the seagulls wheeling in the sky. Duke was walking on the outside of the boy, beside the cliff edge. He felt comfortable enough as long as he didn't look down.

"Nothing."

"It was something about your father being in a spaceship."

"My father is an astronaut," the boy said. "The very last astronaut, or anyway he will be. He's on Mars right now. But he's coming back soon."

"Your father is an astronaut? Your mother told you that?"

"She didn't have to tell me. I know it."

Duke shook his head, perplexed. If the boy wanted to imagine that his father was an astronaut, who was he to object?

And what was it that Martha had told him, back in Montreal, when they were watching the astronauts on TV? *I hung around a little with one of those guys.*

Maybe it was true, what Daniel was saying. Maybe his father *was* on Mars.

Then he remembered the boy's prediction.

"Wait a minute," Duke said. "Didn't you say that an astronaut was going to die . . ."

"That's right," the boy said. "But not my father, not yet. My father still has things to do."

"Things?"

The boy stopped walking and stared down over the cliff face. "You know what?" he asked.

"What?"

"You could die. If you fell off this cliff. I bet you could die."

Duke glanced down uneasily to the waters crashing on the rocks below. "Probably. Except I'm not going to fall."

"I could push you. When you're not expecting it."

Duke looked searchingly at the boy. The boy's expression did not seem hostile, only earnestly interested in his response.

"I don't like that," Duke said. "I don't like you threatening me."

"I didn't say I *would* push you. I only said I *could.*"

Duke stopped walking. "That's enough. We're going back to the house."

"I don't want to go back. I want to walk some more."

"I don't care what you want. We're going back."

"No," the boy said. "Won't."

Duke reached out to grab Daniel's arm, but he jumped out of reach.

"All right. Stay, if you like. But I'm going back to the house." He turned to leave.

"You can't," the boy said. "I'm not allowed out here by myself. You're supposed to be looking after me."

Duke hesitated.

"You can't leave me here," the boy said. "Suppose I slipped and fell off the edge? Suppose I jumped?"

"You wouldn't do that," Duke said, his mouth dry. "You wouldn't do a stupid thing like that."

"I might. I might not."

Someone is going to have an accident . . . Someone could get killed.

Suddenly Duke believed it. Someone was going to die here. Maybe the boy, maybe himself. The boy could see the future. Or else he was going to make it happen.

Again Duke grabbed for the boy. Again the boy evaded him easily. He pivoted away and came to a halt inches from the cliff edge. He stood there, teetering dangerously. "You can't catch me," he said. "Not in a million years."

"You crazy little bastard. You're going to get us both killed."

The boy pulled the Talkie out of his pocket and switched it on. "Hey, Talkie. What's a bastard?"

"A child born outside marriage," said the Talkie.

"That's me, all right. A crazy little bastard."

"Come here," Duke said. "We're going back."

"Come and get me," the boy said. He turned and raced off down the path.

"Wait," Duke said. "Stop."

"Run, run as fast you can," the boy shouted back, weaving close to the edge of the cliff. "Can't catch me, I'm the gingerbread man."

Duke gave chase, but the boy was too quick. The gap between them continued to lengthen. He followed doggedly, keeping his eyes on the path and away from the waters beneath.

Far ahead, the boy stopped and turned to watch him. "Faster," he shouted. "Faster."

Duke increased his pace. And caught his foot in a buried tree root. He felt himself hurtling through the air, arms flailing, towards the cliff edge.

This is it, he thought. This is really it.

And then his hand was clutching reflexively around a branch of a bush growing on the side of the path. The branch cut into his hand, but he held on, his body dangling halfway over the edge of the cliff.

He pulled himself back on to the path. He lay on his stomach on the ground, staring down at the water, imagining himself lying broken on the rocks below.

He looked up to see Daniel standing over him. "It's all right," he said, his tone almost solicitous. "I was only kidding. You're not going to die today."

Duke got up and dusted himself off and they walked in silence back to the house.

* * * * *

Snow was sitting in a rocking chair on the porch of the guest cottage, reading the European edition of the *New York Times*. He nodded to Duke.

"Good walk?" Snow asked.

"Terrific."

Daniel had run ahead to the house. Duke turned to follow.

"Too bad about the Mars thing," Snow said.

"What?"

Snow held up the paper so that Duke could see the front page: *Bad News From Mars: Mission Commander Dead In Freak Accident.*

"Jesus," Duke said.

"Accidents will happen," Snow said. "Particularly with inadequate preparation. They really shouldn't have rushed into this mission. But they thought it was going to be a tremendous morale-builder. They supposed people would be glued to their home entertainment centers, watching this Mars trip, that it would somehow help to bring us together. But it's been a ratings disaster. Too remote, you see. Perhaps things will pick up now, but I doubt it."

He's not coming back, Duke thought. That was what Daniel had said. *I know it.*

But then maybe Snow had it right: Accidents will happen. Maybe it was just a coincidence.

"Not that it was ever really about morale," the psychiatrist was saying. "The whole psychology of the space program, it's driven by the classic *puer aeternus* archetype—the flying boy, the eternal boy, the restless wanderer, the dreamer who rejects being a grounded adult living in the mundane, daily reality of the world . . ."

Snow realized that Duke was staring at him blank-eyed.

"Are you all right, Robert? You look a little pale."

"What? Yeah, I'm fine."

"Going to Mars," Snow said. "Just another piece of denial. Another death rattle of the old order. As if we could learn anything from going to Mars."

"I don't know," Duke said, finally focussing on what Snow was saying. "I think it does mean something, people going there. It's like the fulfillment of an ancient prophecy, somehow."

"An ancient dream," Snow said. "A perfectly primitive dream, dressed up in the latest scientific drag. Another flicker of the emerging world mind."

Duke wondered why he was having this conversation with Snow. Surely it would only lead to another impenetrable lecture. But he was in no hurry to follow Daniel into the house and find him crowing over the news of the dead astronaut.

"Like your crop circles, you mean? It seems to me that you could explain anything that way."

"Anything," Snow agreed. "Because it's all happening for the same reason. It's all driven by our collective unconscious. More and more I'm convinced we're on the brink of some kind of global transformation."

"And what happens when this collective unconscious awakes?" Duke asked, curious despite himself. "Do we all plunge into savagery?"

"Jung sometimes thought as much, although not always. Teilhard de Chardin was far more optimistic. You know his work?"

"I don't believe so."

"A great but largely unsung prophet," Snow said. "Long before the emergence of the Internet, he predicted the appearance of a global mind, joining man and his machines. First there will be an enforced resonance: As all the networks come together we start to think together, feel together. Ultimately we reach a final point of convergence, an Omega Point, a culmination and integration of all things—art, science, philosophy. And here there emerges a kind of super-conconsciousness, enclosing the entire world in a single thinking envelope that Teilhard called the noosphere. A supermind. An Overmind, if you like.

"Of course, if Teilhard was right then this Overmind must already exist, somewhere out there in the world beyond time. The question is whether it is now trying to communicate with us."

"How do you mean, communicate?"

"Teilhard believed that the great human mystics throughout history were able to tune into its emanations. Now, as the moment of convergence approaches, these messages become more urgent. People start to apprehend them everywhere, whether in crop circles, or in dreams, or in songs . . ."

"What songs did you have in mind?"

"I'm not a great student of popular culture, Robert," Snow said. "You'll forgive me if I am less than familiar with your own *oeuvre.* But when I listen to the audio channels I hear such signifiers in the music of many different artists. Perhaps because I am so familiar with her work, I hear them most strongly in Martha's music."

"You're saying that Martha is tuning into this Overmind?"

"I do believe so, yes. Not consciously, of course. But she does seem to be particularly attuned to it."

"And what exactly would this Overmind be trying to tell us?"

"I think it's really quite simple. It's saying, *prepare yourselves.* Prepare for what must come."

Duke shook his head wearily.

"This is all very interesting," he said. "But I don't buy it. Global mind? Point of convergence? From where I sit, people aren't joining together. We're just getting more fragmented all the time."

"The disturbances, you mean? These are only temporary. As we approach the tipping point, primeval images of apocalypse well up from the archaic depths of the emerging collective mind, fuelling anxieties that energize and exacerbate our current divisions. But the Disturbances cannot continue forever."

Snow folded his newspaper neatly, tapped it with his finger. "And meanwhile the government tries to distract us with glorious spectacles."

"Instead of going to Mars, maybe they should just have sent for Martha. Maybe she would bring people together."

"That's a very romantic notion, Robert. But not a useful one. I do hope you're not planning to share it with Martha. It's exactly the type of idea that would feed right into her problems."

* * * * *

Duke found Daniel in the kitchen, sitting on a stool at the counter drinking apple juice and watching the TV panel above the stove. The Time-Fox WorldNews channel was playing. A somber-faced news reader was talking about the tragic death of the Mars mission commander. The picture cut away to a dimly lit shot of a boulder-strewn hill, while the news reader talked on about a fatal rock slide.

"I told you," the boy said. "I told you he would die."

"Yes. You did tell me."

The boy looked at him expectantly.

"You think this proves something?"

"You don't believe me yet," the boy said. "You won't believe me until afterwards."

"After what?"

"After the accident."

"No," Duke said, shaking his head. "I'm not going to play this game."

"Don't you want to know who's going to have an accident?"

"There isn't going to be any accident."

"Yes there is."

The boy seemed very sure of himself. But then, he always did.

"All right," Duke said, despite himself. "Tell me."

The boy shook his head. "That would spoil the surprise."

* * 1 9 * *

It was Denning who found the body. He picked up Wyatt's footprints and followed them into a cave in the wall of a dry river valley. And there was Wyatt, sitting with his back to the wall of the cave, eyes staring sightlessly ahead of him.

Leaning over, Denning checked the dial on Wyatt's wrist that indicated his oxygen reserves. The pointer was all the way into the red zone. The suit had run out of oxygen some six hours before. But the power pack still held a charge, and when Denning flipped on the suit's radio he heard an answering crackle in his own earphones.

The cave was no more than half an hour's walk from the camp. Even if Wyatt had lost his bearings completely, he could have called for help if he had wanted to, long before he ran out of oxygen. But he had not wanted to. He had just sat there in that cave, staring at the wall, until his oxygen ran out.

The cave was unprepossessing: perhaps five meters deep, barely tall enough to stand up in. Denning wondered why Wyatt would have wanted to go in there.

He turned to look at what Wyatt had been staring at on the cave wall. A series of fine cracks ran through the rock, forming an intricate hieroglyphic pattern, almost like a circuit diagram. Some kind of weathering effect, Denning thought, absently. He stepped forward to get a closer look. And there was a flickering at the corners of his eyes, a strangely familiar flickering . . .

His vision darkened. He heard, far-off, a rustling sound. A breeze blew on his face. He tasted metal, then spices. He smelled burning. He swayed, then stumbled to his knees on the cave floor.

He felt a hand on the arm of his suit, pulling him up.

There was light now, and he blinked against it. He saw the hand first, and then the face. The hand was pale and bluish in appearance. It had six long, delicately tapering fingers.

The face that loomed above him was equally pale and similarly blue. It was thin and hairless, with large sad-looking eyes.

Denning climbed to his feet, and the hand released its grip. The blue man towered over him, a full meter taller. Denning wondered why the blue man did not bang his head on the roof of the cave. Then he realized that the roof was gone, and so were the walls.

He was looking out over what, a few minutes before, had been a dry river valley. But now there was water rushing over the dusty river bed, and plants and trees and wild blue grass covering the slopes. And a few miles down the river, he saw a squarish, brightly colored barge, with great white sails flapping in the wind. In the distance was a city on the hill, its delicate, oddly titled crystalline towers reaching towards a dazzling blue sky.

Denning shook his head in exasperation. "And you're supposed to be a Martian, right?"

"Right," the blue man agreed.

"Oh, great. That's just great. I'm hallucinating."

Oxygen starvation, he thought. But when he looked at the readout on his wrist, it showed almost a full tank. Of course, it *would* do that, wouldn't it, if he were hallucinating?

"This isn't even my hallucination," Denning said. "It's Mike Wyatt's. His dream of a Mars that never was."

"True enough," the Martian said, except that he was no longer a Martian. His face was blurring, melting, morphing . . . "But what *is* your dream, Jake?"

The face was his mother, and then his wife. It was his father and it was Bruce Springsteen and it was Cal Ripken. It was a politician, a war hero, a porn star, a preacher, a singer, a serial killer. It was Jesus and it was the Buddha and it was Mohammed and it was Mike Wyatt.

"None of the above?" Wyatt asked. "No dreams at all?"

Wyatt was wearing cutoff jeans and a t-shirt. Of course, Denning thought, Wyatt wouldn't need a space suit. Seeing that he was dead.

Denning blinked, slowly and deliberately. But Wyatt remained standing there.

"Mike . . ." he said. "You're dead."

"True enough," Wyatt said, and Denning realized that it was the same voice the blue man had used. It had been Wyatt's voice, all along. Or not his voice at all. "But you needed to talk to me. The Martian didn't do it for you. Worked for me, but I guess you're more of a skeptic."

"You're not Mike Wyatt," Denning said.

"Yes I am. That's exactly who I am at this moment in time."

"You've read Mike's thoughts, somehow. Scooped out his dreams. Swallowed him up."

"I am what I eat," Wyatt said. "I am what I am."

"You're going to do the same thing to me."

"Maybe I already did."

Denning shook his head. "I'm dying," he said. "Isn't that right? You're some kind of demon, or angel."

"Depending on how you look at things," Wyatt said. "But you're not dying. Not here, not now. You have things to do first."

"Things?"

"Look," Wyatt said. "Look at this."

Denning looked. And for a moment, he saw, all the way through. There was no Wyatt and no Martian, no river, no trees, no barge; and no cave either. There was only light. Waves of brilliant light everywhere.

"What?" he said, blinking at the glare. "What is this?"

"Some call it the noosphere," Wyatt said, as the light faded as suddenly as it had come.

Looking beyond Wyatt, Denning could see that the barge was back on the river, and the city of tilting towers once again stood on the hill.

"The what?"

"The primordial light of creation," Wyatt said. "The consciousness distributed throughout matter. Trapped there until apocatastasis, when it will be released from its black iron prison."

"Apocatastasis?"

"The revelation of all secrets. The restitution of matter to the divine, along with the accumulation of all knowledge. The Jews, they called it *tikkun*." Wyatt sucked meditatively on a piece of blue grass. "I used to read all that stuff back on Earth. But it was only words. I didn't really *see*."

"You're dead, Mike. You can't see anything. This is all just my delusion."

"As you like."

"You're trying to tell me all this is real?" He indicated the river, the barge, the city.

"It's all real, Jake. And all unreal."

"What's happening to me?" Denning asked. "What the fuck is happening?"

"You saw, Jake. You looked into the aleph and you saw. And you're still seeing."

"Aleph?"

"On the wall of the cave. It's a gateway, Jake. To everything, everywhere, every time. I looked into the aleph, and I couldn't look away."

"Until you died."

"I died, yes. That's true enough, from your point of view. But you can still access me. I'm still in here. Everything is in here. There is no time inside the aleph, Jake. No now or then, forward or backward, before or after, alive or dead, you or me. It's all here at once . . . everything that has ever happened, or ever will happen."

Wyatt tugged at his ear in a familiar gesture. "It's the Aleph, but it's also the Omega. And the Eschaton, the final object at the end of time, accumulating everything to itself, sucking up all of human knowledge like a vacuum cleaner."

"Aleph?" Denning echoed. "Omega? Eschaton? What you talking about?"

"You ever read Borges? No, of course not. Or Frank Tipler, or Terence McKenna? Neither did I. But I can read them now. It's all an open book to me. And soon it will be to you. But for now, think of the Eschaton as a strange attractor, pulling us towards it. A singularity, if you like, a spiritual singularity. And it's coming, Jake, it's coming real fast, the New Jerusalem I learned about in Sunday school, the world beyond history."

"I don't understand."

"You don't need to understand," Wyatt said. "Not yet."

"But why is it here? In this cave on Mars? Why should it be here?"

Wyatt shrugged. "Maybe it was always here. Or maybe someone put it here for us. Knowing that we would eventually come here in desperation."

"Put it here? What are you talking about? Aliens?"

"Could have been aliens. Or angels. But that's not exactly the point."

"And what did you mean, 'in desperation'?"

"We *were* desperate, Jake, all of us. We were at an end of something, and we knew it. An end to living with our machines, analyzing everything we touched. Living as tiny, isolated specks of consciousness, every man and woman his own astronaut, cocooned in our own technology. Cut off from the world, from the animals, from other people, from ourselves. We knew there had to be an end to it, but we couldn't face that. We just kept pushing on. All the way to Mars."

"That's not why we came," Denning said. And thought: *I'm arguing with a hallucination.* "We came here to explore. People have always explored, always pushed back the boundaries . . ."

"Bullshit, Jake. People have always tried to escape. That's all they ever wanted to do. But you can only run so far. And this is it. This is the end of the line. We came here looking for some way out of the trap we had built for ourselves, some way out of history. And we found it. Just look inside the aleph, and you'll see."

"But what is it?" Denning asked.

"Like I told you, it's a gateway. And now it's inside *you,* Jake. You're the gateway. The gateway for the light."

Denning stared into the Aleph and saw that it was all laid out for him, his future, all his futures. He saw himself burning up in the ship and he saw himself coming home. He saw himself at a party in a big hotel. He saw the singer, Martha Nova, lying naked beneath him on a hotel bed, and then again up on a stage, blood pouring from her head. He saw a child go under the wheels of a car and the same child staring out a window at a street jammed with people.

And then he was back in the cave, staring at a pattern on the wall, and Chang was screaming into his earphones.

"Denning, where the fuck are you? Denning, will you come in please?"

And it was gone, all of it: Wyatt, the Martian, the light, the river, the barge . . . It was all gone. He tore his eyes away from the pattern on the wall, and he acknowledged the call, and Chang came to help him with the body.

* * * * *

They carried Wyatt out of the cave, and they buried him outside the base dome. They used the flagpole to mark the spot. The flag itself had been ripped apart in a dust storm.

The flagpole would blow away a few weeks later, and then they would no longer know exactly where Wyatt was. But by then it would no longer seem a matter of much importance.

"What the fuck did he think he was doing out there, anyway?" Denning asked, as they stood by the makeshift grave.

"Looking for Martians, I guess," Chang said.

They lied to Control about Wyatt's death. It was Denning who thought up the cover story. It came into his mind all in one piece. "We could say there was a rock slide. Like when we were scrambling up the side of that valley. We haven't transmitted the footage from that one yet."

"Why?" Chang asked. "Why should we do that?"

"Because it's the decent thing to do, of course, for Mike and . . ." He could not recall the name of Mike's wife, but the principle was correct, in any case. "For Mike and his family. To preserve his memory. That's the sort of thing friends do for each other."

"I don't give a flying fuck about preserving Mike's memory."

"What's the point of telling them he went mad?" Denning persisted. "Nobody is going to want to hear that. It'll be very bad PR for the Agency. They'll just take it out on us. They'll say it was our fault, letting him wander off like that."

Chang considered. "Makes sense."

"A rock slide," Denning said. "Struck down tragically in his prime."

"All right," Chang said. "I could go with that."

And so they faked the report. And for a while it made Denning glad, thinking about the thing he had done for Mike and for his wife, whatever her name was. They had been good friends, after all, they had spent many happy hours together.

* * 2 0 * *

Duke sat at the table in the patio, waiting for Martha to return from town. He scanned his e-mail on his notebook—a quarterly financial statement from his accountant, a query about an obscure '00s mini-CD from an online collector magazine—then found himself checking departures from the Corfu airport. There was a RussAir flight that night to Athens, where he could pick up a direct flight to L.A. on Air Japan . . .

Home. He was thinking about going home. But he had no home now, except this one. And he was not sure how much longer he could stay here.

He heard distant thunder. Heavy clouds were gathering in the sky, darkening the afternoon sun. Somewhere a dog howled. As Martha's car came up the driveway, he felt the first drops of rain on his face. As he got up to go in the house to meet her, it began to rain harder.

"How did it go with Daniel?" she asked.

"The truth?"

"That bad?"

"Awful."

"You had a fight?"

"You could say that."

"I'm sorry, Robert. I'm not going to make excuses for him. But you have to know that it's hard for him, getting used to having you around. You have to give him more time."

"I've been telling myself that since I got here. But it isn't getting better, Martha, it's getting worse. Daniel doesn't want me around. And I'm not sure I want to be around him. I hate to say this, Martha. But he isn't just obnoxious, he's *spooky.*"

"Spooky?" Martha frowned. "Why do you say that?"

"It's a lot of things. The way he talks, the strange things he says, the games he plays on me . . . His goddamn *predictions.*"

"What kind of predictions?"

"He told me a few days ago that an astronaut would die. And maybe someone else, right here in this house. Maybe me."

Her face flushed with anger. "You should have told me about this. I'll talk to him, Robert. I'll tell him he can't go around upsetting people like that."

"But why should he listen to you? He picked up this whole fortune-telling act from you in the first place. Like they say: *monkey see, monkey do.*"

Martha cleared her throat, said something so quietly he could not catch it.

"What?"

"I said, *it was no act.*"

"What?"

"I have to be honest with you, Robert. This time around, I have to be. I *could* see the future, back when you first knew me. I can't see it anymore, but it was true, what they said back then. I did see the Seattle fire, the earthquake, all those things. I could see the future then, just as Daniel can see it now."

Duke was shaking his head. "No," he said. "No. This is craziness, Martha. Don't you know how crazy this sounds? No one can see the future, Martha. Not you, and not your son."

"I never talked about it, because I knew that people wouldn't believe me, they would think I was crazy. Or if they did believe me, they would think I was some kind of witch. So I let the songs speak for me. But I could see."

"You started to believe your own publicity, that's all. And now you've somehow handed down your little delusion to your son."

"It's not a delusion," Martha said. "Not for me, or Daniel. And you know it. That's why you're so upset."

"I'm upset about your kid threatening me."

"You're worried that what he said might be true."

"I know it can't be true."

"But he was right, Robert. An astronaut *did* die."

"Coincidence. Lucky guess. And because of that I'm supposed to take his other prediction seriously? That someone here could die?"

"We should take everything he says seriously." She put her hand on his arm. "Did he say who was going to have this accident?"

"He wouldn't tell me. But maybe he'll tell you. Or maybe you could look in your own crystal ball and find out."

She flinched away from his sarcasm. "You're angry. But that's because you're frightened to believe. We should have talked about this before. I guess I was afraid of how you would react."

"You foresaw it, you mean?"

"Maybe I did. Even though I don't see anymore, I can still remember bits and pieces of what I saw. That's how I knew that we would meet again, that you would come and stay with me in Corfu."

"Like a puppet on a string? Like a bird on the wire?"

"That's not how it was," she said, tears filling her eyes. "You came because you wanted to."

"And what if I want to leave here right now?"

"That's your choice, Robert. But . . ."

"But I'm not going to leave? Is that what you were going to say?"

"No," she said. "You don't leave. We get over this, somehow. And you stay here with me. And then my music comes back, and I write some new songs, and I go home to record them. And you . . ."

"Yes?"

"You come with me."

"Don't count on it Martha."

"I know this is hard for you to accept."

"I *don't* accept it. And right now, I have to go. I have to get out of here."

He picked up her car keys from the hall table. "OK if I borrow your car?"

"Where are you going?"

"I don't know. For a drive. The airport, maybe."

"It's pouring." She nodded out the window, at the sheets of rain streaming down.

"Airplanes have radar, Martha."

"You're flying somewhere?"

"I might."

"Anyway," she said. "You don't."

"Don't what?"

"Have radar. You'll need it, to drive in this weather."

"I'll take my chances."

* * * * *

Daniel was climbing one of the big oak trees that lined the far end of the driveway, when the rain began. He raised his face up to the sky to taste it. Within a few minutes his clothes were soaked through to the skin.

It got very dark, very quickly. The lights of the house glowed faintly in the distance.

Daniel didn't mind the darkness, and he didn't mind being wet. But he was hungry. He climbed down from the tree, and began to trudge back up the driveway towards the house.

He heard thunder as he walked, and then a different noise, of a car's engine coming to life just by the house. Headlights shone in the gloom, and then the car roared on to the driveway.

It was maybe five hundred meters up the long and winding driveway from the house to where it met the road. The driveway was slick with rain, and the car was moving too fast.

I should get out of the way, he thought. But he knew he was not going to be able to get out of the way.

He took a half-step towards the side of the driveway. But he felt he was moving as if in slow-motion, as if in a dream, as if his muscles were frozen, as if time itself was shuddering to a halt. The car was almost upon him.

Above his head, there was a burst of light.

* * * * *

Duke was drenched the moment he stepped out the front door of Martha's house. He had not even packed a change of clothes. Oh well, he thought. He could buy some in Athens, if that was really where he was heading.

He sprinted for the car and turned on the engine. The windshield was fogged and the wipers could not keep up with the torrents of rain. It was so dark that he could hardly see his own headlights. But he drove off, anyway, pumping his foot down harder on the gas than he had intended.

The road to town, he recalled, was somewhere up ahead. He strained forward to look for it. He could see nothing.

And then there was a burst of light illuminating the road like the pulse of a strobe. Some weird kind of lightning, he thought. And then he saw the child directly ahead of him in the middle of the driveway, his face looming enormous in the sudden light.

He spun the wheel hard to the right, knowing that it was too late.

* * * * *

Martha pressed her face to the window, straining to see through the rain and the gloom as Duke drove off.

And then she thought about Daniel. She went to the foot of the stairs and called up. "Daniel? Where are you, Daniel?"

But Daniel did not reply. And she knew, suddenly, that he was not upstairs. That he was outside in the rain.

Someone is going to have an accident.

She turned back to the window but she could see nothing, not even the taillights of the car.

Her heart was racing. She could hardly breathe.

Please, she thought. Please let me see.

And then her vision cleared, and she could see everything: Daniel standing in the rain, at the end of the driveway; and Duke in the car, hands clenched on the steering wheel, jaw set, head straining forward in concentration, peering into the darkness, seeing the child in front of him, spinning the wheel desperately. She could see the car swerving, skidding; Daniel's face bathed in light; the trees lining the road like a wall . . . She could see it all.

Once again, she could see everything.

* * 2 1 * *

Until she was nearly six years old, her life was ordinary enough. She went to school, she played with her friends, she loved her parents, and sometimes she hated her little brother Sam. And the future was as much a mystery to her as to everyone else.

And then it changed. It changed the day she saw the dark man outside the school yard, peering in through the wire-mesh fence as she played with her friends. He was staring directly at her.

He was a short man with dark hair. He was dressed neatly, in a gray suit with a red tie, but his hair was a bit disheveled, his eyes were a little wild and scary. But even if his eyes had not been scary, she knew enough not to go near him, knew that strange men were to be avoided.

When Mrs. Roberts from next door came to pick up Martha, along with her own daughter Cheryl and Kenny from down the street, she stayed close to her the whole way home, clinging to her hand while the other children ran on ahead laughing and screaming, the way she usually did.

That night the dark man she had seen outside the school yard came to her house. She was in the kitchen, helping her little brother Sam finish his dinner. Peering out into the hallway as her mother opened the door, she could see that the man had combed his hair. She heard him saying something to her mother, who stood aside to let him in. He was carrying a clipboard in his hand.

"Who is that man, Mommy?" she asked, as they came towards the kitchen. "I don't like him."

"Don't be silly, Martha," her mother said. "He's from the parents' committee at your school. He's raising money to build a new computer lab."

"That's right, honey," the dark man said. "We want to make you as smart as you are pretty."

Up close, she could see that the man's eyes still looked funny, red-rimmed and empty and spooky.

And then the man reached over to pat her on the head. "Learning new things," he said. "It doesn't hurt a bit."

Afterwards she was never sure whether the man had touched her at all, or just passed his hand over her head. For a moment it seemed to her that light pulsed from the man's hand, a thrilling burst of light exploding into her head and pouring down her neck and immersing her entire body. But the moment was so odd, so dreamlike, she could not hold on to it.

Then she felt the beginnings of a terrible headache.

"Mommy," she said. "I don't feel too good. Can I go to my room?"

She went into the bathroom first and splashed water on her head, but it didn't help. She undressed and got into bed and lay there listening to the murmur of voices in the kitchen below.

She heard the man leave only a few minutes later. "I'm sorry," her mother told him, at the door. "I wish we could pledge more, but they're talking about more layoffs at the factory and we really have to be careful."

For hours after that she lay awake, afraid that he would come back. But the dark man did not return that night. She would not see him again for many years.

Eventually she fell into an exhausted sleep. When her mother woke her up for school her headache was gone. But other things were different. Everything was different now, and always would be.

"What's the matter, Martha?" her mother asked, standing over her bed, staring alarmed into her wildly darting eyes. "Are you still feeling sick?" She reached over and felt Martha's forehead. "You're not hot or anything. What's the matter?"

"I . . ." Martha said. "I . . . I don't know."

She put her hands over her eyes, removed them again. She put her hands to her ears, took them away.

"It's awful," she told her mother. "I can't stand it. I can't stand to look at it. I can't stand to hear it."

"What's awful, dear?"

"The voices. The pictures. Make them stop. Please make them stop."

"I'll call the doctor," her mother said.

"It was that man who did this. The dark man. He filled my head with the pictures, with the voices. It was him. It was him."

She screamed then. And then she stopped talking. She stopped talking altogether, and would not respond to her mother's increasingly anxious inquiries. She did not talk again for almost a month.

* * * * *

It was very confusing at first, a chaos of words and images pressing down upon her, filling up her mind. And very frightening, too. It was a bit like watching TV and flipping from one channel to the next and so on without end, everything blurring into one vast jumbled show. It was like watching TV, except that she couldn't turn off the set and the picture had a yellowish tinge. And often it seemed that she was in the show herself, seeing and hearing these things, doing things that were familiar and things that were quite unfamiliar. Except that it wasn't *her,* exactly.

Some of the scenes were quite ordinary, like running down a wintry street, or sitting at a kitchen table drinking coffee, or swimming in a huge azure pool. But her legs were incredibly long as she ran down the street, and she was too young to drink coffee, and it was no swimming pool she had ever seen.

Other scenes were really quite nice, like standing up on a stage and having people cheer her, or sailing in a great white boat under a warm sun, or eating wonderful foods in palace-like restaurants.

But there was much more that was simply mysterious to her, mysterious and scary. A city in flames all around her. A man in a space suit walking on the moon, except that it wasn't exactly the moon. And, here and there, the strange dark man, appearing and disappearing.

The visions raced on inside her head, and they had no end, there was nothing she could do to stop them. And meanwhile she could not speak, she could not begin to describe what was happening to her.

* * * * *

They took Martha away to the children's hospital in the nearest big city. They put her in the psychiatric ward. She would remain there for three months.

Her mother stayed with her the first week, but then she had to go home to look after Sam. Martha barely noticed her departure. Although the doctors and nurses were kind, she did not want to speak to them either.

But she was learning, slowly, how to control the sights and sounds inside her head, how to switch them on and off. As she began to master this trick, the chaos in her mind became less scary, more bearable.

Within a month she was able to speak to her parents when they came to visit, and to the doctors and the nurses. She would talk, too, to the other children in the ward, those who would talk to her, although many wouldn't. Watching them sitting there, rocking themselves back and forth, she would wonder what they were seeing and hearing inside their own heads.

Now that she could talk, the doctors asked her many questions. In particular they would ask about the dark man with the funny eyes, and what he had done to her. They asked the same questions over and over, as if they could not remember her answers from the time before.

"So he didn't touch you, except on the head?"

"No."

"But you were afraid he might touch you somewhere else."

"I was just afraid of him, that's all."

"Did someone ever touch you in a place you didn't like? A teacher, an uncle, a friend of the family?"

"No," Martha would say. "Only that man. Only here." She would touch her head. "I think he touched me here."

It would be too confusing to tell them that she wasn't sure that he had touched her at all: that perhaps she had been touched only by the light that had flooded from his hand and into her body. And she knew they wouldn't believe her in any case. She was not sure she believed it herself.

"But were you ever afraid that someone wanted to touch you?"

"No," Martha would say. "Never."

The doctors rarely asked about the words and pictures inside her head, and she never volunteered information about them. Certainly she never told them what she was beginning to suspect: that the person in those pictures was her, the way she was one day going to be.

Here she was, quite clearly, at seven or eight, only a little taller, her hair a little longer, examining herself in the washroom mirror at school, about to sing in some concert. And here she was again at maybe fourteen, much taller now, hair cut short, in her bedroom back home, sitting on the same old bed, although the walls were mauve now instead of pink, and covered with posters of pop stars. And here she was full-grown, up on a stage in a long white dress, with thousands of people hanging on her every word.

She especially liked those parts of her life to come in which she would be a star, and live in an enormous house, and travel all around the world. She would run through these scenes in her mind again and again, listening in wonder to the music she would one day make, drinking in the acclaim of the crowd.

But she held back from telling the doctors about these strange waking dreams. They were private, and she didn't want to share them, and she somehow knew they would not want to hear them.

As she learned how to control her visions, as she became visibly calmer each day, the doctors began to treat her differently. She caught on, finally, to what they were thinking. They thought that she was getting better.

She realized, too, what they wanted of her but would not ask directly.

"They stopped," she told one of the doctors one morning. "The pictures have stopped. The voices, too."

They discharged her the following week.

"Some sort of late developing childhood schizophrenia," she heard the doctor tell her father. "Fortunately an acute episode rather than a chronic condition. We don't know what triggered it. She may actually have been molested, but there was no evidence of that. We think it more likely she imagined it. She has an amazing imagination for a little girl."

Martha attended the outpatient clinic every six months for the next few years, enjoying her trips to the big city, the visits to the zoo and the science museum and the great turning tower. But as far as the doctors could see, there was no sign of a recurrence, and eventually these visits ceased.

* * * * *

When she came home, she found her watch on the bedside table where she had left it. It was an inexpensive digital watch with a calendar display. It had stopped the very same day her episode began, probably right around the time her headache came on.

Her father got her a new battery for the watch, but it still refused to work. Her mother gave her an old wind-up watch she found in the back of her drawer, but it soon starting losing time. And so it went on.

"Electromagnetism," her father told her, on returning from one of many trips to the watch repair shop. "The man says you must have powerful electromagnetism. Some people do. He says you should ought to try dowsing. People who can dowse often have problems with watches."

"What's dowsing?"

"Finding water underground with a twig, or a metal rod."

"Cool," she said.

It was the light, she thought, the light in her body that had changed her electromagnetism and stopped her watch and possibly given her the power of dowsing. Although she would never actually try to find water. There was more in her future than dowsing.

Eventually her parents gave up trying to find her a watch that worked. Battery-powered or windup or self-winding, they would all start to run too slow or too fast or else just seize up. She would never wear a watch again.

* * * * *

For the most part, she stopped trying to see the future. The present—her friends, her family, her schoolwork—were enough for her. And the future was too much for her to deal with.

Besides, even when she did try to see her own life up ahead there was no guarantee that she would see what she wanted. All too often she would see bad things instead: accidents, illnesses, disasters. It was as if the bad things wanted to be seen and known more than the good things, they sent the loudest signals from the future.

But although she tried not to see, sometimes it would happen whether she wanted it to or not. Someone or something would trigger some kind of connection.

The first time it happened, she was playing with her best friend Elaine. It was a few weeks after her return from the hospital, a cold midwinter day. They were up in her bedroom, putting Barbie through her paces, when she saw it. The edges of her field of vision seemed to blur, and take on a yellowish tinge. The room faded from view. And she saw Elaine drowning.

It would happen on a warm summer's day. They would be at the swimming hole just outside town where they swam every summer. They would be laughing and playing, Martha and Elaine and a few other friends. She would turn her head just for a moment, and when she turned back Elaine would be gone.

"Elaine?" she would shout. "Where's Elaine?"

Someone would see her, then, under the water. They would dive down and pull her up. But by then it would be too late.

"Elaine," she said, as the vision faded.

"What?" Elaine asked, engrossed with the doll.

But somehow she could not bring herself to warn her friend. Elaine would not believe that Martha could see her dying, but she would be upset all the same. She would tell her parents, and they would tell Martha's parents, and they would take her back to the hospital in the big city.

And she was not yet certain that she could see the future. Perhaps it would not happen, Elaine drowning. Or perhaps it would happen only if she talked about it.

But through the rest of that winter, she saw this same scene repeatedly. It would come into her mind while she sat in class at school, or when she was playing in the snow, or watching TV, or lying in bed. She would see it most often when she was with Elaine, playing with their dolls or having imaginary tea parties. And each time she saw it she felt the same black helplessness.

The summer came around, and the long vacation, and her friends would want to go swimming. And she would suggest doing something else, or else going to the public pool in town rather than the swimming hole. Sometimes they accepted her suggestions, but often they did not. And so they went to the swimming hole, and she went with them. Somehow she could not refuse. They went swimming again and again and Elaine did not drown and Martha felt a growing sense of relief. Until one day Elaine did drown.

That was when she knew for sure that she could see the future. And when she first learned that even though she could see the future, she was powerless to change it. No matter how hard she tries, the events rolled on past her like a movie.

Elaine drowning was the worst thing she saw for many years to come. But there were other bad things she could not change. She saw her brother break his arm falling from a climbing frame in the playground, and then he did break it, despite her repeated warnings. She saw herself and her friends getting into trouble at school, letting the rabbit out of its cage and getting sent to the principal. She saw it, but she could not stop her friends from doing it, and she could not stop herself.

She could not change even the good things she knew were going to happen to her. It was not that she wanted to stop them, but she would try to, sometimes, just to change *something.* She was asked to sing a solo in the school concert, for example, something she desperately wanted to do, and she refused. But her music teacher and her parents combined against her and somehow forced her to sing.

It was as though her life was all planned out ahead of her, and there was nothing she could do to break the plan. In that sense, her ability to see the life ahead of her was an entirely useless talent. And yet she knew that it would be a different life all the same, from the one she would have lived if she had not been able to see the future.

* * * * *

A few times she tried to talk about her visions with her mother, but her mother clearly didn't want to hear about them. Nor did she want Martha telling anyone else what she thought she saw. "It will just upset people," her mother warned her. "And make them think you're strange."

It confirmed for her that she was doing the right thing in trying not to see.

It was the last time she would try to tell someone about her seeing until she was well into adulthood.

* * * * *

Even when the visions stayed quiet, there were still the *feelings* to contend with. If she allowed herself to, she could feel what the people around her were feeling. And sometimes, even when she tried to avoid it, she would feel it anyway, she couldn't help herself.

The stronger the feelings, the harder they were to shut out: desperation and anger came in at full blast, but even worse somehow was other people's sadness, seeping into her.

The more people there were around her, the harder it was to screen it out. In the local mall, or at school assemblies, she'd feel overwhelmed and exhausted. Sometimes she would just climb a tree in the park to get away from everyone.

As she became a teenager, she fought hard against seeing, against feeling. She drank and took drugs to dull the sounds and images in her head: downers mostly and sometimes speed, but never grass or acid, which only made things worse.

Then one day she heard a song in her head, and she didn't try to resist it anymore, because she knew it was her own voice, from the future, and she had to trust it, and because she was just so tired of trying to fight it.

* * * * *

She did well enough in high school to go on to college, except that people in her family did not go to college. When she left school at eighteen, she got a job in a local department store. There were still jobs to be found in those days.

She enjoyed these years as much as she would enjoy any period of her life. She enjoyed being an ordinary person working in a store. She enjoyed having ordinary boyfriends with ordinarily futile ambitions. She knew she would not be ordinary much longer.

And then the recession hit home, the one they would soon start calling the Great Deflation, and the department store closed and so did the factory and there were very few jobs of any kind available.

Now she began to hear the songs in her head, the songs she would have to write. She had heard them before, but never with such sharpness or such urgency. It was time to begin the long road towards her destiny.

She moved to the city and began to sing in public, at first in tiny clubs. She met up with Abe Levett, and began her remarkable ascent.

* * * * *

She had always known that Abe would become her friend and her manager and, for a time, her lover. She had been looking forward to meeting him for a long time.

He was different from anyone she had ever known before. She liked the way he talked, fast and excited, waving his hands in the air. She wished it was possible for her to get that excited about anything in her life, now or in the future.

She liked his ambitions, his restlessness, his endless dreams, the way he saw the future as infinitely malleable. She liked the way that her own fatalism outraged him. For Levett, life was a series of challenges to which he was constantly rising, and nothing was impossible. He was wrong about that, but she liked him for it all the same. It was the way things should have been.

She liked his body, too, its strength and compactness and the way he used it to please her. As a teenager having sex for the first time she would sometimes compare her early partners to Abe, to how it would be with him.

But most of all she knew that he would be a friend to her, perhaps the most important friend of her life.

She had been looking forward to meeting Abe, to starting her career, to becoming a superstar. And yet when it happened she could only take it calmly, as she took everything calmly. It was no more than she expected, and in some ways it was less.

In a sense, she had been cheated out of enjoying her good fortune. She had anticipated these events so long, turning them over and over and over in her mind, that nothing was truly new to her, nothing was really exciting. She was never able to immerse herself entirely in the moment. Always a part of her would remain separate, watching the events critically or else thinking about what would come next.

In a sense she had cheated herself.

She watched the development of her career as if from a distance. She had seen it so many times before. For Abe's sake, she would pretend excitement at one triumph or another. But she doubted that he was ever really fooled.

As her career took off, she began to see more and more of her special fans, the ones who called themselves the Children, crowding towards the stage at her concerts, waiting to catch a glimpse of her at airports and hotels. She had been expecting their devotion, but she did not really understand it. She understood the desperation of the times, and she knew that her music in some way provided people with release. But she did not really understand why that should be.

* * * * *

For a few months, she loved Robert Duke. She loved him less for what he was as for what he would become, and there were times when she would forget that he was not yet that man. Briefly, present and future would mingle together.

At other times, she saw him as he was. But even then, she was still amused with him, with his illustrious past and his enormous though fast-fraying conceit.

She was sad when he left, nearly as sad as she had been when her mother died. She had known that these things would happen. But because she had not been able to bring herself to look at them too closely, they hit her hard when they did occur.

She was sad, but she knew that she would see him again.

* * * * *

At the party in the space center in Houston she met the dark man again, as she had known she would. Except that he was not yet that man, only an earlier, paler shadow of what he would become. And at the same time, she saw what he would become, how he would turn the world.

It was quite early in the party, but he was already very drunk. He was small and swarthy, like a coal miner in one of the D. H. Lawrence novels she had read in high school. In no way was she drawn to him. She was not even afraid of him.

He made his routine pass, and was obviously astonished when she took him up on it. They went back to her hotel room, and he kissed her, clumsily, his mouth sour with alcohol. And then the thing that she expected happened, the thing that she had previewed many times but still did not quite understand.

There was a strange flickering light in the corner of her eyes. And the man who had been with her was gone. Someone else had taken his place; someone later.

"Hello, Martha," he said.

His eyes were still funny and empty, but she was not afraid of him anymore.

"Who are you?" she asked, although she knew what he would say.

"I'm Jake Denning," he said. "And then again, I'm not."

She felt a powerful energy in the room, radiating from the dark man, pulling her towards him.

"Where did you come from?"

"Mars," he said. "I was on Mars. Or I will be."

He reached out and put his hand on her arm. His touch was gentle, but she could feel the energy coursing through him.

"You know," he said, as he drew her towards the bed, "what comes next."

"Yes," she said. "I know."

* * * * *

In the morning the dark man was gone, and the other was back in his place. He woke up slowly, not sure where he was. After he had got out of bed to go to the bathroom to hold his head under the tap, he seemed a little sharper.

"Some night," he said.

"Some night," she agreed.

He looked at her strangely. "Only . . ." he said. He did not complete the thought. He shook his head, as if to clear it.

He watched her brushing her hair for a moment.

"How about we go back to bed?" he asked. He sounded like he was trying to persuade himself as much as he was her. "I could stick around a little longer."

"That would be nice," she said. "But I have a plane to catch."

"Oh. All right."

He seemed almost relieved.

"I'll see you, then," he said.

"Yes," she said. "Have a good trip."

"Trip?"

"To Mars."

"That hasn't been decided yet," he said.

"You'll go," she said. "Don't worry about it."

"I hope you're right."

"I'm right. You'll see."

Usually she was careful never to make predictions like that. But in this case she knew that it wouldn't matter. And so she told the astronaut that he would go to Mars, although not what he would find there. She was not very clear on that point herself.

She would see the astronaut again. And the dark man that he would become. She would see them both on the last night of the world.

* * * * *

Her child, Daniel, was born. And even as she lay on the delivery table with the baby in her arms, she realized that the visions were gone. It was as if a curtain had been drawn down over the future.

She had expected this too. She had always known that there would be a time during which she could no longer see. But it did not make it any less shocking.

She was left only with scattered memories of the times to come: Playing a miserable season in a Vegas hotel. A terrible breakup with Abe. A house on an island where she would live in seclusion from the world.

Meeting up again with Robert Duke, backstage in a shabby little theater in Montreal. Recording a song she had yet to write. A New Year's Eve party in New York.

But these memories of the future were curiously hazy. And in time, just like her ordinary memories, they began to fade. She suspected that she was making them fade, that there were things that she no longer wished to remember because she was no longer prepared to deal with them.

Her own death, for example. Had she been able to see that before? She could no longer recall. Before, it would have been an abstraction. But now, as she held the baby in her arms, she could not stand to think about how little time remained to her before the end. She could not bear the thought of being separated from her child.

The songs stopped coming to her, too. There would still be other songs that she would sing. But for now she could not hear them.

There had been times when she wished to be like everyone else, blind to the future. But it was a painful adjustment all the same. She fell into a depression. On the advice of a friend she went to see a psychiatrist.

She told Murray Snow everything and he believed almost none of it. But he was willing to listen to her, and to work with her to regain her creativity. It was nice, finally, to have someone she could talk to.

The child was as great a joy as she had known he would be. But he frightened her, too, the more so as he got older. When he was two years old he told her, "Mommy, I'm going to fall down stairs tomorrow. And I'm going to bang my head. And I'm going to cry." The next day, he did fall down the stairs. And she knew that her child had something of her former talent. It was as if it had passed directly to him, like some strange birthright.

His talent frightened her, exactly the same way her own talent would have frightened other people if she had not usually been careful to conceal it. But he didn't tell her what he saw ahead for her, and she never asked him about it.

* * * * *

She knew that Abe was hurt by her pregnancy, although he wouldn't admit as much. Of course she could not explain it to him. She could not explain it to herself.

It was a pity that he had been unable to develop other relationships. Although she knew that was probably her fault.

She did not want to play in Las Vegas. She did not want to reach a parting with Abe. She did not want him to go through a shattering breakdown.

She had tried to visit him in the hospital, but he had refused to see her. Something told her that this would happen, but it was only a memory of it happening that way, it didn't have the clarity of her old vision, And so she had gone anyway, in case she had remembered it wrong.

Still, she knew that she would see Abe again. That much of the future, at least, she could remember. They would meet again at the party on the last night of the world.

* * * * *

After her break with Abe, she acquired new management, but it was a caretaker arrangement. She made the decisions now. And without Abe to push her, she allowed her career to slowly wind down. She played less each year, recorded less. Finally she stopped altogether.

It did not seem to harm her career, indeed it seemed almost to help. She was content to raise her child and wait for the moment when she would be needed. It would not be long, she knew.

She met Robert Duke again in Montreal one cold winter night, and she invited him to visit her in Corfu. And for a while they were happy together.

She waited for what would come next.

* * 22 * *

With Denning assuming command of the mission, a command that Chang challenged only infrequently, and in an increasingly desultory manner, they took things easier after Wyatt died, easier and easier, until in the end they hardly ventured outside base at all.

Control was pissed off, of course, but being so very far away there was nothing that Control could do about it.

"The dust storms are worse than we expected," Denning would say. "You've seen the footage."

Control did not notice that he was sending them selectively edited highlights of the same dust storms, over and over again. One dust storm looked much like another, after all. Or if they noticed, they did not comment on it.

It could have been very boring, sitting in the dome, waiting for the right configuration of the planets to make the trip home. It could have been very boring, except that Denning had found himself a new interest.

Mostly what Denning liked to do now was to sit down at his terminal and play with cellular automata. He would sit there for hours on end, sometimes altering a rule here or there, often just watching. Watching the patterns enfold and unfold, whole universes marching across the screen.

He hadn't looked at an automaton program since college, and even back then he had never been terribly interested in them. But one morning, soon after Wyatt's death, he had woken up with a pattern in his head. And he had sat down at his computer to find it. He was still looking. But every day he got a little closer.

"You're going to ruin your eyesight," Chang said, emerging from his own sullen reverie during one such marathon session. "Staring at that screen all day."

"Better than staring at you."

"What do you think you're doing, anyway?"

"Looking for the rules, I guess."

"Rules? What do you mean, rules?"

Denning blinked at Chang, trying to focus on the question. What *had* he meant?

"The rules of the universe, I guess," he said. "The underlying program."

"What are you talking about, Denning? The universe isn't a program. *That's* a program." He gestured contemptuously to the display on Denning's screen. "But *this* isn't." He waved his arms around him to take in their tiny home, and whatever surrounded it. "Clear, now?"

"Some people think the universe could be a program. I remember reading that . . ."

"Fruitcake scientists," Chang said. "Like the clowns who sent us here. You're going to believe *scientists?* I'm telling you, it's bullshit. A computer program is *information.* The universe isn't information. The universe is real. Real matter, real energy."

"But suppose it *is* information. Information in three dimensions instead of one. Suppose that matter and energy are actually composed of bits of information. Bits that sometimes arrange themselves to behave like electrons, or whatever."

"Bits? How do you mean, bits?"

"Like in an automaton. Or a movie for that matter. The individual bits of information seem to meld together, one into another, into patterns. But actually the bits are discrete. Maybe the universe is like a lattice of individual cells, each one switching on and off at different points in time to create the patterns we see."

"That doesn't make any sense," Chang said. "*Points in time.* Time flows. It doesn't *jump,* like some fucking digital clock."

"But when you get right down to it, maybe there is no time," Denning said, his voice growing excited. "Maybe that's an illusion, too. Sure, we *think* it flows. But how do we know we're right? Maybe our perception isn't finely grained enough to see the jumps. That could be a limiting factor in the program, an artifact of how it was written. Or it could be intentional."

"Intentional? What do you mean, intentional?"

"Deliberately built-in. By whoever made the rules of the program."

"Made the rules? Oh, I get it. That would be God, right?"

"I didn't say that. All I'm saying is, supposing there *are* rules? What are they? And how does it turn out in the end?"

"How does what turn out?"

"The run. This particular run."

"The universe, you mean? You want to know how the universe turns out?" Chang roared with laughter. "You and every physicist who ever lived. Except that those people have been wasting their time, because *you're* going to figure it out on that ditsy little machine. That's a good one, man, a really good one."

"It's something to do," Denning said. "I never said I could do it. But it's worth trying."

"No, it isn't. Because I can tell you right now how the universe turns out, at least for us. It's like this: We go back to Earth and we're heroes. And we have ourselves a good time for a while. And then we die. As for the rest of it, who gives a shit? What difference can it make? What possible difference?"

"I've got this strange feeling," Denning said. "I don't know where it comes from. A feeling that the run is almost over. This run. That soon we start over."

"Not me," Chang said. "I'm not through with this universe yet. I got a lot more living to do."

* * * * *

It was a pity, Denning thought, that Chang did not share his interest in cellular automata. The man needed something to occupy his mind. Chang did not want to work, but neither did he want to read, or play computer games, or even play cards on the few occasions when Denning would suggest it. Chang was stupefyingly bored most of the time, and his boredom could very quickly cross over into anger.

"I can't stand it," he would say. "I just can't stand it. I never knew it would be like this. What kind of an idea was this anyway, sending us here? We knew that it was going to be like this, we knew what a godforsaken dump this was, but they sent us anyway. And why did we let them do this to us? So we could get our pictures on the evening news? I can't believe I let them do this to me."

Much of what Chang said made sense to Denning. Which didn't mean he wanted to hear it over and over again.

"I wish Control had sent a woman," Chang would say. "It's the least fucking thing they could have done."

There had been women on the mission team, but in the end none had gone. Initially there had been talk of a much larger crew, but when the economics of it forced a compression, the women had dropped out of the running. The sociotech types had figured out that if they were going to send a woman, they would have to send two, because one woman and two men was an almost certain recipe for disaster. But Control could not find it in their hearts to send two women and one man.

"Even the dyke," Chang would say. "Marsha or Louise, that would have been better, but even the dyke would have been okay. She would have got so bored, I bet she would have gone for it."

"Shelly, you mean?" Denning would say. "You don't know that Shelly is a dyke. She just didn't like you very much."

"Or you," Chang would say. "But what the hell, out here I bet I would look pretty good to old Shelly."

Usually, when Chang started up on one of his rants, Denning would try to escape into his books or his programs. Or, he would close his eyes and try to doze off, knowing that Chang wouldn't notice. Except that he found it hard to get to sleep these days. Every time he closed his eyes the pattern would start flashing across his retina, the weird, elusive flickering pattern.

And then one day, in the middle of one of these ritualized conversations, Chang broke the script.

"Hey, Denning," he said, raising his hand in front of his eyes as if to shield them. "What the hell are you doing?"

"Doing?" Denning echoed. He opened his eyes. "I'm trying to get some sleep, what does it look like?"

"You're, I don't know, you're *flashing* man, there's this weird *light* coming out of you . . ."

Looking down, Denning could see that his whole body appeared to be flickering in and out of existence. "Hey," he said, "I think I'm . . ."

And then he was no longer in the dome. He was someplace else, where the light was too bright and the pull of gravity too strong. Incredibly, impossibly, he was back on Earth.

* * * * *

The pattern that he had glimpsed on the cave wall was inside his head now, all the way inside, filling him up with a new knowledge. And there were things he had to do.

He was in a small town somewhere, shivering in a thin business suit on a brisk fall day. He was staring through a wire-mesh fence at some kids playing in a school yard. He saw the one who had brought him here, a small blond girl. She was singing to herself, some skipping song, and he could hear that she had a very nice voice. She looked up and met his glance, then quickly looked away.

Later, he followed her home and talked his way into the house. He passed his hand over the girl's head, and part of what was inside him rushed into her.

He left the house, and felt himself flickering again. Now he was in a hotel room, looking at a man groping drunkenly with a fair-haired woman. It took him a moment to realize that the man was himself—or at least, an earlier version of himself, a few years younger—and that the woman was the singer he had met at the party at the Space Center.

"I'm sorry, kid," he said, reaching out to touch his earlier self on the forehead, feeling the man go rigid and slump to the floor. "Those are the breaks."

He put the younger Denning in the bathroom. And he made love to the singer.

"I don't understand," the singer told him, before he flickered from the room. "I don't understand what any of this is about."

"You will," he told her, "in the end."

Now he was outside, in a torrential rainstorm, flying effortlessly, dream-like, above tall oak trees. The air was warm and smelled faintly of olives.

It was dark, pitch black, and then it was light, a burst of light pulsing from his own body. Looking down, he saw a road running between the trees, and a boy standing on the road. There was a car bearing down on the boy, who made no motion to get out of the way. He just stood there, as if waiting, looking up into the sky, looking at Denning.

The car was swerving, but too late. Denning could see how it would be. The car would smash into the child, tossing him up and over the windshield to fall by the roadside like a broken doll. Then the car would skid off the road, crashing into the trunk of a massive oak tree, the front-end crumpling on impact, the driver's head slamming into the windshield.

Denning swooped down from the sky and lifted the boy up out of the way of the car. The car rushed beneath them, skidding off the road and into the trees. Denning reached out to touch it, so that it passed harmlessly through a gap between the trees, spinning around completely and coming to a halt in the muddy field beyond.

Denning set the boy back on the ground. "You should get home," he said. "You could catch a cold."

Daniel was staring at the car. "He was going to crash. And then he didn't. Can you teach me how to do that?"

"You'll figure it out for yourself," Denning said. "By the way, I'm your father."

"I know," the boy said.

"Of course you do."

The light surrounding Denning had dimmed now to a faint glow.

Duke had climbed out of the car. "Daniel," he called, out of the darkness. "Are you okay, Daniel?"

"I can't stay now," Denning told his son. "But I'll be back."

"On your ship."

"That's right."

He reached out and ruffled the boy's hair. Then the flickering came again and carried him away.

* * * * *

In the dome on Mars, Jake Denning woke from strange dreams with a raging headache, feeling like he had not slept at all.

"Hey, Chang," he said. "Did you see . . ."

"What?" Chang asked, blankly. Clearly he did not remember what had happened, if anything had happened at all.

"Nothing."

He put a hand up to his head. His hair was soaking wet.

Fever dreams, he thought.

There was something he was trying to recall, about a singer and her child and a pattern in his mind. But it was all slipping away from him now.

Maybe it would come back to him.

* * * * *

"Daniel," Duke said, as he emerged from the field on to the driveway. "Thank God you're okay. I thought for sure I was going to hit you."

"But you swerved out of the way."

"And then I was going to hit the tree . . ."

"But you didn't."

"I thought I saw . . ."

"What?"

"I don't know." Duke rubbed his eyes. "It was hard to see *anything.* But then there was this flash of lightning. And I saw you. And I thought I saw this gigantic bird, swooping down on you."

"No bird," Daniel said. "There wasn't any bird."

"We should get back to the house. Your mother will be worried."

"She won't be worried. She saw the whole thing. She knows we're okay."

They began walking up the driveway to the house.

"You think she can see that well?"

"Oh sure. She can *now.*"

* * 2 3 * *

"I'm sorry," Duke told Martha later. "That was stupid of me. I hope I didn't scare you."

"Oh, you did. I thought for sure you were going to die. I saw the car going out of control . . . And Daniel standing in the road, in the way of the car . . . I thought you were both going to die. And then . . ."

"Then?"

"I knew that you would be all right. I could see you and Daniel back in the house with me."

"What are you trying to tell me, Martha? That it came back? Your gift came back?"

"Yes. Because I needed it. I needed to know that you and Daniel would be all right."

He shook his head wearily. "And you expect me to believe you now? Believe that you can see the future?"

"I think you already believe it."

"I guess maybe I do. Daniel was right about the astronaut and he was right about the accident. And if he can see the future, why not you?"

Accepting it, finally, he felt a strange dizziness, as though he were looking down on himself from a great height.

"Are you okay, Robert?"

"Yes. No. I don't know. This is still a little weird for me." Sweat was pouring down his face. He wiped at it with a shaky hand. "You think I'm going to be able to handle it?"

"You'll handle it."

"You predict it, in other words? You predict that I'm going to hang in there with you?"

"I wasn't making a prediction."

"But you see it, don't you?"

"Please don't get upset."

"What's to get upset about? A little thing like losing your free will?"

She gave him a sad smile. "You can learn to live with it. When you've had enough practice."

"I don't know if I can learn to live with a woman who sees the future. And her son who runs around making predictions about it."

"I'll make him stop."

"But he'll still see it. Even if he doesn't tell me about it, I'll read it in his eyes. And in yours."

"Read what?"

"I don't know. Dead astronauts. Earthquakes. Riots. Assassinations. The end of the world . . . I'm really not sure I can live with that."

* * * * *

The next morning, Duke slept in late. He woke to an unfamiliar sound. It took him a moment to recognize it as the tinkling of the synth program on Martha's PDA.

He got up and opened the door through to her study that adjoined the bedroom. He saw her sitting on a cushion on the floor, engrossed in picking out a tune on the tiny touch-board.

She looked up and saw him standing in the doorway.

"That's nice," he said. "What is it?"

"I don't know what it's called yet."

"It's new?"

"That's right," she said. "It's new."

He could hear the happiness in her voice, and the relief, but also another undertone. Sadness, maybe. Although why would she be sad to be writing songs again?

"It came back," she said. "My music came back. I woke up this morning and I heard it in my head. The new music."

* * * * *

Snow left the next day.

"There's no more reason for me to be here," he told Duke, before he departed. "We've achieved Martha's objective in therapy. Or at least, *she's* achieved it."

Music drifted down the stairs from Martha's study. Snow glanced upwards.

"She's going to want to go back, you know," he said.

"I know."

"It would be a good idea if you could stop her. I'm not sure what kind of welcome she's going to find when she returns."

"You think MentHealth will go after her? Try to commit her?"

"Yes, I do. But perhaps you can persuade her to remain here."

Duke laughed. "Everyone seems to think I have influence over Martha. But like I told you before, Murray, she'll do what she has to do."

Snow sighed.

"Take care of her, Robert."

Duke did not challenge Snow's assumption that he would be staying with Martha.

* * * * *

Duke stood with Daniel, watching Snow's cab pull away.

"Yesterday *I* was leaving, Daniel, you know that? That was where I was going in such a hurry. I was heading back to L.A. Maybe I'm still going to do that."

The boy looked uncomfortable.

"What's the matter, Daniel? You feel a prediction coming on, but your mother told you to keep quiet? It's okay, I give you permission, just this once."

The boy said nothing.

"Look, Daniel, I know you don't like me very much. Wouldn't you be glad to get rid of me?"

"No," Daniel said. "You should stay with us. For Mommy."

"And you'll try to get used to me?"

"Yes."

"Tell me something, Daniel. You knew what was going to happen. That you would almost get killed. But you still went out to play on the driveway."

"I wanted to climb trees. And I knew that nothing bad would happen. That he wouldn't let me die."

"He? What do you mean, 'he'?"

Daniel stared at him, unblinking. "My father," he said. "My father wouldn't let me die."

"You father?" Duke echoed, baffled. "Are you talking about . . . God?"

"My father," the boy repeated, in an exasperated tone. "My father the astronaut. I *told* you about him. Don't you remember?"

"But I thought you said your father was on Mars?"

"Sometimes he is," Daniel said. "Sometimes."

Duke shook his head, as if to clear it. "The point is, none of this had to happen. You could have told me that you would be out on the driveway. You could have warned me."

"But it doesn't work like that. It *did* have to happen. You can't warn people. Or if you do, it doesn't make any difference. Whatever is going to happen will happen."

* * * * *

Martha was busy with her music now. Duke would sit watching her for hours as she programmed her sequencers or sang into her wristband recorder. The new songs were coming to her almost effortlessly, as though some inner voice was singing them to her. The new songs were a lot like her old ones, but purer, somehow, almost hypnotically simple, refined down to the very essence of Martha Nova.

"Why now?" he asked. "Why did the music come back to you now?"

"Because it was time, I suppose."

"Time to make a comeback, you mean?"

She hesitated. "It's more than that, Robert. It's because we're at the end. The beginning of the end, anyway."

He felt a thrill of fear. "That's what you see?"

"It's what I've always seen. And now it's coming. Finally."

He shook his head. "I'm sitting here listening to you talk about the end of the world. And believing you."

"Not exactly the end of the world," she said. "But the end of this way of being. The world will go on. People will go on, too, I think . . . But not in the same way. Everything will be different."

"How?"

"I don't know, exactly. I don't see that far ahead."

Duke stared at her, surprised. "Why not?" he asked. Why can't you see?"

"It's like I hit a barrier. It's like . . ." Her eyes filled up with tears. "Actually, it's like I'm dead. I don't see beyond a certain point, because I won't be here to see it."

"What?"

"I'm going to die, Robert. I'm going to die soon."

"No . . ." he said, shaking his head in denial. "That can't be."

Tears were flooding down her face now. She brushed at them with her hand.

"I know it's hard for you to accept. It was hard for me, too. And I've had much longer to get used to the idea."

"No," he said, again. "You can't die, Martha."

She leaned against him, and he held her quietly for a few minutes. Then she drew back and fumbled for a tissue.

"I should start to think about packing," she said.

"Packing?"

"I have to go home soon. I have to record this music."

"Do you?" he asked. "I mean, what if we just stayed here forever?"

"I can't stay, Robert. You know that."

He nodded reluctantly. "Yes. I guess I do know that."

"I was hoping you would come with me. But you're welcome to stay on here as long as you like . . ."

"You know I'm going to come with you, Martha. You told me, remember?"

"I guess I was hoping that you'd *want* to come with me."

"Of course," he said. "Of course I want to."

* * * * *

Chang whooped with delight as the ship swung perfectly into its preprogrammed arc towards Earth. "I can't believe it," he said. "I can't believe we're actually going home."

"Right," Denning agreed. "Home."

Home. It was all he had wanted, ever since they had left Earth, to get back home. Except that he was no longer sure what that meant.

For the first time in a long time he thought about Hilda. He had not messaged her in months, despite Control's urging. And after a while she had given up on her own perfunctory end of the correspondence. Too busy drinking herself to death, probably. If he were lucky.

No, it was hard to get very excited about going home. He was just too tired for that, so very tired. Maybe, on the voyage back, he would finally be able to get some sleep. Maybe he would stop having such weird dreams.

On the screen he could see Earth, a tiny bright speck across the great gulf of emptiness. Waiting for him.

Briefly, a familiar lattice-like pattern flickered across his retina. He rubbed his eyes.

"Glory," Chang said. "Money. Sex. Liquor. Here we come."

"Right," Denning said, again. "Here we come."

The ship raced onwards, closer and closer to Earth.

* * PART SIX * *

Nearer To the Fire

* * 2 4 * *

In the living room of his mother's hotel suite, Daniel watched the talk show on the talk channel. It was the *Bob Milton People In Town Show.*

The talk show host smiled. "Well, Jake," he said, "I guess it's great to be back home."

His guest shrugged. "I guess so, Bob," he said. "I guess I'm glad to be home."

The guest peeled back his lips, as if to force a smile, but the effect was more of a leer. His stare into the camera was level enough, but there was something evasive about his eyes. He looked tired. He looked worse than tired. He was painfully thin.

"You did a great job, Jake," said the talk show host, "a great, great job for all of us here in this country. We're all very, very proud of you."

Applause from the studio audience. It was an audience the singer's child had often seen before, one of the best audiences. He especially liked the three old ladies in the front row with the funny hats, and the fat man three rows behind who put his fingers in his mouth to whistle in appreciation at the talk show host's more notable witticisms.

"Jake Denning, folks," the talk show host said. "The man who came back. Came back from Earth's nearest yet most mysterious neighbor, the actual planet Mars, and came right here to tell us all about it on the *Bob Milton People In Town Show.*"

More applause. Denning, looking vaguely embarrassed, nodded his head in acknowledgment.

"Ah, actually Bob," he said, "that would be Venus. Earth's nearest neighbor, I mean. Or the moon, if you count that."

The host smiled, peeling back his lips to show clenched teeth.

"Thanks for the correction, Jake," he said. "How about 'Earth's most mysterious neighbor?' Are you okay with that?"

"Oh sure, Bob," Denning said. "Mars is very mysterious." He remembered his rehearsal with the Agency flacks. "The question of water on Mars, for example . . ."

"Let's just hold off on the water," said the host. "We don't want to get people too excited. Why don't you tell us all about those little green men?"

The astronaut stared back blankly at the host for an embarrassingly long moment.

"The Martians," the host prompted. "Tell us about those cute little green Martians. What the hell happened to them? I take it you didn't find any?"

"That's right," the astronaut said. "We didn't find any, Bob. No little green men. Not so much as a shred of lichen. Plenty of dust, though, you never saw such dust . . ."

"You must have been disappointed," the host said.

"Disappointed?"

"That there weren't any little green men."

"Little green men?" the astronaut echoed, as though the subject was new to him. "On Mars, you mean?"

The host's smile had frozen on his face.

"On Mars, that's right. You must have been disappointed not to find any Martians."

The astronaut looked puzzled. "We knew that already. We knew that there were no Martians, so we weren't really disappointed. We knew that as far back as Mariner One, that nothing could survive on Mars except just possibly some kind of microorganisms. It's the UV, the ultraviolet light, streaming down with hardly any atmosphere to stop it, sterilizing everything."

"But surely," the host persisted, "surely you *hoped* that all the scientists were wrong. In your heart of hearts . . ."

"Oh sure," the astronaut agreed. "Sure we hoped."

* * * * *

Two men dead, Denning thought, and he wants to talk about Martians. No doubt they want to keep it light, for the holiday season.

He shook his head, as if to clear it. He had been drinking all afternoon, on the airplane coming in from Houston and then in the TV studio, and yet he did not feel drunk, only very tired. He had felt that way ever since reentry. All through the debriefings, and then again through all these press conferences and interviews. It wasn't a matter of wanting to sleep. Sleep didn't help at all. In fact it made things worse.

"Too bad," the host was saying. "Too bad there were no Martians. Really too bad."

"It depends," Denning said, seized by a sudden impulse. "It depends on how you look at it. Maybe, if you looked at it *just so* you would see one. Whether you wanted to or not."

What am I saying? Denning wondered. He did not know what he was saying. He listened to what he was saying with much the same interest, and unease, as the talk show host.

"See one?" the host echoed. "How do you mean?"

"Now that I think about it, I did see a Martian one time. Tall, blue. Six fingers on each hand."

"You saw a Martian?" The host gave a little choked laugh. "That's a good one, Jake."

Denning shook his head. "I'm not joking, Bob. I saw a Martian. Really I did."

"Then why didn't we hear about this before? Was it some kind of secret?"

Denning scratched his head. "Guess I forget to mention it."

"Where did you see this Martian?"

Denning frowned in concentration. "In a cave, I think. Yeah, a cave. It spoke to me. It spoke English, strangely enough. Or maybe it was some kind of telepathy."

"And what did it say?"

"That we were blind men, basically. Blind men chasing our own tails, all the way to Mars. Except . . ."

"Except?"

"Except as it turned out," Denning said slowly, remembering now, "it wasn't a Martian after all. It was Mike Wyatt."

"We're talking about the commander of the mission?" the host asked. "Mike Wyatt. Tragically killed in a rock fall."

"That's right, Bob," Denning said. "That's who we're talking about. Awful thing, just awful."

"So Wyatt was pretending to be a Martian? As a gag, you mean?"

"A gag? No, it was no gag. Mike didn't play gags, he wasn't that sort of guy. Besides . . ."

"Besides?" the host asked, as he signaled frantically to move to a commercial.

A stricken look came over Denning's face. "Besides," he said, and his voice fell to a whisper, "he was already dead."

* * * * *

After the commercial break, Bob Milton was joined by the mud wrestling champion of the world. The astronaut was nowhere to be seen.

Daniel turned off the wall screen. He looked around the room. His mother was in her bedroom, getting ready for the party. Robert had fallen asleep in his armchair.

The child turned on his Talkie. "I just saw my father," he told the machine. "On the screen."

"Is that so?" the Talkie responded. "No kidding?"

"He's starting to remember what happened to him on Mars."

"Oh," said the Talkie. "Had he forgotten?"

"Yes he had. But it's all coming back to him now. And he thinks he's going mad."

"And is he?" the Talkie asked.

"That depends," the child said, "on how you look at it."

* * 25 * *

It was nearly ten on New Year's Eve, almost an hour past curfew, and the limousine—a big, black electrically-powered armor-plated late-model Cadillac—moved noiselessly down an almost deserted Fifth Avenue. From the back seat, Levett peered uneasily at the desolate streets, through the tinted bulletproof glass of the window.

It was more than two years since this current curfew had come into force, more than two years since Levett had ventured out so late. The downtown area, with its gutted buildings and boarded-up windows, looked unfamiliar in the darkness, like the streets of some quite different city.

It was a quiet night so far, and this was one of the best policed areas of the city. But venturing out after curfew, even with a special police permit on the windshield of his car, caused Levett considerable unease. What if a Guard patrol should mortar first and ask questions later? Such incidents were not uncommon. Only the month before, a member of the city assembly had been killed near Times Square by a nervous watch detail.

He worried, too, about being seen in this big black limousine. It turned him, at least in his imagination, into a moving target. It made him look important, and these days it did not pay to look important.

His anxiety persisted, became more acute. His heart raced in his chest, the palms of his hands were cold and damp, his vision field seemed to narrow in upon him.

Anxious, he thought. I'm anxious. Last week I was depressed and now I'm anxious. Is that an improvement? His therapist would no doubt think so. Anxiety, his therapist had told him, at least showed involvement with the future.

Now he tried to damp down on his racing heart, practicing the relaxation exercises taught him by his therapist. He tensed and relaxed the muscles of his jaw, stomach, thighs. Some relief came, not much.

Why, he wondered, am I so uptight about seeing Martha again?

He had thought about her often since his breakdown. At times he had imagined seeing her again, perhaps even managing her again. But he had made no efforts to contact her since his release from the clinic. Better, he had decided, to let the past lie. Better not to stir things up again.

He had convinced himself that he was all finished with Martha Nova. Until the MentHealth operatives came to call.

* * * * *

Following his release from the clinic, Levett had moved to New York. He lived there in a one-bedroom condo in a new but rapidly decaying medium-priced high-rise on West Houston. Graffiti already scarred the sham wood panels of the elevators, which often shook alarmingly in their ascent and descent. The door of his apartment was scratched and dented by the carelessness of a succession of medium-priced moving men.

He could have afforded better. In the years of his greatest success, he had spent freely on houses and paintings and parties and women. Afterwards he had run up huge medical bills. But he was still a wealthy man. There was still plenty of money left from his one-time share of the most valuable entertainment commodity in the world.

He could have afforded better. But this was the first place he had looked at on coming to New York, and he could not summon the energy to look further. Dulled by his long confinement and continued medication, he regarded his living situation apathetically.

He lived there as a man in a trance. He watched the screen, he programmed his meals, he took his medication, he went to see his therapist. He made no attempt to contact friends or family. He never listened to music.

Once he had been busy, so very busy. But not now. His busyness, his therapist told him, had been only a manic defense against depression. And these days, there was nothing for him to be busy with.

When the MentHealth operatives came to call, at first he thought they were regular-duty Intervenors. They looked the part, in their blue serge suits. And they acted it, too, pushing him back through his doorway into the apartment.

"I'm registered," he said. "I'm registered with an approved therapist and I've been taking my medication."

"That doesn't concern us," the taller agent said. "We're in special operations. Actually, we've met, Abe. You don't remember?" He flashed identification. "I'm Olson. This is Webb."

"Olson?"

Levett's memory had been patchy since his breakdown. Part of the problem, his therapist explained, was repression, a deliberate forgetting. Those memories might come back in time. Others had been lost forever in the electroshock therapy.

"We had such a nice chat," Olson said. "About Martha Nova's tour plans."

"Vegas," Levett said, remembering now. "You made mc book her into Vegas."

"Worked out well, too. But now we need another little favor from you."

"Favor?"

"The details of this conversation will remain confidential. We'll be monitoring you from here on in, however this goes. We can have you pulled in as AP anytime we like."

AP: *Ambulatory Psychotic.* Under the Mental Health laws, unregistered psychotics had virtually no civil rights.

"I'm not psychotic," Levett objected. "I'm depressed."

"I'm not interested in your symptoms," Olson said. "That's entirely your affair."

"I don't understand what you're doing here. What do you want from me?"

"We want your help."

"What could I do to help you?"

"You can get to Martha Nova."

"This must be some sort of mistake." He felt dizzy in the head, his knees were weak. He sat down. "I haven't seen Martha in five years. I don't want to see her, she wouldn't want to see me. I have nothing to do with her anymore."

"We're aware of that. But we think she will see you, for old times sake."

"But what do you care about Martha? She's retired. She doesn't perform, she doesn't record, she doesn't even live here anymore. She's history, that's all she is. Over. Finished."

"You're wrong," Olson said. "She's coming back. She has a new release scheduled, and her record company is throwing a party to launch it right here in New York. You may be able to see her before the party. If not, we'll swing you an invitation. Either way, you'll be able to get close enough to talk to her."

"Talk to her about what?"

"About staying retired," Olson said. "We think that would be best for everyone. Pull the record, cancel the party, go away somewhere no one can find her."

"Why would I want to tell her to do that?"

"Because if you can't stop her, we'll have to find some other way."

"Some other way? You mean, send her to one of your Recovery Centers?"

"That would be an option," Olson said. "To be honest with you, I don't know what Plan B is. I don't need to know it. But I wouldn't rule out something more *drastic*."

"Drastic?" Levett stared at Olson. "You mean you're going to kill Martha, if I can't stop her from making this comeback? Is that what you're saying?"

"Like I said, I don't know. But at this stage of the game, that's what it may come down to."

"But you can't ask me to do this. I can't see Martha, I just can't . . ."

Webb, the shorter of the agents, who had been silent all this time, now spoke up.

"Don't get excited, Levett," he said. "If you don't want to do it, don't do it. Our psych specialists were pretty sure you would want to. Occupational therapy, so to speak. Give you a sense of purpose. Get back to rolling that rock. But we don't need you that bad, we can probably find someone else to warn her. And if we don't, it doesn't matter much anyway. Fuck it, we're already on our way into dust. Decaying."

He pulled a loose thread from the lapel of his jacket.

"You sound like some kind of Nova Child," Levett said.

"But I am a Nova Child," Webb said. "I believe it all. This world is nowhere, it's nothing, nothing at all. It's a prison, a prison for the light. We've been cast out, into this dead stuff . . ."

His voice grew dreamy, far-off.

"But we will be released. Any day now. It's coming, coming very soon. It's like Martha promised us: the light is breaking through. Every morning I wake up and turn on the screen and see if it's started yet. Because we're very close now, very near the end. Look at the wars, the crime, the vandalism, the terrorism, the craziness, the desperation . . . The worse things get, the more excited we get. We expect things to get worse. We would be disappointed if they didn't."

"Don't give me that crap," Levett said. "I've already heard enough of it to last me a lifetime. Don't forget, I *made* Martha Nova."

"No, you didn't," Webb said. "No you didn't. *We* did."

"We who? We the government?"

"We the Children," Webb said.

Levett turned to Olson. "This guy is nuts."

"A man's religion," Olson said, "is his own affair."

* * * * *

There was a huge mob outside the hotel, streaming all the way back down the Avenue. Levett had not seen so many people collected in one place in many years. He found it frightening.

Around the hotel, squads of city police and state troopers held an uneasy line. This was clearly a massive violation of the curfew, and yet the security forces seemed powerless to enforce the law. There were just too many of the Children, and this was their big night. Tonight, they would allow nothing to stand in their path.

Tonight, in this hotel, at a small and very exclusive New Year's Eve celebration, Martha Nova would make her first public appearance in five years. She would communicate with representatives of the international media in order to promote her long-awaited new album. And then she would perform her new songs. The show would be seen on the giant screens mounted on the roof of the hotel, and around the world.

It was for this new music that the Children waited, that they had waited for so long.

As the limousine moved towards the hotel checkpoint, an arm of the mob swung away to wrap itself around the car. Faces pressed up against the darkened glass. Levett was momentarily terrified that they would break the windows, tear the car and its occupants apart. But then, disappointed, they fell back. Obviously they did not know that Martha Nova was already inside this hotel.

Usually the Nova Children were so calm and quiet. But tonight they seemed overexcited. It was as if they expected something enormously significant to happen. More significant even than a new album by Martha Nova.

Levett pressed the button to roll down the side-window and peered out to get a closer look. The Children looked happy, smiling, full of joy. They were singing. The whole crowd was singing, Levett realized, chanting the same thing over and over again.

"Getting near / Getting near the end . . ."

It was the chorus of one of Martha's old songs, one of her most famous. Dimly, Levett recalled her singing to him, sitting at her kitchen table in her tiny studio apartment back in Toronto, the day they had met. Before the albums and the tours, before all the craziness.

The chanting, soft and eerie and compulsively repetitive, disturbed him. He rolled up the window.

"I don't understand it," Levett's driver said. He shook his head from side to side. "I just don't get it. All this craziness, all for some *singer.*"

"It's not the singer," Levett said. "It doesn't matter who the singer is. It's just a hunger, a great hunger. A hunger for religious ecstasy. That's what it is."

He had read that in a news magazine piece, and it had stuck in his mind. *A hunger for religious ecstasy.* It was a pretty good way of putting it. He couldn't do better than that himself.

The limousine passed through the checkpoint and down into the underground parking facility of the hotel. Here, Levett immediately felt safer. He boarded the elevator to the penthouse floor.

✶ ✶ 2 6 ✶ ✶

Denning studied his reflection in the mirror of the hotel bathroom. He straightened his tie with the Space Agency logo, brushed back his hair.

I look, he thought, like a fucking wreck.

"A party," he muttered. "Just what I needed."

"What?" Edison asked. "You say something?"

Edison was the Agency flack appointed to guide him through this little victory tour. He was a tall black man with big shoulders and stern eyes and a business card identifying him as a Public Relations Representative.

Edison would be reporting back to the Agency on his every move. So far the report would not be a glowing one. Edison had not been pleased with his performance on the *People In Town Show,* not in the least.

"You saw a Martian? Only it turned out to be Wyatt? Only he was dead? What the fuck was that?"

"Just trying to lighten things up a little, that's all."

It was possible, he thought, that Edison already suspected the truth that Denning was no longer even sure he wished to conceal. That he was going mad.

"Let's move it along," Edison said, already halfway to the door. "I got some reporters lined up for you."

"I bet they can hardly wait."

✶ ✶ ✶ ✶ ✶

The Agency had not been happy with their lone returning astronaut.

"Why didn't you film the rock slide?" they asked. "The one that killed Wyatt?"

"We did. We sent you the footage."

"The video showed the site after you took the body out. Why didn't you film it before you dragged Wyatt out of there?"

"We thought he might still be alive. We didn't have time to think about shooting video."

"And why didn't you keep Chang restrained? If you knew he might do something crazy?"

"Well, you're right, I should have. I accept full responsibility. But I wasn't thinking clearly, you understand, with all the pressure, and with what happened to Mike . . . I didn't know Chang would do that, just open the airlock and step out. I couldn't have known he would do something like *that.*"

"And these dust storms. The folks in Planet Science find it very hard to believe you had so many of the suckers."

"Then let the folks in Planet Science go see for themselves."

Clearly, the Agency did not want to buy any of it. They kept asking the same questions over and over again, and then they trussed him into a lie detector to repeat the entire performance. They didn't tell him the results. But he could sense from their frustration and irritation that he had somehow passed with flying colors.

The Agency did not want to buy his story, but in the end they had no choice. The world's media were lining up, and they had to throw them something, quickly.

It was fortunate, in a sense, that the world's media had other things on their mind than the man from Mars. Things had got worse since he had last listened to the news from Earth, which had been long before Chang smashed the radio. Things had got worse, and no one seemed to believe they would get better.

The unemployed now officially outnumbered the employed. The cities were almost unmanageable. There were small wars everywhere, national and regional conflagrations, some involving limited nuclear exchanges, some threatening to widen. Ghastly things were happening to the environment. Everywhere you looked there was drought, flooding, famine, plague, pestilence.

And then, just recently, there had been the sudden and unexpected return to public life of Martha Nova, an event causing tumult among large sections of the global teenage public.

If it had been a slower period for news, the media might have pressed harder for access to the sole surviving astronaut. As it was, the Agency was able to keep him under wraps for two days, pleading the effects of full gravity after the weaker gravity fields of Mars and the ship.

Actually, Denning had surprised the doctors with the speed of his recovery. Coming off the ship he had hardly been able to walk, but within hours he was showing unexpected strength, and the next day he was walking around unaided. The Agency canceled the plans for a brief sit-down press conference, and began to work on a more ambitious itinerary.

* * * * *

His wife, they told him, had entered an alcohol treatment center shortly after his departure. The treatment had been successful. She did not want to see him again. She had filed divorce papers the day before his return to Earth. The Agency had done their best to persuade her not to, but her mind was made up.

They broke this news to him at the end of the debriefing. They did so carefully and circumspectly. He roared with laughter.

The last president, the one who had tormented him on the way out with those ceaselessly banal exchanges, had not been reelected the month before. It served him right, Denning thought. Obviously, Mars had failed to work the trick for him.

The trip had not been a crowd-pleaser. No one was much interested in Mars, not even with two dead astronauts. The first batch of journalists he met were practically nodding off with boredom.

Oh sure, they would ask plenty of idiotic questions. But they weren't really interested in the answers. No one was much interested in *anything* anymore. Like Denning and Chang, back in that dome in the awful empty wastelands of Mars, they were just going through the motions.

* * * * *

At first he resisted going out on a publicity tour.

"I talked to a lot of journalists already," he told Linda Maxwell, the Agency's chief PR person, scowling at the schedule in front of him. "Couldn't I take a few days and rest up?"

She shook her head. "I'm sorry, but we've got to move fast on this, before everyone forgets all about you. Interest is pretty low as it is."

Linda Maxwell was tall and blond and certainly the best-looking woman he had seen in nearly three years. He thought briefly about asking her to join him for a drink, but it seemed like too much work.

"Maybe it would be better," Denning said, uncertainly, "if we did let people forget the whole thing."

"You went to Mars," Maxwell said. "You went to another planet, and you want people to forget that? You should be proud, Jake. You shouldn't want to hide yourself away."

"Oh, I'm proud all right."

"And when this is over, you're going to find a lot of doors opening to you. Business, politics, you name it."

"Right," Denning agreed. "Doors."

"And people really need this, you know. Some good news, for once. It'll help take their minds off things."

"Good news?"

"It's a triumph of the human spirit," she said, moving into full PR flight. Denning was glad, now, that he hadn't asked her to go for a drink.

She was just too alarmingly perky. "The climax of the space age. The pinnacle, in a sense, of our whole civilization."

"Our whole civilization?" Denning echoed, dubiously. He wondered what kind of medication this woman was on. *Everyone* around him seemed to be on medication: scientists, journalists, janitors, nurses, all popping their little yellow or green pills right in front of him, like candy.

"I mean, sure there were difficulties, tragic difficulties," she said. "But the important thing is, you made it back. After walking on another planet. Think of it, another planet. It doesn't get any better than that, Jake. I mean, I for one would call that very good news."

Denning looked back to the itinerary. "New York? Is that safe?"

"You'll be well protected," she told him. "This time of year, for maximum media impact you've got to be in New York. For the New Year, you know."

"New Year?" he echoed. "Right, the New Year." He had long ago lost track of the date. "That would be the year 2024, right?"

"Right," she said. "Another magic number. First it was January 2000, then it was December 2012. Now they're shooting for apocalypse in 2024."

"What's so special about 2024?"

"I'm not really up on this stuff . . . Someone figured that they needed to add another solar cycle to the old Mayan Long Count, the one that was supposed to end in 2012. And someone recalculated the McKenna Equations based on a new translation of the *I Ching* . . . It doesn't really matter how they explain it, it's like people can't wait for the world to end. We've got Evangelicals waiting for the rapture, Orthodox Jews waiting for their messiah, rumors of one Antichrist in the Middle East and another in Old Russia . . . witches and white magicians and Nova Children and who knows what else. It's crazy out there all year round. But New Year, that's always the craziest. You can bet they'll be out there again, all those crazies, waiting for the end of the world."

"Great," Denning said. "Just great."

"But you don't have to worry about any of that," she said. "You'll be at the best party in town."

"In Times Square, you mean?"

"Times Square?" she echoed, incredulous. "Times Square is a definite dead zone these days. What they do now is, they drop that ball inside a studio against a computer-generated backdrop of Old Times Square. With a replicant Guy Lombardo providing the soundtrack. But you're not going there. You're going to the Martha Nova party."

"The singer?" Denning asked, feeling an obscure alarm. "That's the best party in town? What's the big deal about a singer's party?"

"She's putting out a new album. Everyone will be there, all media, there's huge interest."

"And I'm supposed to compete with her?"

"Compete?" She laughed. "No way. But maybe we'll catch a few scraps from the table."

"I don't know if I like the idea of this party."

"It'll be really good PR for the Agency."

Fuck the Agency, Denning wanted to say. But he did not. He was still afraid of what they might do to him.

"And we need it," she said, as though reading his thoughts. "We really need some good PR. Losing two out of three crew members, that wasn't good copy anyway you slice it."

"It wasn't my fault. You know that. They were my buddies. I would have done anything I could to save them."

He looked away from Maxwell, rubbed an imaginary tear from his eyes. Or perhaps it was a real tear. He was getting good at this.

"We know you've been through hell," she said, her voice softening. "We're just asking you to soldier on a little longer. And who knows, maybe you'll even enjoy this party. You deserve a break. You deserve something to take your mind off things."

"Did Martha Nova invite me to this party? Personally, I mean?"

"No. We arranged the invite with her record company. Why? Do you know her?"

"I met her once, a long time ago. I spent a little time with her."

"That could be a good angle," she said, taking notes. "*Auld lang syne,* and like that."

Denning shook his head. "She probably wouldn't even remember me. I hardly remember it myself."

Except that the flickering was back now, in the very corners of his eyes. And although he didn't want to, he was beginning to remember. He was beginning to remember a great deal.

* * * * *

"Why did we go to Mars?" Denning said, echoing the journalist's question. "I'll tell you why we went to Mars."

And he would tell this sniveling excuse for a journalist exactly why they had gone to Mars. He would tell him in exact detail. He was angry enough now to spill the whole show.

He was angry with being pushed and pulled and programmed full of answers by the boys and girls at the Agency; angry with people bugging him all the time, grabbing and jostling and tearing away at him. And angry when they ignored him, too, the way they were mostly ignoring him at this party. This party for some dumb *singer,* of all things. A singer who wasn't even, as far as he could recall, a particularly good lay.

What kind of world is this, he wondered. A world where an astronaut just back from Mars, *Mars* for chrissakes—Earth's almost nearest and certainly most mysterious neighbor, as Bob Milton had so eloquently put it on the *People In Town* show just three hours before—was strictly second-best compared to a lame-ass singer. What kind of a world is this? Where, he wondered, is our sense of values? Where is our pride, for chrissakes? Where?

He hadn't wanted to come to this party in the first place, but he had been dragged here all the same. And now he was playing warm-up act for Martha Nova, the real star of the show. Even while they were asking him their ridiculous questions the media people kept looking over their shoulders to make sure they weren't missing the start of the real action.

"I'll tell you why we went to Mars," he told the assembled knot of reporters. "I did a lot of thinking about that and some day I'm going to lay it all out in my memoirs. But for now I'll put it simply. Fear. Fear and hatred. That's why we went to Mars."

"Fear?" The journalist who had asked the question blinked. "Hatred?"

"Hatred of what we fear. Hatred of nature, good old Mother Nature. Hatred of the Earth and the sun and the moon and Mars and the whole fucking universe."

"I don't understand you," the journalist said. "You're suggesting that people hate nature? Surely that's not true. People love nature."

"You're absolutely wrong," Denning said. "There's nothing they hate more."

Edison, who had been standing beside him during this exchange, now leaned forward as though to whisper in his ear. Denning shook him off.

"But the countryside . . ." The journalist faltered. "The national parks, the campgrounds . . ."

"Simulations," Denning said. "Simulations of nature, that's something else. Simulations are safe. Nature is scary. Nature wants to kill us. And it will, eventually, every one of us. Nature is raw. Nature is senseless, arbitrary, uncontrolled. Control it, and it isn't nature. Pave it over, put electric sockets on the trees, smash your rockets against the sky."

"Technology," the journalists said. "But people hate technology."

"Naturally we hate it," Denning said. "That's the whole point. We can't stand excitement and we can't stand boredom. That's the whole point."

"I don't understand," the journalist said. "What does this have to do with going to Mars?"

He looked uneasy. He was, after all, only a show biz columnist, not a science correspondent.

* * * * *

The lights in the room began to cycle up and down in illumination.

"It's show time," Denning heard someone say. And then the crowd of journalists around him melted away.

Edison shook his head slowly.

"Smooth," he said. "Real smooth."

"Nobody wants to hear the truth."

"Truth?" Edison echoed. "Did someone ask you to tell the truth? What's the matter with you, Denning? Get a grip for chrissakes."

"I've got a grip," Denning said. "Don't worry about that. So let's just enjoy the show, okay?" He turned away from Edison, to watch the stage.

* * 27 * *

Somehow Duke was not surprised to see Murray Snow at the party. He stood alone, looking distinguished in a gray suit, quite unperturbed as the people swarmed around him in their high fashion clothes and corporate uniforms.

"Having a good time?" he asked, having to shout above the din in the room.

"Yes indeed," Snow said. "I find this all quite fascinating. Although in some ways, what's going on *outside* the hotel is even more interesting."

"How do you mean?"

Snow led him towards a balcony that overlooked the street. They stepped out into the cool night air.

"Listen," Snow said.

"Listen to what?"

But he was already beginning to hear it, welling up over the traffic noise and the sirens and the distant sound of explosions: the singing coming from the masses of the Children who surrounded the hotel and spread far up and down the Avenue.

"To the sound of the world-mind," Snow said. "Awakening."

The singing was powerful and it was eerie. It sent shievers of apprehension up Duke's spine.

"And Martha is the trigger," Snow said. "My intuition told me as much all along. But I became overprotective of her, I tried to hold her back.

Perhaps, in a way, I was afraid of this moment arriving, even though I had so long expected it." He gestured towards the crowd. "And I still fear for her. But she was right to come back all the same. She knew what was necessary, and I did not."

* * * * *

Too many people. Too many bodies packed into one space, breathing the same air, battling to maintain and extend their own territory. Levett was seized by a renewed panic. He stood frozen by the wall, watching the partygoers ebbing and flowing across the floor.

A small stage had been set up across the room, with instruments and mikes and a computer deck. But the stage was vacant.

The sound system in the room was playing a Bach fugue. It was barely audible over the buzz of conversation.

Looking around the room Levett noticed one man attracting some attention. He was talking very loudly and emphatically, and could well have been drunk. Levett heard him shout something about Mars.

A second knot of people had formed around an older man, whose deeply lined face was somehow familiar: Robert Duke.

Duke and Martha were an item again. Levett knew that from the stack of briefing material that Olson had given him to update him on Martha's life.

It was the first news of Martha he had scanned in years. He didn't follow the entertainment news, or watch the music channels. He avoided, as a matter of policy, hearing any news of the world outside his apartment. It was just too depressing.

Much had happened to Martha since Levett had last seen her. She had sold millions of records without once setting foot on a stage or in a recording studio. Her cult had grown more enormous than ever. But this news of Martha's life in the years since he had last seen her was somehow unreal for Levett. For him nothing had happened in between, nothing of any importance, it was all just a meaningless blur.

* * * * *

The lights in the room dimmed and the sound system shut down. Spotlights picked out a man in a bright yellow blazer standing on the stage. On the crest of the blazer was the familiar corporate logo of RealTime Records, a series of concentric green circles around the globe of the Earth. Levett didn't recognize his face. Once he had known all the faces.

The executive picked up the microphone. "Hello everyone," he said. "Hello world." There was quiet. "Usually, people are slow to recognize greatness. Michaelangelo, the Wright Brothers, Jim Morrison. People don't approve of you until you've got where you're going, or else been and gone.

"But to every rule there is an exception. And tonight RealTime Records is proud to present the first new music in five years from a very exceptional woman. I give you Martha Nova's latest, greatest masterwork. I give you . . . *End of Time.*"

Still milking that apocalypse *shtick,* Levett thought. Which must be getting kind of tired by now, even if her fans do still eat it up. It's time she moved on. She has the talent, but she doesn't seem to have the motivation. She needs someone to guide her, someone to push her to think about some new ideas, to sing some new kinds of songs. If I were still her manager . . .

But he could not afford to think such thoughts. Simply being here in this hotel, so close to her, was disturbing enough.

A promotional video was showing now, a collage of photographs of Martha, at first silent. Then music swelled to fill the room. There was still no sign of Martha: just her image on the screen, and her voice, rising and falling through the giant speaker system.

The music was familiar and the music was strange. It was as though he had never heard anything like it before, but also as though he had been hearing it all his life. Levett shivered, in the grip of profound apprehensions.

It was electric music, a full band pulsing in the mix behind Martha, a lusher sound than he had ever heard from her. But it was a sweet electricity, sweet and soft and insinuating, rolling and shuffling around her voice.

"*Dance . . .*" the voice said, and Levett strained to make out the words. "*Is this a dance or still a dream?*" And later: "*And who is dreaming?*"

A dance tune, he thought. She cut a dance tune. The desolation shuffle.

He closed his eyes, and it was as if he could see the dance, the slow undulating dance. Beginning in the streets below with the Children, snaking its way across the city, moving out across the country, the continent, the world.

* * * * *

The brightness of the video hurt Denning's still-sensitive eyes. And the music bothered him too. The music was too cool, too slithery. The music was like being in space.

Leaving Edison watching in rapt attention, he turned and made his way through the crowd to the door. In the corridor outside were a pair of bored-looking security guards and a small boy staring out of the window.

"Hey, kid," Denning said. "What's happening?"

He followed the child's gaze down into the streets below. The streets were choked with people. Denning had not seen so many people in one place since the launch, when more than one million had surged into Florida to watch their boys take a shot at Mars. Those scenes had been incredible, just incredible. And now it had come to this.

It looked like a real wing-ding of a New Year's Eve party out there. But he was too tired and too aroused to make any sense of it. He turned away from the chaos below.

"Some party, huh?" he said.

"It's not a party," the child said. "It's a transformation. Can't you feel it coming on?"

Big words for a little kid. Denning did not follow the child's meaning at all, although it disturbed him at some level he had no wish to explore.

"Look, kid," he said. "You want my autograph?"

The child turned to face him. "I don't collect autographs," he said. "I collect snowballs. You know those plastic domes with cities inside, and snowflakes that you shake up? I collect them. I have snowballs from thirty-six cities."

"That's terrific," Denning said.

Denning did not much like children in general, and he was by no means sure that he liked this one in particular. But you had to try and be nice to them, you had to try and reach the children. The children were the whole future of this country. The children were what this thing was all about.

"You know who I am?" he asked. "I'm Jake Denning, the astronaut. I just got back from Mars. You probably saw me on your media wall. I bet you just can't wait to tell all your buddies how you met the man from Mars."

"I saw you," the child agreed. "I saw you start to remember."

"Remember?" Denning asked. "Remember what?"

But the child had turned back to the window, to watch the coming transformation.

* * * * *

Levett did not see Duke approaching him across the darkened room. He was too deep into the music to notice.

A hand touched his arm. He jerked it back involuntarily.

"Hello, Abe," Duke said. "How have you been keeping?"

"Good," Levett said. "Real good." He mopped the sweat from his forehead with the sleeve of his jacket. "Goddamn hot in here."

"Hot," Duke agreed. "Yes, it is." He looked speculatively at Levett. "So, how do you like the music?"

"I don't know," Levett said. "I don't know if I like it."

"What brings you here, Abe? You came to see Martha?"

Levett nodded. "I need to talk to her. There's something I have to tell her."

"And I'm sure Martha wants to see you, Abe," Duke said, guardedly. "But I don't know if tonight is the best time. Maybe you could make an appointment through her management . . ."

Levett shook his head vigorously.

"No," he said, his voice shrill. "It has to be tonight. I have to talk to Martha tonight."

Again, he mopped at his brow with his sleeve.

"You okay, Abe?"

"I'm fine," Levett said. "It's just the heat."

Duke looked at his watch. "Eleven thirty," he said. "Martha will be down soon. She's scheduled to start at midnight. Why don't you stick around?"

* * * * *

"How come you're not listening to the music?" the child asked the astronaut. "Don't you like the music?"

"No," the astronaut said. "I don't like the music."

The music, in fact, still echoed at the back of his mind, down deep somewhere he could not dislodge it. In his mind the music played on, and it made him shiver.

There was something spooky about the music. Just as there had been something spooky about the singer, that one night he had spent with her, something that had cut right through his drunken haze. There was something very spooky in the way she looked at a person.

"If you don't like the music," the child said, "you're not going to enjoy what comes next."

"What do you mean?" Denning asked. "What do you mean, I'm not going to enjoy what comes next?"

* * * * *

Emerging from the elevator into the corridor, Martha Nova saw the astronaut talking to his only son. She had previewed this scene, of course, imagined it in detail for many years. And still it brought her close to tears.

"Things will be different," her son, Daniel, was telling the mad astronaut, his father. "Things will be very different."

She saw the future. But she saw it only up to a certain point, a point in space and time beyond which she could not move. And now she had almost reached that point.

She had concluded long ago that this point must mark the moment of her own death. She presumed that her death would be very sudden, since she was unable to preview how it would happen. Her last memory of the future left her frozen on stage in the middle of a song and after that, nothing.

She believed her son could see further ahead than her, into the future beyond her death. But she had never discussed what he saw with him. Now she listened carefully to the conversation between Daniel and his father, even though she had overheard it so many times before.

* * * * *

"What will be different?" the astronaut asked the boy. "How will things be different."

"Everything," Daniel said. "Everything will be different. The whole world will change. There will be a transformation. But first there will be a burning."

"A burning what?"

As if in answer, the child nodded out the window. Denning followed his glance. For a moment, it seemed as if the whole world was on fire. He could see no roads, no sidewalks, no buildings, only the sky burning red from horizon to horizon.

The astronaut took a step backwards from the window.

He blinked, and the fire was gone. He saw that the buildings still stood, that the sidewalks below still swarmed with people.

"What was that?" he asked. "What the fuck was that?"

"Many things will burn," the child said. "But nothing important, nothing we'll need. The burning is the end of the old time. Afterwards comes the new time."

It was daylight outside the window and it was night and it was day and it was night again . . . The time rushed past and Denning saw it all change. He saw the people streaming out of the city, through streets choked with abandoned automobiles. He saw the waves of fire that swept on through, consuming some buildings entirely and leaving others charred and empty. He saw the rain fall, and keep on falling, for many days and nights.

He saw grasses grow up through the cracked concrete of the empty city, and then bushes and trees, an entire forest seemingly overnight. Deer grazed below him on what had once been a sidewalk. Wild turkeys strutted by.

The pace of the visions slowed. It was daylight outside the window, a soft but brilliant daylight streaming down from a cloudless blue sky.

Now people were returning: Some who walked and some who flew, some who were naked and some in elaborate costumes. They ate the fruit that grew on the new trees and drank from the springs that burst from the ground. They talked and sang and danced and bathed in the information that rained down upon them from the golden cloud that hung over the city, a cloud that was actually a swarm of tiny brilliant lights.

The vision faded. The astronaut shook his head.

"What does this have to do with the music?" he asked.

"The music precedes the transformation," the child said. "The music imagines the transformation."

"The music imagines the transformation," the astronaut echoed. "What the hell does that mean?"

* * * * *

What the hell does that mean? Martha, standing at the other end of the corridor, was seeing herself back in the Children's Hospital, watching this scene for the first time in complete bafflement. *What the hell does that mean?*

And again, as a teenager, tracking obsessively through her last days, trying to see her own death. *What the hell does that mean?*

And later, at the Space Center, meeting the astronaut for the first time and remembering the last time.

What the hell does that mean?

The future spoke through her. And now they were getting very near the end.

"Through the music," Daniel was saying, "we sing the transformation. We sing the new world."

"We?"

"We the children."

The astronaut was still staring doubtfully out the window. He had seen something out there, Martha knew. Some glimpse of the world to come. He had seen it through his son's eyes.

She walked towards them.

"Hello, Jake," Martha said.

The astronaut turned.

"Are you coming to see the show?" she asked.

The astronaut and the child followed behind her, silently, as she walked through to the backstage area. The child took a last backward glance through the window.

Down below in the streets, the dance had already begun.

* * * * *

Memories. The memories engulfed Levett. Standing frozen in the backstage area to which Robert Duke had led him, with the stage crew swarming around him, waiting to see Martha, he understood at last how it was that he came to be in this time and place.

He had forgotten so much. He had made himself forget. But the memories were back now. He remembered the last time he had seen Martha Nova. He remembered the last thing she had said to him: *I'll see you later. I'll see you at the party.*

And then he had run from her suite in the hotel, the superbly air-conditioned hotel that stood alongside the other hotels in the middle of the desert. He had run out into the street, out into the heat.

And he remembered why he had run. He remembered his moment of recognition.

"Abe."

He looked up, startled. Martha was smiling at him.

"You made it," she said.

"You look good, Martha."

"Thank you."

"You said that you would see me later," he said. "You said that you would see me at the party."

"Yes. I said I would see you at the party."

"I ran away from you," he said. "I was afraid of you. I couldn't handle it, knowing that it was true. Knowing that you really could see . . . that everything was coming to an end, just the way you said. That I was going to lose everything, my houses, my cars, my paintings." He shook his head. "As if any of that stuff ever made me happy. *Nothing* made me happy, actually, except hearing you sing. All the rest, all the money and the deals and the hype, was just bullshit."

"But you did good, Abe. Taking care of business for me. I could never have done it without you."

"Or someone like me."

"There's no one like you, Abe."

"You were waiting for me. Out on the ice, years ago. Waiting for me to fall at your feet."

"Because you were the one who was going to make me Martha Nova. No one else could do that."

"And you were waiting for me tonight."

"Yes."

"They sent me here to warn you," he said. "Some goons from MentHealth. Either you call off this comeback, or they stop you some other way."

She nodded, apparently unimpressed.

"Do you understand what I'm saying, Martha? You go ahead with this, they're probably going to kill you."

"I know."

"And you don't care?"

"Sure I care, Abe. But there's nothing I can do about it. It's too late to stop now."

He shook his head slightly. "You won't listen. I knew you wouldn't listen. So why *am* I here, Martha? What am I doing here tonight?"

"You came to see me again, Abe. And to say good-bye."

"Good-bye? But why? I mean, we just got together again . . ." But then he looked into her eyes, and he understood. "You mean . . . this is it?"

She nodded.

"The end?"

"Yes. Almost."

"The end," he repeated. It was not a question this time. He believed her. And wondered why, believing her, he felt so calm.

"But first, we get to have a party."

"Martha . . ."

She wrapped her arms around him and hugged him.

"It's all right, Abe. Really, it's going to be all right."

A stagehand was motioning towards her.

"It's time," she said.

She kissed him briefly on the lips, then released him.

"Enjoy the party," she said.

* * * * *

She took Duke's arm and began to walk with him towards the stage.

She looked radiant, Duke thought.

He felt terrified.

His eyes were red and raw. He had been crying earlier that evening, for Martha, and for himself. He had learned that from Martha, crying in advance.

"I don't believe this," he said, more to himself than to her. "I just don't believe it."

"It will be okay, Robert, you'll see. I think it's going to be wonderful."

"But you won't be here to see it."

She stopped and turned towards him.

"You'll see it for me."

"I don't want to," he said. "Not without you."

"I know it's going to be hard, harder for you than for me. But you have to go on, Robert. Because the world goes on, the dance goes on. Only the music changes."

She hugged him. "Take good care of Daniel."

"I will."

"Now," she said. "Let's dance."

* * 2 8 * *

The crowd on the street outside the hotel swayed to the new music. Kevin swayed with them, gripped by a profound happiness.

This is the way the world ends, he thought. And begins.

He felt a hand touch his arm, turned to see a woman. She was dressed like one of the Children, in a long white robe. But he knew that she was not one of the Children. Her face was intent, preoccupied. Her eyes were hot and fierce, burning through his bliss. A nerve in her face twitched.

He had seen her somewhere before.

He had a brief, jarring, moment of double vision. He was sitting in the MentHealth field office back in the mall, and this woman was sitting across from him at a metal desk, fitting his head into the hood of a machine that would shine lights into his eyes.

It was his MentHealth field worker, Mary Whitestone. But what was she doing here, dressed like one of the Children? He stared at her, frozen with fear and confusion.

"Kevin," she said. "It's time."

"Time?"

But he was already falling out of the moment, out of the crowd.

"Yes." She stared at him, unblinking. "Time to save Martha."

"Save her."

"To keep her love forever . . ."

“By sending her to eternity,” he completed.

“Eternity,” the woman echoed. “Yours for eternity.”

She began to sing.

“*Now that you’re mine / I want to stop time . . .*”

He began to sing with her. Colored lights sparkled in his eyes. He put his hand in his pocket and gripped the handle of the gun.

“*Keep your love forever / Send you to eternity . . .*”

The woman took his arm and began to steer him through the crowd, towards the hotel. “This way,” she said.

They reached the police cordon at the perimeter of the building. As they approached, the cordon momentarily broke open to admit them, then reformed behind them. The woman led him through a back door into a huge, bright clattering kitchen. At the far end of the kitchen was a service elevator.

“You have the gun?” she asked, as the elevator groaned upwards.

He nodded.

The elevator heaved to a halt, and they emerged into a long corridor. At the far end of the corridor, two security guards were standing peering through a crack between a set of doors. Music was coming out of the room behind the doors.

The woman reached in her robe and produced an aerosol can. Kevin heard a hissing sound. The guards slumped down to the thickly carpeted floor.

“Okay, Kevin,” she said. “You know the rest.”

She turned and got back in the elevator. Kevin walked down the corridor to the doors, stepping lightly over the prone security guards.

He knew the rest.

* * * * *

“Hey buddy.”

Denning glanced sideways. Mike Wyatt was standing beside him in front of the stage. He was dressed in a bright-green leisure suit.

Somehow Denning was not surprised to see him. Somehow he was glad to see him.

"Gonna be quite a show," Wyatt said. "Biggest show on Earth."

"You came to see it?"

"Came here to see *you*, buddy. Thought you might like some company. Doug's here, too."

"Doug?"

"Right here."

Denning turned to see Chang standing on his other side. Chang was wearing faded blue jeans and a black tank top.

"How's it going, Jake?" Chang asked.

"Going okay. Going just fine."

"You made it," Chang said. "You went all the way. Scooped the big enchilada."

"That's right," Denning said. "I got it made now."

"All kinds of doors opening for you?"

"All kinds," Denning agreed.

He stared curiously at Chang's unmarked throat. "So what's the deal? You didn't die?"

"Everybody dies," Chang said. "Nobody dies."

"Look Doug, I'm sorry . . ."

"It's okay," Chang said. "Forget it. I can't tell you that I enjoyed it, you killing me. But you had to do it. Otherwise I would have killed us both."

"Thank you," Denning said. "Thank you for telling me that."

"You're welcome, Jake," Chang said. He punched Denning lightly in the stomach. "What else are friends for?"

In the crush of bodies behind Denning, Edison watched his charge talking to himself.

This time, he thought, there could be no doubt about it.

The astronaut had truly lost it.

* * * * *

"Things end," Martha Nova said, as she stepped up to sing. "End and begin and end again. A beginning from every ending."

She began to sing.

"*We are home / We are back home . . .*"

A new song, or a back-catalogue item? Levett could not quite recall. But he felt a sudden rush of pleasure. To see Martha sing again . . . There was nowhere else he would have wanted to be tonight.

* * * * *

Out on the street, Martha Nova's image filled the giant screen on the roof of the hotel. Her voice echoed away down the avenue.

Out on the street, the Children were dancing. The Children were celebrating the coming transformation.

Inside the hotel, Kevin pushed his way through the crowd towards the stage. He was holding the gun concealed under the long sleeve of his white tunic.

Eternity, he thought.

Eternity.

* * * * *

Wyatt tugged Denning's sleeve.

"Something I've been meaning to tell you," he said.

"What?"

"Truth is, you're dead Jake, just like me . . . you burned up on reentry, the way you always dreamed you would. Except you didn't. We changed the scenario a little to get you home. But it's only what you might call a temporary reprieve."

Denning nodded slowly. "Okay," he said. "Makes sense."

"You ready?" Wyatt asked.

Denning felt it coming on now for real, the flickering. He had been feeling little flashes of it for hours, and now it was all the way back. He was filled with the knowledge, filled with the light.

For a moment, he was back in that cave on Mars, staring into the aleph. In the aleph, he saw the Earth. He saw mountains and oceans, forests and rice fields, deserts and petrochemical plants, highways and cart tracks, mirrors and radio telescopes, dinosaurs and trilobites, ants and people and porpoises, he saw it all, every living thing and every dead one, every grain of sand . . .

He saw himself as a child, riding a tricycle in the park behind his house, and as an adult flying bombing runs over Brazil. He saw his mother polishing the silver and his father frowning over a crossword puzzle. He saw himself fucking his first girlfriend and he saw himself burning up in the module. He saw every moment of his life and of every other life.

He tasted ginger and asphalt and mushrooms and sand. He smelled ashes and orchids and dog shit. He heard symphonies and machine-gun fire, Moroccan drummers and jet plane engines, groaning windmills and the songs of Martha Nova.

He saw and heard and smelled and tasted it all, past, present and future, all moments coexisting and coalescing in time, everything that had ever happened, all the way down to the end of time, all the way to the aleph.

He saw the aleph, too. The aleph was inside him and he was inside the aleph. And he felt the energy coursing through him, a great tide of light bursting through him and out into the world.

"Ready?" he echoed.

"For the change," Wyatt said. "It's coming at us, Jake. It's almost here. A giant wave, sweeping backwards in time to meet us. Backwards from the Eschaton, from the end of history, from the final flash at the end of time.

"The Eschaton is like a black hole, absorbing everything to itself, all of human history winding backwards, like a line in a fishing pole, like an old-time video cassette in reverse. It changes everything it touches, turns everything around."

Denning licked his lips. He could still taste the sand, and the bitter mushrooms.

"You talked about that before," Denning said. "Back on Mars."

"That's right, Jake."

"But who made this Eschaton?"

"*We* did. Or we will. In the end, people come together into the new mind. The Overmind. A mind so powerful it can reshape the world, even reach back in time."

"But why? Why would it do that?"

"Because we're summoning it," Wyatt said. "We're calling out to it to release us from this prison we've built for ourselves. And it hears us. It feels our desire for an end to history, to all our misery and despair. We're pulling it towards us, Jake."

"When? When does this change come?"

"The moment is almost here. Everything quickens as we approach the end, all the boundaries dissolve. Soon everything will go so fast that the rest of the future will happen in a few seconds."

"This Overmind. Is it . . . God?"

"Same difference."

"And you're part of it?"

"So are you, Jake. Or you will be. Everyone is here. Although who we were before isn't really the point. I'm just the messenger here. You're the one who has to take it all the way home."

"But how do you know all this, Mike?"

"Because *you* know it, Jake," Wyatt said. "I'm only a projection. Get right down to it, we're *all* projections. Holographic shadows, unfolding into the moment. And now it's time to change the movie . . . So, you ready?"

Denning nodded slowly. "As I'm ever going to be."

"Attaboy."

Wyatt was the Martian again, tall and blue. But at the same time he was still Wyatt, winking and nodding with Wyatt's expressions, speaking in Wyatt's voice. The Martian was still Wyatt, and then again he was neither of those things.

Chang had turned into a huge golden bug.

The flickering was getting faster, as if in time to the music. Denning felt the light begin to pulse out of him, surrounding him with a bright aura.

A boy in white clothes brushed past him, eyes intent on the stage. The boy raised his arm.

"Watch out," someone yelled. "He's got a gun."

* * * * *

"*He's got a gun.*"

Levett looked up. He saw Duke standing behind the stage, pointing towards him. He looked down stupidly at his own empty hands. He realized that Duke was pointing at the boy in white who was standing right in front of him, at the very edge of the stage, raising his arm.

There was an odd strobe-like illumination in the room now, much brighter than the stage lights. As Levett reached out to grab the boy's arm, he seemed to be moving in slow motion. Then his hands were wrapping around the gun.

* * * * *

He's got a gun.

She had forgotten this part of it. Or perhaps she had never been allowed to see it.

The future had ended for her, like an old-time movie snapping in the projector. There was no more of it that she could see.

She felt a great relief.

She smiled as she watched the gun swing towards her.

She watched, momentarily puzzled, as Abe struggled with the boy with the gun.

"No," she heard Abe shout.

And then the gun went off.

* * 2 7 * *

Tilt, Denning thought. Reset. This particular game of pinball is *over.*

Except that he was no longer Jake Denning. Or no longer *just* Denning. He was much more. He was Wyatt and he was Chang, he was the tall blue Martian and the great golden bug. He was Martha Nova and he was her child. He was Martha's lover, Robert Duke, and her killer, the boy in white firing the gun. He was Edison and he was Levett and he was the parking-lot attendant thirty-eight floors below. He was the Children dancing on the Avenue, all of the Children. He was everyone. And he was no one.

The gateway was open now, all the way open. Light continued to flood out of it. To flood out of him.

Denning glanced at the child standing behind the stage. His child. The boy showed no surprise as the gun shot rang out, as his mother staggered and began to fall, only grief.

But the child would be all right. He would be all right in the new world, the one about to dawn for him and for all of the children.

Denning took one last look at his son. And then he was up on the stage, kneeling beside the singer, enveloping her in his light.

"Time to go, Martha," he said.

* * * * *

Time to go.

There was a moment of terrible pain. And then she was lying on the stage and a man was kneeling beside her. It was the one she had always thought of as the dark man, although now he was bursting with light.

"Go?"

"End of the line for us, Martha. This is where we get off."

He touched her on the forehead.

She experienced a final moment of vision. The barrier fell and she saw beyond it at last, saw it shining ahead, the world that would follow the change.

And then she died.

* * * * *

For a moment, Edison thought he saw Jake Denning up on the stage, kneeling beside the fallen singer.

There was a final burst of light in the room, so bright that he reflexively squeezed his eyes shut. When he opened them again, he saw the melee in front of the stage, as several spectators grabbed the boy who had fired the gun. But up on the stage, Denning was gone. And so, Edison realized, was the singer.

They had taken the singer away fast. Rushed her to hospital, maybe. But Edison's main concern was to find Denning. He had to find the astronaut and get him out of the room, before any further damage resulted . . .

Except, he realized suddenly, that Denning was dead. Had been dead ever since he had burned up in that botched reentry.

Then what am I doing here? Edison wondered. What the fuck am I doing here?

A great golden bug skittered past him, heading for the exit.

* * * * *

Duke felt the change coming.

He watched as the man on the stage turned into some kind of creature of light, a gigantic bird enfolding Martha in his wings, carrying her up with him towards the ceiling.

And then the whole room seemed to shimmer, to shake, to spin, to soften, to *melt*... Shading his eyes against the brilliance of the light, Duke watched the walls and the furniture and the people in the room *flow*, somehow, wavering this way and that.

It lasted only a few moments. And then the light was gone, and the melting stopped, and everything looked the same as it had before. But everything was different.

* * * * *

Duke looked up to see Levett approaching him.

"He was standing right in front of me," Levett said. "I could have stopped him."

Duke shook his head slowly. "I wish you could have. But you couldn't."

As always, Martha had called it correctly.

Levett was staring at the blood on the stage. "But where did she go?"

"She went into the light."

"But is she dead?"

"Yes," said a child's voice from behind them. "She's dead."

It was Daniel. He looked as though he might have been crying. But he was calm and composed now.

"Daniel . . ." Duke said.

The boy took Duke's hand. "We should go."

"The police . . ." Duke said.

Daniel shook his head. "There are no more police."

He led Duke from the room.

* * * * *

Two men were holding the boy in white, who was crying quietly to himself. Levett recognized one of them as the record company executive who had introduced the video.

"You can let him go now," Levett said.

"Let him go?" the executive echoed. "But he has to stand trial . . ."

Levett shook his head. "I don't think so. Anyway, he had to do it." He turned towards the boy in white. "You had to do it." The boy's eyes showed no understanding.

"I've got to get back to the office," the executive said. He released his grip on the boy's arm. "Got to plan out how to handle this."

Levett shook his head again. "No more plans. No more office."

The other man released his grip on the boy in white. The boy began to stagger, dazed, towards the door.

Most people had already left.

It was time for Levett to go too.

* * * * *

At the door of the hotel, Duke hesitated, seeing the Children massed outside like a human wall. The massed ranks of police who had been holding them back seemed to have melted away into the night.

The Children were no longer singing. They were crying, most of them, sobbing in an eerie unison.

"It's all right," Daniel said, taking his hand and leading him out on to the sidewalk.

The Children on the sidewalk parted to let them through. And as Daniel walked among them, a calm began to settle.

Daniel began to sing, in a high clear voice, as they walked away from the hotel. He sang one of Martha's new songs. And the Children began to sing with him.

* * * * *

In the parking lot underneath the hotel, Levett picked out a car with keys in the ignition. He drove out slowly, carefully, through the crowd of Children.

The Children were leaving. They were walking down the Avenue, singing, their voices merging into a single chord.

At the head of this procession, Levett glimpsed the singer's child, along with Robert Duke.

Long after the Children had vanished in his rearview mirror, Levett could still hear their singing echoing behind him.

He had tried to save Martha. But Martha could not be saved. Perhaps she had not even wanted to be saved. Because she would have known it was coming, the way she knew everything else.

As Robert Duke had said, he couldn't have stopped that boy from shooting her. They had been like actors in a play—himself, Duke, the boy—forced to play out the final scene. He had tried to save Martha and he had failed, and his failure had been written in stone.

But now the stone was shattered.

History was over. He was free, they were all free.

Levett was no longer anxious about the future, because the future was already here. He faced it with an eager expectation.

Sometime later, the burning began.

Out on the Interstate, driving fast, Levett did not immediately notice it. And when he did notice it, he paid it no attention. He drove on along the burning highway while the radio played its sweet new music. He drove on, through the fire, on that very last night.